# If You Can't Be Good

"Any Ross Thomas novel is fast-paced, smoothly written and brightly observant."
   —*New York Times Book Review*
"[Thomas] is without peer in American suspense and is peer of the best of British."
   —*Los Angeles Times*
"Ross Thomas is our best Washington novelist.... He writes clever, fast-paced, tightly constructed stories about people who misuse power, sex, and high explosives."

   —*The Washingtonian*

# ROSS THOMAS

# IF YOU CAN'T BE GOOD

**PERENNIAL LIBRARY**

Harper & Row, Publishers
New York, Cambridge, Philadelphia
San Francisco, Washington, London, Mexico City
São Paulo, Singapore, Sydney

A hardcover edition of this book was published in 1973 by William Morrow & Company, Inc. It is here reprinted by arrangement with William Morrow & Company, Inc.

First PERENNIAL LIBRARY edition published 1984. Reissued in 1986.

Library of Congress Cataloging-in-Publication Data

Thomas, Ross, 1926–
    If you can't be good.

    Reprint. Originally published: New York : Morrow, 1973.
    "Perennial Library."
    I. Title.
PS3570.H5813    1986        813'.54        83-48392
ISBN 0-06-080832-2 (pbk.)

86  87  88  89  90  OPM  10  9  8  7  6  5  4  3  2  1

# If You Can't Be Good

# 1

It began the way that the end of the world will begin, with a telephone call that comes at three in the morning. This one came from Larry Kallan who suffers from insomnia and assumes that everyone else does, too. It will be Kallan, I suspect, who'll bring me the news of how things turned out at Armageddon.

Instead of saying hello or how've you been or even repent, for the end is at hand, he said, "How'd you like to go to work for the most feared man in Washington?"

"Mr. Hoover's dead and gone," I said.

"I mean Frank Size."

"Oh," I said, "him."

"Whaddya mean, oh him?"

"You know Frank Size?" I said.

"Sure, I know him. He's a client of mine. What's wrong with him?"

"Well, for one thing," I said, "he lies a lot."

"Yeah, but when he does he always apologizes. He prints a nice retraction."

"'With no harm done to anyone.'" At three in the morning I only hummed it to him, but I was still off key.

"What was that? What was that you were humming? I didn't get that."

"A snatch of song. Nothing more."

"What song?"

"Bob Hope's theme, 'Thanks for the Memory.' He sang it to Shirley Ross in *The Big Broadcast of 1938.* I think it was thirty-eight. He must be sick of it by now."

"That was the year you were born. Nineteen thirty-eight."

"That's right."

"You're not getting any younger."

"Jesus, Larry, you can sure make a body think."

"That's what you'd better do—think about your future. If you don't start thinking about it now, well, you're gonna have plenty of time to think about it when you're fifty and standing around on some corner with four-bits in your pocket and no place to sleep."

Now fifty himself, Larry Kallan probably was Washington's most successful investment counselor. He seemed to know all of the gossip first and everyone it concerned and apparently most of them were his clients. He also was a true child of the depression. It still haunted him and he liked to paint vivid word pictures of assorted fifty-year-olds standing around on street corners with nothing in their pockets but a quarter, three nickels, and a dime. Sometimes he could add a little wet snow and wind.

"What's Frank Size looking for?" I said

"An investigative reporter, like him."

"I'm not an investigative reporter; I'm an investigative historian."

"You're a snoop," Kallan said. "A federal snoop and

they won't even give you permanent civil service status. You're a consultant."

"A hundred-and-eight-dollar-a-day consultant," I said. "In point of service, I'm this town's most enduring consultant. I go back all the way to Camelot.'"

"And Billie Sol Estes."

"And the Peace Corps Pot Affair in Nigeria," I said. "We swept that one under the rug rather tidily."

"In twelve years you've had twenty-one different jobs," Kallan said

"Appointments, Larry. I serve only at the pleasure of my President."

"No job security," he said "No pension. No hospitalization insurance. And besides that your politics are all wrong. How you ever survived these past four years is still way beyond me."

"Simple," I said. "I just dug up some of the bodies that I'd once helped bury. I can probably provide the same service for the next administration. If there ever is one."

"I think you oughta talk to Frank Size."

"Did Frank Size mention anything interesting such as money?"

There was a short pause. "Well, I didn't actually talk to Frank."

"Who did you actually talk to?"

"Well, I talked to Mabel Singer. She's Frank's private secetary. You know Mabel?"

"I've heard of her," I said. "Did Mabel mention anything interesting such as money?"

"Well, no, but she did mention one thing you oughta be interested in."

"What?"

"You can work at home."

"You mean no nine to five?" I said.

"That's right."

"You're sure?"

"That's why I called you," Kallan said. "It oughta give you time to track down that Frenchman you're always writing letters about. What's his name, Bon something?"

"Bonneville," I said

"Yeah, Bonneville. He's been dead a while, hasn't he?"

"About a hundred years," I said.

# 2

In late 1959 I had been a candidate for a doctoral degree in history at the University of Colorado when Bobby Kennedy had swung through the West looking for people who might like to see his brother nominated President. Although only twenty-one at the time and a nominal Socialist, I had set up an organization that called itself Republican Students for Kennedy. It had made a lot of noise, but not enough to prevent John Kennedy from losing Colorado in the 1960 election by nearly 62,000 votes. I'm not a Socialist anymore. After twelve years in government, I think I'm an anarchist.

But the Kennedys, devout believers in the spoils system, had been grateful for my efforts and so I was invited to Washington. When I arrived in early February of 1961 nobody was quite sure what to do with me so they made me a $50-a-day consultant and assigned me to something called Food for Peace, which was run out of a small suite in the old Executive Office Building next door to the White House by a young ex-congressman called George McGovern who didn't quite know what to do with me either.

It was finally decided that since I was a budding historian it would be nice if I made a historic record of the first shipment of Food for Peace from the time that it left Baltimore with appropriate fanfare to when it entered the bellies of those whose hearts and minds it surely would win to Democracy's side. I suppose everyone was still a bit naïve back in 1961.

The first shipment of food was 300 tons of wheat destined for the bellies of the citizens of one of those countries on the west coast of Africa that had just shrugged off a couple of hundred years of British colonial rule. A third of the wheat disappeared into the black market the same day that it was unloaded. The rest of it just vanished only to turn up a few weeks later when a Dutch freighter, flying a Liberian flag of convenience, dropped anchor in Marseilles.

Some six weeks after that selected elite units of the new African nation's army were sporting the French-made MAT 49 nine-millimeter submachine guns and I arranged to have some awfully good pictures of them taken which I turned in with my 129-page report that I entitled, "Where the Wheat Went, or How Many 9mm Rounds in a Bushel?"

After that I somehow became an unofficial Cupidity and Corruption Specialist, always temporarily assigned to or inflicted upon one government agency or other that had managed to get itself into hot water. I usually pried and poked around for two or three months, digging through records and asking questions and looking grim and mysterious. Then I would write a long report that invariably told a rather sordid tale of greed and bribery on the part of those who sold things to the government and of avarice in the hearts of those who bought them.

And almost always they sat on my reports while

somebody else scurried about and patched things over. The reports of mine that did surface were major scandals that were already bubbling so fiercely that it was impossible to keep the lid on. Of these the Peanut Oil King Affair comes to mind. So does the one where some Madison Avenue sharpies ripped off the Office of Economic Opportunity. That one I entitled, "Poverty Is Where the Money's At."

The Republicans kept me on as window dressing, I suspect. When they came back to power in 1969 I was once again summoned to the old Executive Office Building, back to the same suite, in fact, where it had all begun eight strange years before. There I was informed by yet another ex-congressman, whose name I can't even recall, that I was welcome to stay on in my present capacity, whatever the hell that was, although there really wasn't going to be any great need for my services because the new administration was going to be "as clean as a—uh—as a—"

"Hound's tooth," I supplied.

"Exactly," the ex-congressman said.

So I stayed on, switching from one agency and department to another and finding no more nor no less corruption and chicanery in places both high and low than I had found before.

But I traveled less, far less, and that enabled me to spend most Saturdays at the Library of Congress in the company of Captain Benjamin Louis Eulalie de Bonneville, late of the United States Army's Seventh Infantry, West Point graduate, protégé of Tom Paine, mountain man, friend of Washington Irving, bankrupt, and—I suspected—a sometime secret agent for the Secretary of War.

Captain (later general) Bonneville was the subject of the doctoral thesis that I had been researching when summoned to the New Frontier. I was still trying to track down his daily journal that had once been in the possession of Washington Irving and now, twelve years later, I thought that I might be getting close. It was of no great matter though. Not to Bonneville anyhow. He already has a dam and some salt flats named after him. And a Pontiac car. He lives.

But I still clung to the idea that I could complete my thesis and armed with a Ph.D. repair to some freshwater college where time had stopped and Ronald Colman was president and the short-haired students, fresh scrubbed and shining, all drove convertibles and were uptight only about such relevancies as whether old Prof Morrison would give the Boomer a passing grade in Chemistry 103 so that he could play against State at Homecoming.

I had kept this back-lot-at-Paramount fantasy of mine carefully nurtured as a harmless antidote to the poisons of the Great Swamp of Bamboozlement that I had slogged through these past twelve years. I needed some free time to complete my thesis and if Frank Size was affable enough to let me work at home, then I would repay his kindness by stealing the time from him. Twelve years in government had left my own morality a bit flexible.

I was telling Frank Size most of these fascinating details about myself—except for my plot to rob him of some time—over the lunch that he was buying me and his secretary, Mabel Singer, at Paul Young's restaurant on Connecticut Avenue.

Size must have been around forty-six that spring. He was the sole proprietor of a seven-day-a-week column that was syndicated to more than 850 daily and weekly newspapers throughout the United States, Canada, and for all I knew, the world. The column was written in his own God-ain't-it-awful style and he must have wanted it to come thundering out of Washington. Instead, it came out gobbling like some old tom turkey who's just spotted the fox. Still, the column could destroy a reputation in a paragraph and there were many who blamed it for at least two suicides.

There wasn't much striking about the way that the most feared man in Washington looked. Except for his eyes, he had one of those faces that can always be found at the head table of the Tuesday noon luncheon. He had a wide, turned up, joke-telling mouth; a big jaw that had grown some pink, fat jowls; a surprisingly thin nose; and neat little ears that were ringed by what was left of his hair.

The rest of him had gone to hell and he looked soft and flabby with a potbelly that rolled out over his belt and hung there, as though looking for a place to lie down. But when you looked at his eyes, you knew that he didn't care what his gut looked like. Or that he was bald. Or slump-shouldered and sway-backed. If contempt had a color, it would be the same shade of gray as his eyes, the pale, cold, glittering gray of polished granite in winter rain. They were eyes that seemed to have priced the world and found it to be a cheap and shoddy place filled with undesirable tenants who were always late with the rent.

"Well, you've had a hell of a twelve years, haven't you?" Size said, forking a big chunk of potato into his mouth. It made me hungry. I hadn't tasted a potato in three years. Unlike Size, I still had some vanity left.

"It wasn't all bad," I said. "There was a lot of travel." I took the third bite of my own lunch which consisted of a chef's salad and a lone martini. I wondered what effect my ordering its twin would have on the job interview. Frank Size didn't seem to drink, but fortunately Mabel Singer did.

"I'm going to have another drink," she said. "You want one?"

"Sure he does," Size said. "You drink a little now and then, don't you, Mr. Lucas?"

"A little."

"Order the drinks, Mabel, and then hand me that stuff you brought."

If you write a column that's the next thing that half the nation turns to after the sports page each morning, you don't have to worry about what kind of service you get in restaurants. Mabel Singer had only to lift her head and a spaniel-eyed waiter was at her elbow, straining to be of assistance. She ordered a Manhattan for herself, a martini for me, bent down, picked up a slim, zip-around leather case, took an oatmeal colored file from it, and handed it to Size.

"What do people call you, Mr. Lucas?" he said.

"Mr. Lucas."

"I mean they don't call you Decatur, do they?"

"My mother did. Almost everybody else calls me Deke."

"Like the fraternity," Mabel Singer said. "I once went with a Deke at Ohio State. I was a Phi Gam. I bet they don't even have those things anymore. Christ, but that was a long time ago."

I guessed it to be about sixteen years ago. Mabel Singer was a big, strapping woman and she must have been a big, strapping coed, smart and brash and full of fun, but usually stuck for a date unless her sorority sisters bribed one of the basketball squad to bring her along. She was still Miss Singer at thirty-seven or thirty-eight and she had the reputation of being the best private secretary in Washington as well as the most highly paid. I knew that the United States Government couldn't afford to hire her and it had tried often enough.

"So you think you might like to go to work for us, huh?" Size said, leafing through the file that Mabel Singer had handed him.

"I'm not sure," I said. "We haven't talked about money yet."

"We'll get to that," he said. "It says here that you're thirty-five and divorced and that your wife's remarried and that you didn't have any kids and that your credit rating isn't bad and that some of your neighbors think you drink too much and that your morals are a little loose and also that you belong to some pretty strange organizations such as the Sacco and Vanzetti Fife and Bugle Marching Society."

"Where does it say all that?" I said.

"In this," Size said, tapping the oatmeal colored file.

"What the hell is that?"

"Your FBI file."

"Shit," I said.

"Surprised that I'd have it?"

I shook my head. "No. You must have a pretty good leak over there."

"You don't like it much though, do you?"

"I don't like it at all," I said. "The FBI collects garbage. It doesn't sort it, it just collects it, and it sits there until it stinks out loud."

"I agree," Size said. "I've written the same thing in the column. Lots of times. But when I hire somebody, I use the FBI files. It saves a lot of money and time. References aren't worth a damn. You wouldn't list anybody as a reference unless you knew he was going to say something good about you, would you?"

"Probably not."

"That's why I use the FBI."

"Can you get anybody's file?"

"Just about anybody."

"That must be handy."

"I don't take them home for bedside reading like Lyndon Johnson did. I only use them when in my judgment the story warrants it."

"In your judgment, huh?"

"You don't think it's infallible, do you? My judgment, I mean."

"I don't think anybody's is."

"What about your own?"

"It's not infallible either."

"But you depend on it."

"Sure. I depend on it."

"Yeah, well," he said, "that's how I make my living. Depending on mine."

The waiter brought the drinks then and I took a swallow of mine before we started getting into the ethics of the thing. I wasn't sure that Frank Size would know what I was talking about. For that matter, I wasn't sure that I would either.

"Why don't you tell him about the job?" Mabel Singer said. "That's why you invited him to lunch."

Frank Size grinned and it was the merry grin of a mischievous nine-year-old pasted across the sagging face of a middle-aged man. It would have been charming, but for the eyes. The eyes took all the fun away.

"Okay," he said. "Let's talk money first. You don't mind talking money, do you, Deke?"

"It's a favorite topic," I said, wondering how much the pally, first-name basis was going to cost me a year.

"The job'll pay twenty-two thousand a year, which is about what a real top-flight reporter gets in this town."

"I'm a real top-flight historian and I'm making twenty-eight thousand now."

"I know how much you make," he said. "I can't pay twenty-eight. But I can throw in some stuff that you're not getting now. I can throw in a noncontributory pension plan. You're going to need a pension one of these days."

"That's what Larry Kallan says."

"Our mutual friend," Size said. "Well, he helped

me set it up. He says that for somebody in your bracket it would be worth a couple of thousand a year."

"What else goes in the pot?" I said.

"Profit sharing." He turned to Mabel Singer. "How much was that worth to you last year?"

"About two thousand. Maybe a little more."

"Okay," Size said "That's nearly four. Hospitalization insurance. I got the best plan going since I have to pay for it anyhow. It oughta be worth about thirty or forty a month to you. That's another four hundred bucks in the pot."

"I'm getting interested," I said.

"Bonuses," he said. "I don't pay a yearly bonus for a hell of a good job. I expect that. But I will pay a bonus if you do a hell of an outstanding job, a superlative one. And it'll be a fat one."

"How fat?"

"Fat enough to make you smile for a week."

"We're just one happy family," Mabel Singer said.

"Happy as clams," Size said. "I got a small staff. Six reporters or legmen, and Mabel and me. I don't count the accountants and the lawyers because they're on retainer. Now I've only got a couple of rules, but you might as well hear them. The first is I don't accept excuses. Reasons, yes. But excuses give me a pain in the ass. The second rule is, I can fire you on a minute's notice—not a month, not a week, not a day, but a minute. You can quit the same way. That might start some people screaming about job security, but I don't look at it that way. If you're doing a damn good job, I'd be a fool to fire you. But if you're doing a rotten job, I'd be an even bigger fool to keep you on. I don't worry about people who just do mediocre jobs. They don't go to work for me."

"What would I do, if I went to work for you?"

"Well, it's something I've been thinking about for a long time," Size said. "Every so often a story'll come along. I hear about it and maybe I'll give it a column or two. Maybe even three or four and that's the end of it. But what I use in the column is just the tip of the iceberg. There's more to it than that, a hell of a lot more, but another story breaks and I have to go after that. I'm in a goddamned competitive business and it's seven days a week, three hundred and sixty-five days a year. What I want to do is go after those stories that I just sometimes skim. And that takes digging, solid steady digging. You know the kind I mean."

"I've done a little," I said.

"Yeah, I've seen some of those reports you've turned in."

"I remember one you managed to see. It had top secret stamped all over it and the Justice Department was damned curious about where you got your information."

Size grinned. "Maybe I should've given you credit."

"Maybe you should've."

"Well, that's what I've got in mind—going after complicated stories that take a lot of time and effort—more time and effort than we can give them the way we're staffed and still fill up the column seven days a week." He made his column sound like a bottomless tub. I suppose it was. "You interested?" he said.

I took the final swallow of my martini. What you really want to know, I thought, is whether I'm interested in helping you go after a Pulitzer. Three times Frank Size had been nominated for a Pulitzer Prize and three times it had been denied him. Sometimes the judges seemed to feel that the Size stories smacked too much of guile and not enough of craftsmanship. Or that they reeked of midnight meetings and pilfered files instead of scholarly, sobersided reporting. Or, most damning of all, that the methods Size had used to obtain his stories were ones in which, in the judges' minds at least, questionable practices had been employed. In other words, if Frank Size couldn't get the news by any other means, he sometimes cheerfully stole it. Or had it stolen.

"I'm interested," I said.

"How soon can you go to work?"

I thought about it for a moment. "Next week. They'll be glad to see me go."

"We might even give it a little plug in the column," Size said.

"You can also give it to me in writing," I said.

"See what I mean, Mabel?" Size said. "He's our kind of folks."

Mabel Singer nodded. "I'll see that he gets a letter off to you this afternoon."

"Why don't you come back to the office with us," Size said, "and you can give her the stuff she'll need like your Social Security number and I'll give you some deep background on the story you'll be working on."

"Deep background on who?" I said.

"Ex-Senator Ames."

"Jesus."

"What's the matter?"

"Nothing," I said. "It's just that I didn't think that a guy could be crucified twice."

Size grinned. "You'd be surprised," he said.

# 3

---

The crucifixion of former Senator Robert F. Ames, a Democrat from Indiana, had begun about seven months ago when he arose on the floor of the Senate one rainy November afternoon and bored hell out of the four other senators present with a long, dull thirty-minute speech about what a noble thing it was that a minor conglomerate called the Anacostia Corporation was going to swallow up yet another victim called Can-Am Mining.

The next day a Washington lobbying firm had air-mailed reproductions from the *Congressional Record* of the senator's speech to all of the stockholders concerned. Fifteen days later the Anacostia Corporation swallowed Can-Am Mining without even a burp.

On Christmas Day, Frank Size's column presented what he claimed was incontrovertible evidence that the senator from Indiana had been paid $50,000 to make the speech by the Washington lobbying firm. Size branded it a bribe and claimed to have the serial numbers of some of the $100 bills that had been used.

He wrote that twenty of the bills had been traced from the Riggs bank where the lobbying firm had an account to the personal account that the senator had with the First National Bank of Washington. The rest of the $50,000 was still unaccounted for.

Other newspapers and the wire services picked up the story and set their reporters off in a yapping pursuit. They looked into the Can-Am Mining takeover and found that it was one of those deals in which a company with a lot of liquid assets pays for its own demise—to the detriment of just about everyone concerned except a few key stockholders.

The story began gathering momentum and taking on other ramifications and by January when Congress came back into session, the Senate reluctantly decided that once again it would have to look into the ethics of one of its own. A hearing was scheduled, but before it could begin Senator Robert F. Ames resigned—after having served exactly five years and four days in what some still call the most exclusive club in the world. The Justice Department, after a couple of weeks of noisy throat-clearing, decided that it didn't have quite enough evidence to prosecute. Two days later Senator Ames left his millionaire wife and took up light housekeeping with a twenty-seven-year-old blond who was an employee of the lobbying outfit that allegedly had handed him the bribe. Senator Ames had just turned fifty-two.

"He's dead," I said, closing the file. "Somebody just forgot to bury him."

Size shook his head. "There's more to it than that."

"What?"

"One, why would he take a fifty-thousand-dollar bribe? He's got money of his own. His wife settled a million dollars on him as his fortieth birthday present."

"Maybe he spent it all."

"He's got plenty left. So if he didn't need the money, why take the bribe?"

"Maybe he didn't take it."

"Crap," Size said. "He took it."

I looked around Size's office. It wasn't much, not for a national celebrity who got $3,000 a speech when he could work one into his tight schedule. He had a suite at 1700 Pennsylvania Avenue, just a block from the White House on the sixth floor of a fairly new building that had once had a putting green on its roof until it started leaking on the tenants below. Mabel Singer held down the entrance to the Size suite. To her left was the bullpen where the six legmen worked. Behind her was Size's office which had a green nylon carpet, a brown desk that was probably walnut veneer, six straight-backed chairs upholstered in green plastic, one of which I was sitting on, some green glassy drapes, and a manual typewriter on a metal stand. That was all. No pictures on the wall of him and Presidents he had known. No mementos on his desk.

I stood up. "Okay," I said. "You want the whole story."

"That's right. The whole story."

"How much time do I have?"

Size shrugged. "Whatever it takes."

"What if there is no story?"

"There will be. You're forgetting about my infallible judgment."

"You're right," I said. "I was. I work at home, right?"

"Unless you want a desk in there," he said, nodding toward the bullpen.

"No thanks."

"Anything else?"

"Just one thing. When do we get paid?"

"Every two weeks."

"Fine," I said. "I'll see you payday."

Three weeks later the phone rang just as Martin Rutherford Hill narrowed his eyes, let a small cruel smile play around his pink wet lips, took careful aim, and dumped his bowl of Cream of Wheat on Foolish, the cat. Foolish, a five-year-old, fifteen-pound brawler, licked once at the cereal, decided he didn't like it, leaped up on the high chair and swatted two-year-old Martin Rutherford Hill across the nose with a sheathed claw. The child screamed; Foolish grinned, dived from the high chair, and streaked for the living room, his claws clicking furiously on the kitchen vinyl. It was another minor skirmish in an old war that neither was winning.

I put down my *Washington Post*, looked up at the ceiling, and yelled to an unseen presence: "Will you come get the goddamned kid!" To Martin Rutherford Hill I said, "Shut up; you're not hurt." The child wailed and threw his plastic spoon at me as I picked up the wall phone on its fourth ring.

After I said hello a woman's voice said, "Mr. Lucas?"

"Yes."

"Frank Size's office gave me your number." She had a young voice, I thought, not more than twenty-five and probably closer to twenty.

"How can I help you?"

"My name is Carolyn Ames. I'm Robert Ames's daughter."

"Yes, Miss Ames."

"You've been asking questions around town about my father." It wasn't an accusation the way she said it, but a melancholy admission of fact. She would probably use the same tone if she were to announce that her puppy had died last night.

"Yes, I have been asking some questions," I said. "In fact, I'd like to ask you some."

There was a brief silence and then she said, "Are you an honest man, Mr. Lucas?"

"Average," I said after a pause. I'd had to pause to think about the question because no one had ever asked it quite like that before.

"If you got the real story about my father, would you write it?"

"Yes," I said without any hesitation this time, "I'd write it."

"Would Frank Size print it?"

"Yes, I'm almost sure he would."

"Even if it proved that he was a liar?"

"You mean Size?"

"Yes."

"He usually admits it when he's been wrong. In fact he does it kind of cheerfully."

"This isn't a cheerful matter."

"No," I said. "I suppose it isn't."

There was another pause and when she spoke again it sounded as if she were reading it or as though it had been carefully rehearsed and she wasn't much of an actress. "I have certain information that will prove that my father was a victim of circumstances. This proof is carefully documented by tapes and other written material, including a fifty-page summary that I wrote myself. In order to clear my father's name, and place the blame on those who rightly deserve it, I am prepared to turn this material over to you at three o'clock this afternoon."

She's taping it, I thought, and decided to be just as careful and just as formal. "I'm prepared to accept the information you described. Where shall we meet?"

She mentioned the name of a sidewalk café on Connecticut Avenue not too far from the Shoreham.

"Outside?" I said.

"Yes, outside. I prefer a totally public place."

"How'll I recognize you?"

She gave me a brief description of herself and added, "I'll be carrying a green attaché case." Then she hung up.

By now the unseen presence and mother of the child had arrived and was busy cleaning up the Cream of Wheat that Martin Rutherford Hill had dumped on the floor. The child watched Sarah Hill wipe up the mess, smiled when she finished, and said, "Glock."

"We'll glock later," she said as she rose. "Who won," she asked me, "the goddamned kid or the goddamned cat?"

"It was a draw."

"Well, he ate most of it."

"He wouldn't part with it if he were still hungry."

"You want some more coffee?" she said.

"Please."

Sarah Hill poured me a cup and then one for herself. She sat down at the round maple breakfast table, rested her elbows on it, held her coffee cup with both hands, and stared over the cup at the garden that lay beyond the open French doors. The garden was her domain and it was quite narrow and deep and the dogwood and azalea blossoms were out and shouting for attention. The roses would be coming along later, in June, but a couple of late-blooming beds of jonquils were still following the sun around. There was no grass in the garden, only plants and shrubs and a bricked path that meandered from one side to another in no particular hurry to get anywhere. A trio of tall old elms provided shade and a bit of dignity. It all looked a little wild and a bit unplanned and even haphazard and Sarah Hill had worked hard to make it look that way.

"Hollyhocks," she said.

I turned to look. "Where?"

"In that corner by the little pink dogwood."

"You're right. They'd do fine there."

"You can catch bees in them."

"In hollyhocks?"

She nodded. "You can fold them up inside and listen to them buzz."

"What do you do with them then?"

"Let them go, I guess. My brother used to step on them."

"I always thought he was a mean son of a bitch."

Sarah Hill and I had been living together for a little more than a year. We had met at the Library of Congress one Saturday afternoon and I had invited her home for a drink and she had just sort of stayed, moving her books and her baby and her cameras in the following week. Without ever really discussing it we divided up the household chores with her taking over the garden and the housecleaning while I cooked the evening meal after she let it be known that she didn't much care to do it. I also did the grocery shopping until she discovered that I was the world's greatest impulse buyer.

She was a free-lance photographer, specializing in natural light portraiture. Her talents were in much demand by various organizations that headquartered in Washington and that wanted something new in the way of publicity shots of their officers and board members. Often using nothing but an old Leica with some fast film, Sarah turned out striking, informal portraits that made her mostly middle-aged subjects look warm, wise, witty, and flatteringly human. She also insisted on paying me $200 a month for her share of the rent and the household expenses. I banked the money in a savings and loan account under the name of Martin Rutherford Hill.

All in all, we got along quite well together and we were genuinely fond of each other. We may even have been in love; at least we tried to be, but after a couple of sour marriages on both sides we had learned that it was something that had to be worked at.

"Who called?" she said.

"The senator's daughter."

"Can we get some Saturday?"

"Some what?"

"Hollyhocks."

"Yes, I think so."

"I still don't think he did it."

"Who?"

"Senator Ames."

"You mean took the bribe?"

"Yes."

"Why?"

Sarah moistened her paper napkin with her tongue and used it to wipe some dried oatmeal from her son's mouth. The child smiled happily and said, "Hrap." She made a face at him. He giggled and said, "Hroo." She made another face and said, "He doesn't look like he'd take a bribe. He looks too dreamy with all that wavy gray hair and sad brown eyes and that only-you-and-I-know expression of his. I just don't think he took it."

"Because he's got sad brown eyes?" I said.

"Because his wife's got money, smartass. She's worth eighty million dollars."

"More like eighteen million," I said and looked at my watch. "Well, I've got to go."

"To the library?"

"Right."

"Are you going to take the car?"

"I'll come back and get it later."

The house that Sarah and I lived in was a narrow, two-storied red brick affair with a flat front that had been built on Southeast Fourth Street some eighty years ago within easy walking distance of the Library of Congress and almost around the corner from where J. Edgar Hoover had been born.

Five years before it had been bought, gutted, and expensively remodeled by a rich young freshman congressman from San Francisco who thought that his constituents would like it if they knew that he had chosen to live in one of Washington's mixed neighborhoods.

The congressman's constituents, mostly black, apparently hadn't much cared where he lived because they hadn't sent him back for a second term. So the ex-congressman now rented the house cheaply to me on the condition that I would move out within a month after he got himself re-elected. I had lived in the house for three years now and from the way that the ex-congressman's last campaign had gone, I could probably live in it forever.

"You be home for lunch?" Sarah asked as she rose and gathered up the coffee cups.

I got up, too. "No, I'll probably eat downtown somewhere. What're you going to do today?"

She turned and looked at me and smiled. It was her dangerous I'm-getting-sick-of-it-all smile. "Oh, my day is fully scheduled with a number of exciting events designed to enrich the mind as well as the spirit. My son and I, for example, get to go to the friendly, neighborhood ghetto chain store where we'll be overcharged approximately five percent for the vittles that you'll cook tonight."

"What're we having?" I said

"Beef ribs."

"Good."

"For conversation, of course," she went on, "I have a two-year-old who speaks in an unknown tongue—plus Mrs. Hatcher next door who usually wants to know if she can borrow a cup of gin. But today's high point, however, will be the changing of the kitty litter box so that Foolish can crap in comfort and if things don't change for the better around here soon, I'm going to find myself a fancy man who'll bring some excitement into my life such as taking a run over to Baltimore on a Sunday afternoon."

I nodded. "I wonder what she's got?"

"Who?"

"Senator Ames's daughter."

"Oh."

I am a little over six feet tall but I didn't have to bend much to kiss Sarah who was a little over five-ten and slender with a striking face whose interesting planes and hollows prevented her from being called beautiful. She had wide-set green eyes and long hair that reached nearly to her waist and was a glossy blue-black in color. Injun hair, she called it, and told everybody that she was one-quarter Choctaw although she was actually only one-thirty-second.

"Hmm," I said, giving her a hug, "nice tongue work."

"You didn't hear one damn thing I said, did you?"

"Sure I did," I said. "You're going to find yourself a fancy man to change the kitty litter box."

# 4

The senator's daughter was late, twenty-four minutes late now, and that made whatever there might have been of the teacher in me think of it as tardiness, something I could never abide, so I squirmed on the sidewalk café's hard green metal chair and sorted through my collection of devastating remarks that I knew I'd never use. At least not on her.

She came into sight at 3:25 P.M., more than halfway up the block on the east side of Connecticut Avenue, in the Sheraton-Park's direction, hurrying the way some women hurry when they're inexcusably late: eyes tunneling straight ahead, chin up and chest out, mouth slightly parted in half-framed excuse, and moving with quick small steps that threatened to turn into a trot.

When she was a little more than fifty feet away I could tell that she matched most of the description she had given me. She was taller than average, around five-nine, and blond, and she wore a dark beige pantsuit with a brass-buckled belt that sort of drooped down below her navel. She also wore a brown leather draw purse slung over her left shoulder and carried a green leather attaché case in her right hand.

She hadn't told me that she would be quite so pretty, nor that the sunlight of an almost perfect May afternoon would play tricks on her hair and make it look as though she wore a cap of frothy gold. She had told me that she would be wearing glasses, big round wire-framed ones with purple lenses, but she wasn't. Still, everything else checked so I stopped sorting through my collection of searing remarks and started wondering about her eyes and whether they would turn out to be brown or blue or possibly even green.

I never found out. When she was less than forty feet away there was a sharp, cracking sound, a bit more muffled than a gunshot, and the green leather attaché case disappeared. One moment it was there and the next moment it wasn't and the girl's hair was no longer golden, it was the color of fire, and the flames shot up a foot or so above her head and then lapped back down, drenching her in hot orange.

She danced in place for a moment, a wild, panicky jig step, and then she screamed, but only once, although I now think that I can sometimes still hear it. After the scream, she tried a dash for the street, as though she felt that she could cool off in the stream of traffic, and she actually took a couple of quick, lurching steps before she crumpled to the sidewalk where she died, twisting herself up into what looked like a big charred knot that was just beginning to smoke.

There were some loud shouts and yells and some oh-my-Gods until a paunchy, gray-haired man, a quick-thinking type, stripped off his suit coat and flailed away at the flames that were beginning to die out anyway. The paunchy man beat them all the way out and even after they were all gone he still flailed away with his jacket although there was nothing to beat at but the charred, twisted thing that curled on the sidewalk and smoked a little in the May afternoon.

The paunchy man's efforts slowed, became hesitant, and then stopped. He was crying now. He held up his coat and looked at it. Then he knelt and used it to cover the girl's head and shoulders. He rose, but bent back down to remove his wallet from the coat. He stood there for a moment, crying and staring down at the girl. Then he looked up and in a loud, distinct voice asked, "What the fuck are we all coming to?" When nobody could tell him he turned and pushed his way through the crowd and wandered off down the street.

I rose carefully from my chair at the table of the sidewalk café. I took a dollar bill from my trouser pocket and slipped it underneath my glass of iced tea. I noticed that my hands were shaking so I shoved them into my coat pockets and skirted the edge of the crowd that had bunched up around the dead girl. I don't know why now, but I tried not to hurry as I walked up the block toward the parking lot.

"Whatta you got?" the attendant said as he stuck my parking stub into the time meter.

"A brown Pinto."

"One buck. What happened down there, some kinda accident?"

"I don't know," I said.

I had to wait before I could turn north on Connecticut Avenue because the traffic was jamming itself up as passing gawkers slowed and even stopped their cars to inspect what lay on the sidewalk. When they moved off, they seemed to move off reluctantly. In the distance a police siren began to wail in petulant afterthought.

As I waited for an opening in the traffic I wondered about the attaché case that was supposed to have been packed with tapes and documents and a fifty-page summary that Carolyn Ames, the senator's daughter, had written herself, and I wondered whether she had typed it or had written it by hand, and then I wondered what the something else was that the attaché case had been packed with. Napalm, probably, because nothing else burns so brightly.

After I finally maneuvered the car out into the traffic, I wondered about Carolyn Ames and what had made her 25 minutes late and whether it had been something minor and totally inconsequential like a chatty phone call or an unwound watch or a missed bus.

It wasn't until I had driven the nearly four miles all the way out to Chevy Chase Circle that I could bring myself to think clearly about what would have happened if the senator's daughter hadn't been late. When I did think about it I had to stop the Pinto and slide over and open the right-hand door and throw up all over someone's nicely kept lawn.

# 5

Even if you have lived in Washington for a very long time, you might not know that less than two miles from the White House and down back behind the Shoreham Hotel there are some wild wet woods that have a narrow ribbon of asphalt winding through them that is called Normanstone Drive. The woods look as if they should be chock full of 'possums and rabbits and raccoons and maybe even a deer or two and they well might be although I never saw any and I've been there often enough.

For Normanstone Drive is where Frank Size lived in a big, sprawling three-storied house with a wild roof line that made it look as though its architect couldn't quite resolve his love affair between Romanesque and English Tudor.

The house perched on the side of a steep wooded hill and Size lived there with his wife and five children and three servants, one of them the lean young man with the tight, small mouth and the still eyes who ushered me into Size's study after coming all the way down from the house to unlock the big iron gates. The gates were the only way into the grounds that were surrounded by a nine-foot Cyclone fence that was topped off by three strands of barbed wire. The fence had gone up after someone had once tried to kidnap Size's youngest daughter.

Size's study was tucked away underneath what I took to be a groin vault in a Romanesque wing of the house. Five deeply inset windows looked out into the woods. Except for a manual Remington typewriter on a metal stand, the room's decoration consisted mostly of books. They lined three of the walls from floor to ceiling. They were piled six and seven deep on a long library table. They nearly covered Size's desk that looked a little worn and beat-up, although it may have been an antique. More books, open and closed, lay about on a fine, old Oriental rug. I took a pile of books out of a chair so that I could sit down.

"It's the way I work," Size said more by way of explanation than apology.

"Looks efficient," I said.

I had called Size from a drugstore near Chevy Chase Circle and told him about how the senator's daughter had died. I had told him in detail because he had kept asking questions. He was good at it and after he had asked all he could think of we had agreed that I'd better come see him so that we could decide what I did next.

"You'll have to talk to the cops," he said, leaning back in his chair.

"I know. They'll probably be curious about why I didn't stick around."

"Tell 'em you panicked."

"I'm not sure I'd be lying."

"Well, if you did, you recovered soon enough."

"There's one thing I'd like to figure out."

"What?" he said.

"Whether that napalm was meant for me or for Carolyn Ames."

Size picked up a yellow pencil and opened his mouth so that he could tap its eraser against his teeth. I assumed that it helped him think. "Her," he said finally.

"Why?"

"Because if she knew what it contained and when it had been set to go off, she sure as hell wouldn't have been late, would she?"

"No."

"So we have to assume that she didn't know what was in it."

"And that someone switched cases on her," I said. "I've already got that far."

"Yeah," Size said, "I see what you mean. It must have been meant to kill her though, not you. She had all the facts in her head and maybe a copy of that report or summary that she said she wrote."

"And of the tapes," I said.

Size brightened. "Yeah, the tapes. If there are copies, I'd sure as hell like to get my hands on them."

"So would whoever killed her."

"What about the timing on the thing? It went off at three twenty-five, but she made her appointment with you for three. That bothers me."

"Not as much as it does me," I said. "If they did mean to kill her and not me, then all I can figure is that the timing mechanism must have been out of whack."

"Unless whoever it was wanted to get you both."

"That's crossed my mind."

Size grinned but it didn't mean anything. "You scared?"

"Then or now?"

"Both."

"I was goddamned scared then, but it's worn off. A little."

Size tapped the eraser against his teeth again. "I'm tempted. Sorely tempted to use it in the column." There was a pause while he thought about it some more. "But I won't," he said with more than a touch of regret. "It's breaking news and that's not what I'm after on this one."

"You still want the entire story, wherever it goes?"

"That's right. I want it all. If there're copies of those tapes, I want 'em. I want her written report, or whatever it was, if that still exists—or if it ever did. And I want to find out who killed her."

"Twenty-four hours before the cops do, right?"

Size smiled again, a bit grimly this time. "I just want it first. You think you can do it—or come close?"

I shrugged. "I don't know. I never poked around in a murder before. I'm not even sure I know how, but I've got one advantage, I guess."

"What?"

"I saw it happen."

He nodded. "There's that. You need any help? I can turn a guy loose, if you need him."

"Not yet."

"Okay. How've you been working the story, up until now, I mean?"

"Through that lobbying outfit that supposedly handed over the fifty-thousand-dollar bribe."

"The Bagger Organization," he said. "I've got a file on them at the office. I'll have Mabel send it over to your house by messenger."

"Okay."

"You think you got an angle?"

I nodded. "Maybe. At least I'm going to try it out at ten o'clock tomorrow morning."

"On who?"

"On Wade Maury Bagger."

"The colonel himself."

"Uh-huh."

"He's slippery."

"That's the kind I'm used to."

"All right, when you leave here you'd better go see the cops. There's a guy I know in Homicide, a Lieutenant Sinkfield. I'll call him and tell him you're on your way down. Sinkfield owes me a couple of favors, one of them a big one. He can use it up by being nice to you."

I rose. "Okay," I said, "unless something else exciting happens, I'll see you next payday."

"It's nice of you to keep in touch," he said.

Lieutenant David Sinkfield of the Metropolitan Police Department's Homicide squad was a chain smoker of about my age who said he went through four packs a day which made me feel terribly superior because I'd given it all up two years before.

I'd told Sinkfield and his tape recorder everything that I could about the death of Carolyn Ames. We were sitting there in silence in a grimy room on the third floor of the District Building at 300 Indiana Avenue while Lieutenant Sinkfield probably tried to think of something else he should have asked me and I tried wishing that I didn't want a cigarette.

"What was she," I said, "twenty-three?"

"Twenty-two. Just. Her birthday was last month."

"Got any ideas?"

He looked at me with a pair of blue eyes that held nothing but suspicion. He had a questing thin nose and a pipe smoker's big jaw. His hair had already gone pewter gray and he might have been a little vain about it because he wore it fairly long and brushed just so. His mouth was thin and usually a bit pursed, but when he smiled, which he had done once during the hour I had been there, he managed to smile suspiciously.

"Have I got any ideas about what?" he said.

"About who killed her."

"We've got damn all," he said. "So far we got you' and that's about it."

"That's not much."

He seemed to agree with that and we sat there in some more silence until he stubbed out his cigarette and said, "Somebody got to her apartment."

"Oh?"

"Yeah. They turned it inside out. Probably looking for those tapes you mentioned. It wasn't burglary. She had a portable color TV set. They didn't touch it except to rip off its back and look inside. She had a couple of tape recorders, too. One of them was the kind that you can attach to the phone."

"Where'd she live?" I said.

"Over in Georgetown," he said. "On R Street. Had a hell of a nice little pad—wood-burning fireplace, one of those atrium things, great big kitchen. Her rent must have been about what I make every two weeks."

"Well, I guess she could afford it."

"What does that mean?"

"It means that she's got a rich mama."

"And papa," Sinkfield said. "I understand he's not hurting for money either. I can see my wife handing me a million bucks. Yeah, sure I can. You're not married, huh?"

"Not anymore."

"Stay that way." He seemed to brood about his own domestic life for a moment before he said, "Guess what Carolyn Ames's mother gave her for her twenty-first birthday?"

"A million bucks," I said

Sinkfield seemed a trifle miffed that I knew. "You've really been snooping around, haven't you?"

"As I said, I'm on the story."

"Yeah, well, the million was in trust. She had to live off the income until her thirtieth birthday—which she isn't going to have. How much do you figure that'd be a year?"

"I don't know. Sixty thousand at least, the way interest rates are now. Maybe even seventy-five."

"That'd be tough, wouldn't it? Trying to make it on sixty thousand a year." He paused. "And single, at that."

"It's a problem I'd like to fool around with."

Sinkfield frowned. "Old Frank Size must be paying you pretty good. He's making plenty."

"He's not paying me anywhere near sixty thousand."

"Half?"

"Not even half."

Sinkfield stopped frowning. My news made him feel better. He must have decided that he could even afford to be a little generous, now that I was down around his own income bracket because he said, "We did find one funny thing in her apartment."

"What?"

"A will. You don't run across many twenty-two-year-olds with a will made out. At twenty-two you think you're going to live forever—plus a couple of weeks."

"How many twenty-two-year-olds have you run across who've got a million-dollar trust fund to worry about?"

"Not many," he admitted. "Not any, in fact."

"When did she make it out?" I said

He nodded. "Yeah, there might be a little something in that. She made it out three weeks ago."

"Who'd she leave it to?"

"The ex-senator. Dear old dad."

"So you've got a suspect after all."

"Why in the hell don't you just go on home," Sinkfield said.

# 6

As arguments went I would have to give it a six on the Lucas Scale for measuring the intensity of domestic squabbles. Possibly a seven.

It had started the night before when I came home and made the mistake of telling Sarah about the interesting thing that had nearly happened to me that afternoon up on Connecticut Avenue.

She had been alarmed at first, so alarmed that she had insisted that we go to bed right away, at least for a while, so that she could comfort me in the way that she knew best. So we had gone to bed for three-quarters of an hour and comforted each other in splendidly erotic fashion.

Then the fight began. It raged through the martinis and Walter Cronkite, reached its roaring peak at dinner (braised beef ribs, Boston lettuce salad, and buttered carrots), and then settled down into cold, occasional sniping for the rest of the evening. By breakfast (hard fried eggs, underdone bacon, soggy toast) we had cut off all lines of communication except for a rattled newspaper or a slammed-down cup.

"All right," I said finally, "I'm sorry I almost got killed. I apologize."

"Always the wiseass," she said, staring out into her garden.

Martin Rutherford Hill, noticing that we were once again speaking, joined in the conversation with, "Harath sone plock." Or maybe he said, "Plog."

"You could at least have called me and told me you were all right."

I was tempted, but for only a moment, to go into the logic of that. "I'm sorry," I said. "I'll remember next time."

"What do you mean next time? Is this what that job with Frank Size is going to be? When you took it, you said it would let you work at home. You've been home only two days in the past three weeks. The rest of the time you've either been down in Georgia or out at the Pentagon with that crazy major."

The crazy major was Carl Sommers, a U.S. Army historian, who was making his doctoral thesis—unbeknownst to the army—a comparative study of GI black-market operations in the European theater during World War II with those that had gone on when the war in Vietnam was at its peak. He was coming up with some extremely juicy stuff. When he completed his thesis, he planned to turn it into a book, retire from the army, and join me on the faculty of Paramount U. Sarah thought he was crazy because he walked ten miles to and from work every day, ate nothing but lean meat and cottage cheese laced with a little wheat germ, and on Saturday nights wore a red wig and hung out in Georgetown trying to pick up anything below sixteen years of age. Major Sommers could make it only with fourteen- or fifteen-year-old girls and he said that it worried him a lot, but not enough to do anything about it. The major was thirty-six.

I smiled at Sarah reassuringly, I hoped, and said, "I've got what I needed at the Pentagon. I'll be home a lot more."

"I'm trying not to sound like some nagging dumb broad," she said, "but when you told me that you almost got yourself killed, it worried me at first. It worried me terribly because I care terribly about what happens to you. Then it made me angry. I can't help it. It just made me mad as hell."

"Okay," I said. "Let's forget it."

She looked at me with hard, level gaze. "You really like it, don't you?"

"What?"

"Digging through the muck. The slimier it is, the better you like it. The more depraved and twisted and warped the people are, the more fascinated you become. And you're good at it, too. That's what bothers me sometimes."

"I'm just a historian," I said.

She nodded. "I think I know where you'd really like to work."

"Where?"

"In hell. You'd be happy as mud as the devil's historian."

Headquarters for the lobbying outfit that called itself the Bagger Organization, Inc., was a fairly old town house on Q Street just west of Connecticut Avenue, a couple of doors or so down from the Krishna kids and a few doors up from a quartet of doctors who were making a wad of money by administering to the shakes of the city's more affluent alcoholics.

The building was a narrow, three-story, red brick structure with a basement and something of a history, but not enough of one to inflate its value or to bother the District of Columbia Historical Society should it be announced that it was to be torn down and turned into a parking lot. It seemed that President Harding had once lodged his mistress there for a brief time until he could find her more discreet quarters a bit farther out at 2311 Connecticut Avenue.

I paid off the cab, entered the building's tiny foyer, pushed a black button that was labeled "RING," and then waited for something to happen. In a moment a voice with iron vocal cords said, "Yes," and I said, "Decatur Lucas."

"Right," the voice said and a second later a buzzer sounded. There was no knob on the brown metal door so I just gave it a push. When nothing happened, I rang the bell again and the iron voice said, "Push hard." I pushed hard and the door swung easily open as if it were counterweighted. I rapped it with a knuckle just to see whether it was solid steel. It was.

I entered a wide hall that was paneled with old, carefully polished light oak. On the right a flight of stairs curved up toward the second story. On the left, a young, pretty girl sat behind a brown metal receptionist's desk.

"Mr. Lucas?" she said, smiling brightly.

"Yes."

"Go right through that door into Mr. Cutter's office."

The door that she indicated was behind her and to the left. I found myself in the large office of a short man who was striding across the room to meet me. He had his hand stuck out.

"I'm Johnny Cutter, Mr. Lucas," he said. I shook his hand and it turned out to be thick and wide and hard. "Mr. Cutter," I said.

"Sit down, won't you," he said. "The colonel will be off the phone in a moment and if you don't mind, I'll just go ahead and sign some letters."

I told him I didn't mind. I sat down in a leather chair and Cutter went behind his carved desk where he seemed to crouch like a hard, muscular toad who'd been assigned to guard the sleeping prince. I watched him sign his letters. He did it carefully, even painstakingly, and he smiled a little as if he still liked the look of his name.

I glanced around the room. Despite the ornate mahogany desk, the clubby leather furniture, the thick Oriental rugs, and the fabric-covered walls, Cutter's office offered all the warmth and coziness of an infantry-company orderly room, which wasn't particularly surprising since Cutter had spent twenty years in the army, the last ten of them as a sergeant major.

When Cutter finished signing the letters he looked up at me and blinked twice slowly, the way a toad would blink. Then he rose and strode over to the door. He seemed to stride everywhere he went. He gave the door two sharp raps and I wondered in how many places in how many countries he had knocked just like that to bring Colonel Wade Maury Bagger tidings of either fortune or disaster or just the news that it was five o'clock and time to go home.

When a voice said, "Come," Cutter opened the door and barked, "Mr. Lucas is here." He had a harsh, deep voice packed with authority and intimidation, the kind of a voice that collection agencies dream about.

Cutter was built like an upside-down triangle. He stood against the door with his shoulders back as though they were nailed to the wood. A nod of his head that was almost a jerk indicated that I should go in.

The room that I entered was elegant, but not as elegant as the man who stood behind the Persian walnut desk, his hand out, a glistening smile on his face. He was Colonel Wade Maury Bagger (USA-Ret.)

and I had spent two days down in a place called Ocilla, Georgia, finding out what I could about him. They remembered Wade Maury in Ocilla, all right, although he hadn't been back home since he left to join the army in 1942. He came from good stock though, at least on his mama's side. She could trace her ancestry to back before the Revolutionary War, back to the Wades of Virginia. The Maurys, of course, had supplied the South with two generals during the War Between the States and the folks down at Ocilla reckoned that Colonel Bagger could claim direct kin with both of them. As for the Baggers, well, the least said about them the better, but it had been Lyon Bagger who must have sweet-talked the pretty little schoolteacher from Macon into the back seat of his Moon touring car on a warm spring night back in 1922 and even married her three months later only to disappear forever, probably up north, after just two weeks of it. The only legacy that his father had left Wade Maury Bagger was a big-boned, six-foot-three-inch frame, a pair of map green eyes, a soft deep southern baritone, and the flashing, white, shit-eating grin that the folks down at Ocilla said that all the Baggers had.

After we shook hands and said hello Wade Maury Bagger kept standing until he made sure that I was seated and comfortable. After that he sat down in a high-backed leather chair, the same model that is much favored by Supreme Court justices, cocked his feet up on the desk and let me admire the burnished gleam on the soft, supple leather of his black loafers that I thought I could match if I wanted to spend eighty-five dollars, which I didn't. My feet and those of Cutter, who was sitting next to me, rested on a thick, tobacco-brown carpet. We sat in deep, soft chairs of pale leather. There was a matching couch against the wall. In front of the couch was a long, low table of inlaid wood. It had gracefully curving legs and looked very old and very expensive. On the walnut paneled walls hung four paintings that at first glance seemed to be representative of the better efforts of some of the lesser French impressionists. On second glance, they turned out to be exactly that and I later learned that the Bagger Organization had them insured for $95,000.

Bagger smiled at me again and then turned his head so that he could look out through a window at the one-way traffic on Q Street. Construction of the new subway jammed the traffic up and made some of the drivers lean on their horns, but Bagger couldn't hear them in his soundproof office any more than he could hear thunder, low-flying planes, or for that matter, the end of the world.

Still looking at the traffic Bagger said, "I hope Mr. Size is keeping well."

"He is," I said.

"I've asked Mr. Cutter to sit in with us, if you have no objections."

I said that I had none.

Bagger turned his head so that he could look at me once more. It was quite a head, long and narrow with thick, wavy hair, white as old bones. His green eyes were set underneath heavy black brows. He had a good straight nose and beneath it was a carefully tended tar-black moustache. His strong chin even had a nice little cleft in it. You wouldn't want to call it a dimple. It was a proud face, even haughty, the kind that could have worn a monocle and no one would have dared say a word.

"You're a new addition to Mr. Size's staff, aren't you?" Bagger said.

"Yes."

"I thought I knew most of them from when they descended upon us like locusts last Christmas. Wouldn't you say locusts, Johnny?"

"Yeah," Cutter said, "locusts."

"What did you wish to see me about, Mr. Lucas?"

"The Anacostia Corporation, for one thing."

"And the other?"

"There are really a couple of others, maybe even more than a couple."

"And they're what?"

"They're the president of the Anacostia Corporation, Frank Highsmith, and Senator Ames."

"It was a shocking thing about the senator's daughter, wasn't it?" Bagger said, sounding as if he meant it. "I've been told that he's taking it hard. Very hard."

"He's having a bad year," I said. "But let's talk about Frank Highsmith and his Anacostia Corporation first."

"All right," Bagger said. "Let's."

"He's had an amazing career, hasn't he?"

Bagger nodded. "Amazing is an accurate description. I think we have a brochure around here that gives a brief biography of him, if that would be of any help."

"I've read it. It wouldn't. I used to buy ice cream cones from him in Denver when I was a kid. That was back in 1949 when he was first starting out with a couple of trucks that he and his wife drove. By fifty-three he had forty ice cream trucks and the Teamsters got interested. He bribed one of them to lay off, got caught, and went to jail down in Florida."

"None of this is exactly news, Mr. Lucas," Bagger said. "Mr. Highsmith paid for his mistake."

"Sure," I said. "His wife ran the ice cream trucks until he got out of jail. Then he sold the business and that gave him about a hundred thousand dollars in cash. He used the money to buy stock in a Denver aluminum siding company called Denside, Inc. He somehow got control of it—nobody's quite sure how— and then borrowed every dime he could and bought into a Chicago cosmetic company called Mirofair which had once done around four million dollars' worth of business a year. When Highsmith bought in, its net worth was down around $9,524—if my memory's right."

"I'd say you have a hell of a good memory," Cutter said.

"Thanks. Well, after that Highsmith merged with a string of other small companies, all of them losers. In sixty-one he made his big jump. He found himself a real white elephant, the Boisdarc Pottery Company of Tulsa which had lost more than a million dollars in 1960 and sixty-one and whose liabilities were up around seven million dollars. As I said, a real loser."

"Losers can also be winners, Mr. Lucas," Bagger said

"Sure they can and by now your client had strung together a mini-conglomerate of them. He called his string the Anacostia Corporation. I don't know why. Maybe he just liked the name. He went looking for a profit-making company to merge with. He had a lot to offer—thanks to the tax-loss carry forward provisions. If a profit-making company merges with a big loser, it can cut its taxes enormously, but you know that, don't you?"

"It has come to our attention," Bagger said in a dry tone.

"Well, your client Highsmith looked around and found just the thing—the South Plains Company of Dallas. South Plains had just got through selling off its major assets, a couple of oil refineries, and it was fat. It had liquid assets of around forty-five million— nearly half of it in cash. It was making a nice yearly profit. So Highsmith made a deal with its chairman and its principal directors. He offered to buy their stock at a big premium. It was going for twenty-two dollars a share then. He offered them thirty-one. All they'd have to do is resign and let themselves be replaced by Highsmith and some of his buddies. The deal was made. Highsmith planned to borrow the money from one of his pet Boston banks. When the merger took effect, the new company would assume the indebtedness of the loan from the bank. In other words, South Plains would pay for its own take-over."

"It's done all the time," Cutter said.

"Sure it is," I said. "But this time some South Plains stockholders got wind of it and set up a squawk. That was bad. So Highsmith came looking for help. He came to you. He needed something to soothe the stockholders until he could get to those who were setting up the squawk. What would be better than a United States senator getting up on the floor of the Senate and delivering a speech that praised the approaching merger?"

I paused. It had been a long recital. No one said anything. Bagger gazed at me, his lips curved in a slight smile. Cutter blinked at me a couple of times.

"Now comes my question," I said.

"Yes," Bagger said.

"What did you and Cutter here do with the two hundred thousand in cash and the two sacks of gold bars that you stole from the salt mines in Merkers, Germany, back in April of 1945?"

# 7

It was the questioning technique that I had developed over the years. I would drone along either reciting old facts or asking tired questions for which they had ready answers. Then I would throw in the zinger and watch what happened. Sometimes they blustered. Sometimes they fell apart like wet Kleenex. And sometimes they thought you were bluffing and decided to call. That's what Bagger did.

Nothing in his face changed. If he had been wearing that monocle, it would have stayed in place. Next to me I could feel Cutter grow very still. I glanced at him and he looked like a toad ready to pounce. A mean toad. At a nod from the colonel he might have broken my arm. Probably the right one.

But the colonel didn't nod. He smiled instead. It was a slight smile, just enough to let me know that he appreciated my little joke although he didn't feel that it was in the best of taste.

"Something tells me, Mr. Lucas," he said, "that you've been extremely busy for quite some time."

"About three weeks," I said

"Merkers," he said, the way people say a name when they're trying to be helpful, but can't quite dredge it up from memory.

"Germany," I said. "April fourth, 1945. You were a first lieutenant. Cutter was a buck sergeant. The records show that you were with a special mobilized intelligence and reconnaissance outfit of platoon strength that was out in front of your division. The Ninth. You were in a jeep. Right so far?"

Bagger looked at Cutter who shrugged. "We were out in front," Cutter said. "I remember that. I don't remember any place called Merkers."

"It's not on most maps," I said. "It's too small. But according to testimony that was taken later from three German civilians an army jeep carrying two American soldiers arrived in Merkers at thirteen hundred hours and the soldiers asked directions. The Germans didn't speak English; the soldiers didn't speak German. The Germans thought you wanted the salt mines because that's all there was there. This is from the CID report. The CID never did find out who those two American soldiers were. I did."

"Really?" Bagger said. "How?"

"By cross-checking rumor with hunch. The rumor was that you and Cutter made a lot of money out of the black market in Germany and later in Korea. Just rumor though. But by digging out the records of the special mobilized I and R platoon, I can almost pinpoint you and Cutter as being in Merkers at one P.M. on April fourth, 1945. It had to be you. Nobody else was in a jeep and nobody else was that far out in front of the Ninth Division."

"I see," Bagger said.

"You want the rest of it?" I said.

The colonel shrugged. "Why not?"

"Only one person had stayed on to guard the salt

mines. He was an old man. A German civilian. His name was Wilhelm Vesser. He was sixty-two. He also ran the fifteen-man double-decker elevator that went down into the mines, twenty-one hundred feet down. That's where they kept it."

"Kept what?" Cutter said.

I had memorized it. "That's where they kept four thousand cloth sacks stamped with the Reichsbank's name. Each sack contained twenty-five pounds of gold cast into small bars. In addition to that there were sealed cases of foreign currency. They contained twelve million American dollars, one million French francs, a hundred and ten thousand English pounds, and four million Norwegian crowns. You know how the Germans kept records."

Neither Bagger nor Cutter said anything. They just looked at me. I gave them the rest of what I had. "The two American soldiers took a hundred thousand dollars and two sacks of gold each. That was about all they could comfortably carry. Maybe the old man helped them. At least that's what was missing when it was finally checked out. The elevator started up. It creaked. Maybe it was halfway up when it happened. Maybe only a third. But one of the soldiers took a forty-five automatic out of its holster, put it up against the old man's back, and nearly blew him in two. They later dug the slugs out of the elevator. The old man was shot twice."

That was it. That was all that the crazy major and I had been able to put together. It was part hunch, part conjecture, and very little fact. Whether it was true depended on what Bagger said next.

He looked at me for what seemed to be a long time before he said, "What do you want, Lucas?"

"The facts about Senator Ames."

"What facts?"

"What have you got on him?"

"What makes you think we have anything on him?"

"You'd have to," I said. "Why else would a man get up on the floor of the Senate and proceed to wreck his career? Not for fifty thousand dollars. He didn't need it. He's worth at least a million. So he must have been blackmailed into doing it. It doesn't make sense any other way."

Bagger smiled again. "That's because you're not in my business," he said.

"What business? The buying and selling of U.S. senators?"

"Let me tell you a little story," he said. "It's not one you can use because it could never be proved. And it doesn't really matter much if you could, because the man's dead." He looked at Cutter. "I'm going to tell him about Judge Austin," he said.

Cutter nodded. "Yeah, that's a good one."

Bagger leaned back in his chair, locked his hands behind his head, and stared at the ceiling. "You can take this for what it's worth," he said, "but let's say that some friends of ours were once given the assignment of corrupting a federal circuit court of appeals judge. Judge Theodore Austin. Ever hear of him?"

"I think so," I said.

"Well, he had quite an education, did Judge Austin. He had bachelor and master degrees from Rutgers and a bachelor of divinity degree from Baylor University in Waco where he remained for two years teaching Sanskrit, Greek, Latin, and classical Hebrew. After that, he went to Northwestern and spent a year studying there. Then to the University of Bonn where he studied two more years. After all that study he became an ordained Baptist minister and watched over the flock of a small church in Grove City, Pennsylvania. But his intellectual curiosity still wasn't satisfied so he began the study of law at the University of Pennsylvania and when he got his degree, he started practicing in Philadelphia. He got interested in politics and was elected to the Pennsylvania State Senate. A few years later Harry Truman made him U.S. District Attorney for Pennsylvania and when an opening occurred on the U.S. Court of Appeals, Third Circuit, well, the job went to our friend the Sanskrit scholar. He retired several years ago with full honors and benefits, his reputation unsullied. A tough man to corrupt, wouldn't you say?"

"I'd say impossible."

"That's what our friends thought, but they also thought that they'd try anyhow—in a most subtle manner, you understand. So they made an appointment with Austin and began what they hoped was their oblique approach. The judge cut them off after five minutes. Guess what he said?"

"I have no idea."

Bagger smiled. "He said, 'Just how much money are we talking about, gentlemen?'" Bagger laughed. "'Just how much money are we talking about, gentlemen?'" he said again as if to make sure that I had got it. "After that our friends could buy the judge for twenty-five thousand dollars a decision and sell him for fifty. They were sorry to see him retire."

"That's a hard story to believe," I said.

"Why?" he said. "Because 'The Place of justice is an hallowed place, and therefore not only the bench, but something, something ought to be preserved without scandal and corruption.' That's a quote, or part of one."

"It's the introduction to the canons of judicial ethics of the American Bar Association," I said. "But what's your point?"

"Christ, it's obvious," Cutter said. "I never even finished the ninth grade and it's obvious to me. The point is that nobody ever asked the judge before whether he'd like to be corrupted."

"Exactly," Bagger said.

"You mean nobody ever tried to corrupt Senator Ames before?"

Bagger didn't answer. Instead he rose and walked over to the window and looked out to see how the Q Street traffic was doing. After a moment he turned and looked at me. "That fanciful tale you told earlier. About—uh—Merkers, Germany, wasn't it?"

"That's right," I said. "Merkers."

"There's nothing to it, of course."

"No?"

"No. But you're using it to trade with, aren't you?"

"Maybe," I said.

"If Frank Size printed it, he could never prove it."

"He could print it and let the army worry about proving it," I said. "There's no statute of limitations on murder. They could dig up the same old records I dug up. They could turn the army CID loose in Germany. They haven't got much to do there anyhow. They might dig up some witnesses. I didn't even try. I haven't got much, but it's enough for Size to go on. He's never worried too much about facts. You could sue him, of course. But you'd have to get in line."

"What do you want, Lucas?" Cutter said.

"You already asked me that," I said. "I want the real story on Ames."

Cutter nodded. "And if we give it to you, you'll lay off the other—all that crap about Germany."

"I might," I said. "It depends on how truthful I think you're being."

"Tell him," Cutter said.

"He's bluffing, Johnny," Bagger said.

"Yeah, well, I don't want those CID guys digging around in my record. That's all bullshit about Merkers, or wherever it was, but there're a couple of other things they might stumble over." He grinned at me. It was a tight, hard grin. "None of us are perfect," he said.

"I bet."

"All right, Mr. Lucas," Bagger said, easing himself down into his chair. "I'll tell you about Senator Ames, but I'm afraid that you're going to be in for a disappointment."

"I'll try to live with it."

Bagger leaned back in his chair and made his fingers form a steeple under his chin. He looked a little like I hoped the president of Paramount U would look. "There was no fifty-thousand-dollar bribe," he said.

"I said I wanted the truth."

"You'll get it, if you'll just listen," Cutter said.

"It's true that we had withdrawn fifty thousand from the bank to buy ourselves a tame senator," Bagger said. "But we would not be so naïve as to hand this same sum of money over to our—oh, I think I'll call him our corruptee."

"That's a good name," I said.

"If he had insisted on cash, we would have furnished it to him in untraceable bills. Or we could have arranged a bank loan for him. An unsecured bank loan, of course, that he could have defaulted on after a couple of years of paying interest. With no harm to his credit rating, I might add. Or we could have arranged for a fifty-thousand-dollar contribution to his favorite charity—or to his campaign fund. Unless one is terribly green in this business, well—you know what I mean."

"I think so," I said. "That still doesn't explain the two thousand dollars in hundred-dollar bills that was traced from your account to his account. When Size broke the story, you claimed that it was a personal loan. Nobody believed you, of course. They thought the senator had used the two thousand to top off his personal bank account and then squirreled the rest of the fifty thousand away in a safety-deposit box or under his mattress."

Bagger sighed. It was a long, patient sigh. "It *was* a personal loan," he said. "We met in his office on a Saturday morning. He had a speaking engagement in Los Angeles that evening. He discovered he'd forgotten his wallet and his airline ticket—that was after he'd agreed to deliver the speech for us. At least he said he'd forgotten them. He asked if we had any spare cash at the office—enough to pay for his ticket and his expenses. I had the fifty thousand in cash with me so I lent him two thousand."

"Why didn't he go home and get his ticket and his billfold?" I said.

"You know where he lived then?"

"In Maryland on the Chesapeake Bay."

"His flight was from Dulles. He would have had to go all the way out to Maryland and then over to Virginia to catch the plane. He didn't have the time."

"But he didn't spend the two thousand," I said. "He put it in his bank account."

"He didn't make the speech out in California either," Cutter said. "He canceled out at the last moment."

I found myself shaking my head. "The man sounds like a fool," I said.

"Or as though he wanted to get caught," Bagger said.

"That's a possibility," I said, "but not much of one. Okay. There're a hundred United States senators. Why'd you pick him?"

"We didn't," Bagger said. "Without mentioning names there are at least four U.S. senators who would turn handsprings for fifty thousand dollars. At least one of them is in the Senate for the money he can make and so far he's made a hell of a lot of it. We were planning to go to one of them—we weren't quite sure which one—when we heard about Senator Ames."

"What did you hear about him?"

"That he was—uh, shall we say ripe?"

"Who'd you hear it from?"

"From one of our employees whose assignment was the Senate."

"Where'd he hear it?"

Cutter glanced at Bagger. Both of them smiled. "I'd say *she* heard it in bed, wouldn't you, Johnny?"

"Flat on her back," Cutter said.

"Is this the blond that he's shacked up with now?"

"The very same," Bagger said.

"What's her name?"

"Connie Mizelle."

"How long has she been working for you?"

"Well, she's not working for us any longer," Bagger said.

"Did you fire her?"

Cutter snorted. "She quit before we could."

"How long did she work for you?"

"How long, Johnny?" the colonel said. "A year?"

"About that."

"What do you know about her?"

Colonel Bagger shrugged. "She was from California. She went to high school in Los Angeles. Hollywood High, I think. She won a scholarship to Mills in Oakland. After college she worked up and down the coast. She was with a small ad agency in Los Angeles, then a top-forty radio station in Burbank, and after that she worked for a lobbyist in Sacramento. That's why we hired her, because she had some legislative experience."

"How'd she get to Washington?"

"She was doing publicity for a self-styled artists'

manager who had a rock group. He pushed them too hard and too soon and they bombed out here in the DAR hall with four-fifths of the seats vacant. She was stranded. So she came looking for a job. We hired her."

"How old is she?"

"What is she, Johnny—twenty-five, twenty-six?"

"Twenty-seven," Cutter said.

"And she's with the senator now?"

"Yeah," Cutter said. "They got themselves a little love nest in the Watergate."

"How'd she get him to do it?" I said.

"Make the speech, you mean?" Bagger said.

I nodded.

"She told us that she simply asked him to do it. They were pretty good—uh—friends by then. So when she asked him to do it, he agreed. She said that when she told him that there'd be fifty thousand dollars for him in it, he'd said no, that he didn't want it."

"And you believed her?"

"Wouldn't you—if you could save fifty thousand?"

"When did she tell you that he didn't want the money?"

"On our way over to his office."

"After you'd already taken the money out of the bank?"

"We'd taken the money out of the bank on Friday. It was the money we were going to use—not the money we were actually going to give him. But sometimes they like to look at it. Even touch it. We figured the senator might be one of those."

"But he wasn't," I said.

"No," Bagger said. "He wasn't."

"How long has Connie Mizelle been shacked up with him?"

"How long, Johnny?" Bagger said.

Cutter seemed to think about it for a moment. "Must be five or six months now. Ever since he resigned."

"What about the senator's wife?"

"What about her?" Bagger said. "That's not our worry. If you want to know about Ames's wife, why don't you ask her? You might want to wait until after her daughter's funeral. But I don't know. Maybe you wouldn't."

"Bereaved parents are my speciality," I said.

The colonel looked at his watch. "Is there anything else?" he said. "If not—" He didn't finish the sentence.

"Not right now," I said. "There might be something later."

Cutter rose from his chair beside me. He clapped a hand on my left shoulder. I looked up at him. "You know something?" he said.

"What?"

"All that stuff about Merkers or wherever it was in Germany. I wouldn't push that too far if I was you, pal." His fingers dug into my shoulder and I fought back a yell or maybe even a scream. "You know what I mean?" He gave my shoulder an extra squeeze and again the pain shot through my arm.

"I wouldn't do that again if I were you," I said.

"You wouldn't?" Cutter said.

"No," I said. "Somebody might get hurt."

"That's right," he said, "somebody might."

# 8

The next morning at ten-fifteen I stood on the steps of St. Margaret's Episcopal Church at 1800 Connecticut Avenue and helped Lt. David Sinkfield of Homicide count the mourners as they filed in for the funeral of the senator's daughter, Carolyn Ames. The services were being held eight blocks south of where she had died and seventy-two persons attended not counting myself, Lieutenant Sinkfield, his partner, Jack Proctor, and a man who looked like a prosperous banker but who was actually a prosperous private investigator, Arthur Dain.

I watched while Sinkfield buttonholed him. It was a pleasure to watch the way Sinkfield worked.

"Hello, there, Mr. Dain," he said, moving casually so that the man would have to step to one side out of the way. "Remember me, Dave Sinkfield?"

I could almost see Dain's mind working. "Yes, how are you, Lieutenant?"

"Fine. Just fine. This is my partner, Jack Proctor."

Dain nodded at him. Proctor said hi-yuh and went back to counting the mourners.

"Girl had a lot of friends, didn't she?" Sinkfield said.

"It would seem that way."

"You a friend of hers, Mr. Dain?"

"Not exactly."

"Then you must be working."

"After a fashion."

"Must be a pretty important client to get a busy man like you out of his office."

"All my clients are important to me."

Sinkfield nodded. "I bet they appreciate that. You know, we've been working on this case for only a couple of days now, but one thing we've found is that the Ames girl had a lot of friends."

"Did she?"

"Oh, yeah. A lot of 'em. I'm surprised that more aren't turning up for her funeral, but you know something?"

"What?"

"I don't think that people like to go to funerals anymore. Not the way they used to anyhow."

"I suppose not," Dain said. He was about forty-five, I thought, and getting tubby. He held his apple chin up whenever he thought of it to keep the second one from showing too much. He had smart, cool green eyes that looked out from behind wire-framed bifocals. His mouth was thin and wide and the upper lip overshot the bottom one and made him look either impatient or mean, I wasn't sure which. His nose was only a nose and his hair wasn't getting any thicker, but as a concession to this decade and the last he wore fuzzy gray sideburns. The rest of him was strictly 1955 from the button-down white shirt with its neat sober tie to the dark blue suit and the black wing-tipped oxfords. Or maybe that was what he always wore to funerals.

"We go to a lot of funerals, Proctor and me," Lt. Sinkfield was saying. "You know, it's kind of our job to go, us being in Homicide and all. We go and sort of check out who turns up and who doesn't. But, hell, I don't have to tell you, Mr. Dain. You're in the business, kind of."

"Yes," Dain said, moving a little as if trying to edge away.

Sinkfield blocked him again, this time with a casual move of the shoulder. "For example," Sinkfield said, "here we are at the Ames girl's funeral and you turn up. That's interesting. Is that why you're here, Mr. Dain, looking to see who turns up and who doesn't?"

"I'm merely representing my client," Dain said.

"And I don't suppose you're gonna tell me who your client is?"

"I don't think that's necessary."

"Mind if I guess?"

Dain sighed. "No, I don't mind."

"Well, I figure since it's you who's out on the job the client's gotta be pretty goddamned important or else you'd have sent one of those hillbillies of yours all dressed up in his first coat and pants that ever matched. But since you're here yourself the client's gotta have money—a whole lot of money—so I'd say that your client is the senator's wife, Mrs. Ames, on account of she's got ziggety-three million bucks."

"You've talked to Mrs. Ames," Dain said.

"She your client?"

"Yes. She's my client."

"Well, yes, we have talked to her," Sinkfield said. "Right after her daughter got killed. She didn't mention anything about you though. She hire you to look into her daughter's death?"

"You know that's privileged information, Lieutenant."

"I don't know any such thing of the kind. It might be privileged if you're digging up stuff so she can get a divorce. That'd be privileged all right. Is that what you're doing, working up a divorce case?"

"Believe what you like."

Sinkfield smiled. It was his suspicious smile and as far as I knew it was the only one he had. "Okay, Mr. Dain. It's been nice talking to you."

"Yes," Dain said and moved on into the church. Sinkfield turned to me. "You eavesdrop pretty good, don't you?"

"I try."

"You get all that?"

"I think so."

"He's doing pretty good for an ex-accountant."

"I thought he used to be with the CIA."

"He started out with the FBI then switched to the CIA. You know what he's got now?"

"Dain Security Services, Inc.," I said.

"He's got two hundred guys working for him," Sinkfield said, "and most of 'em ran out of bus fare on their way up to Detroit from South Carolina. He gives 'em a uniform and for two-bucks-twenty an hour they wander down long stretches of ten-foot-high steel fence at night with a Dain Security patch on their arm and a loaded thirty-eight on their hip. He charges four-fifty an hour for their services. Turns a nice little profit, wouldn't you say?"

"Not bad," I said.

"Know how he got started?"

"No."

"It was just five years ago. He was forty then and still with the CIA and not going anywhere. A couple of his superiors out there along with a couple of guys that he used to work for at the FBI got together and took him to lunch. The Jockey Club. Hell, I don't know where it was. Maybe it was a whole series of lunches."

"It doesn't matter," I said.

"Yeah. Well, anyway, they told him that they happened to know that there were some awfully prosperous people and corporations and organizations around who, through no fault of their own, you understand, sometimes ran up against problems that needed a real skilled investigator, the kind that was halfway honest and who wouldn't upset 'em with his grammar or bother 'em with his manners."

Sinkfield paused to light a cigarette from the butt of the one that he was already smoking. "They told Dain that these people and outfits would have delicate problems that needed a delicate touch, problems so delicate, in fact, that the ordinary law shouldn't even be bothered with 'em. They told him that these people even had problems right now and it sure was a pity that there wasn't somebody in town that these guys could recommend. But if Dain set up his own firm, then there would be, and these guys could almost guarantee him a steady flow of clients with real delicate problems. And if Dain was short on capital, well, hell, these guys that he used to work for would look at it as a privilege if he'd let them invest a few thousand each just to get things off the ground."

"I've heard he's pretty good," I said.

"He ain't bad," Sinkfield said. "He ain't bad and he's getting awful rich. Those hillbilly guards of his will shoot at anything that moves as long as it's black. They give us a lot of business."

Sinkfield's partner, Jack Proctor, touched his arm. "Mrs. Ames is just pulling up," he said.

We turned and watched a long, black Cadillac slide into place in front of the church steps. A young, lithe man with an olive complexion and a dark gray suit that wasn't quite a uniform got out from behind the wheel and hurried around to open the rear door.

The woman who emerged from the car was wearing black and when the young man offered her his arm she shook her head no. She also wore a small black veil. She walked up the steps, looking neither left nor right. She held her head high. Through the veil I could see a strong-boned, handsome face that once might have been extremely pretty. I guessed her age at around forty-three or forty-four, although she didn't look it.

"Where's the senator?" I said.

"Probably in that one," Sinkfield said, nodding at another Cadillac that had pulled up behind the one that had brought Mrs. Ames. The senator got out first. He glanced around as if he weren't quite sure where he was or what he was doing there. I thought that he looked the way senators are supposed to look—even corrupt ones. He was tall and fit-looking and strong-faced with a ledge of a chin. I couldn't see his eyes behind a pair of dark glasses, but I knew that they were a mellow brown that some called sad and some called warm. His hair was longer than it had been when I had last seen him, which had been on television, and its brown waves seemed to have more gray in them. A lot more.

He paused for a moment and then looked down as if trying to remember something that he was supposed to do. He turned back toward the car and held out his hand, his left one. He helped her out of the car and I remember wondering what the strange hissing was until I realized that it was my own sharp intake of breath. It was the sound that I made the first time I ever saw Connie Mizelle.

It probably would be sufficient to say that she was blond and beautiful and brown-eyed and let it go at that. It would give you an idea of how she looked.

Just as you would have an idea of what they looked like if somebody were to tell you that the Taj Mahal is a pretty white building and that the Mona Lisa is a nice painting of a woman with a funny kind of a smile.

The thing about Connie Mizelle, though, was that she had no flaws. Not one. Not as far as her looks went. That's not to say that her features were perfectly regular. If they were, she wouldn't have been beautiful. Now that I think of it her forehead might have been a little high. Her nose may have been a shade too long and her mouth too generous. Her eyes, with some kind of fire in the bottom of them, were probably too large and too velvety brown. And some might have argued that her legs were too long and slim and her hips too round and her breasts too proud. But put all these mistakes together and it added up to a throbbing sexual beauty that bordered on walking lasciviousness. To top it all off, she looked smart. Maybe too smart.

"Close your mouth," Sinkfield said, "unless you want to chew flies."

"I'm not hungry. I'm in love."

"First time you've seen her, huh?"

"Right."

"First time I saw her I had to take off from work and go home and throw a fuck into the old lady. In the middle of the afternoon, for Christ's sake."

"I'd say you're normal."

"Huh," Sinkfield said. "You haven't seen my wife."

Connie Mizelle nodded at Sinkfield as she and the senator went past us into the church. The senator stared straight ahead. He looked as if he might have been in mild shock or dead drunk. They both produce the same glassy, unseeing gaze and slow, too careful walk.

Sinkfield didn't nod back at Connie Mizelle. Instead, he stared at her with what can only be described as honest lust. He shook his head after she was inside. "I shouldn't be thinking things like that," he said. "Not in church at a funeral."

"As I said, you're normal."

"I think I'm oversexed," he said. "You know it's tough being that way and married to what I'm married to. You know what she looks like, my wife?"

"What?"

"Like a middle-aged boy." He shook his head again. "I don't go for that."

A Diamond cab pulled up in front of the church and a tall, lean young man got out. He wore a dark suit with a blue shirt and a black tie with small white polka dots. His hair was a shining dark bronze color that clung to his head in crinkly waves. He was a remarkably handsome man with sharp, bright features that made him look as if he were newly minted. His skin was a light, golden brown, the color of coffee that's half cream.

"Now if I liked boys," Sinkfield muttered, "I'd go for something like that. Pretty, huh?"

"Who is he?"

"The boyfriend. Chief Ignatius Oltigbe."

"Chief?"

"He's a paramount chief in Nigeria, whatever that is, except that he's an American citizen because his mother was American. His father was Nigerian. I don't know. It's all a little mixed up."

Ignatius Oltigbe looked about twenty-eight or twenty-nine. He moved up the church steps with a lithe stride and gave Sinkfield a brilliant white smile. "Hello, Lieutenant," he said, "am I late?"

Sinkfield glanced at his watch. "You got a few minutes."

"Time for a cigarette then," he said and produced a dull silver case. He offered it to Sinkfield who held up his right hand to show that he already had one going. Oltigbe turned to me. "Would you care for one, sir?" He had a fine British accent, the kind that one learns through being taught received pronunciation. It seems a casually effortless way to speak until an American tries to imitate it.

"I don't smoke," I said.

"Good for you," Oltigbe said and because he stood there and kept looking at me Sinkfield finally bestirred himself and said, "This is Decatur Lucas. Ignatius Oltigbe."

"How d'you do," he said without offering his hand. That was all right. I don't much like to shake hands either. "Are you a friend of Carolyn's?" he said.

"No. I'm not."

"He's a reporter," Sinkfield said.

"Oh, really," he said and dropped the cigarette he had just lit on the steps and ground it out with his shoe. "That must be interesting."

"Fascinating," I said.

"Quite," he said, all British to the core, smiled again at Sinkfield and brushed past us into the church.

"You've talked to him before, I take it," I said.

"Yeah," Sinkfield said. "He doesn't know anything either. Or says he doesn't. But whattaya expect of somebody who claims he's an African chief, was born in Los Angeles, and talks like an English butler? I bet he gets more ass than a rooster."

Sinkfield's partner, Jack Proctor, wandered over and said, "I think I'll go on inside, Dave." He was a tall, heavy man with a strangely kind face. Everything seemed to turn up at the corners, even his eyebrows.

"Might as well," Sinkfield said.

"You comin' in?"

"Yeah, in a minute."

We stood there on the steps of the church while Sinkfield smoked a final cigarette. Just as we were turning to go in a woman dressed in a plain brown suit walked up the steps and paused near us. The suit had eight big buttons up the front, but they didn't come out right because she had buttoned them up wrong. Her hair was long and dark brown and slightly tangled on the right side. She wore some pale lipstick and she had overshot her lower lip with it. Her eyes were hidden behind big round dark glasses but the Clorets she'd been chewing couldn't hide the Scotch on her breath. It smelled expensive.

"Is this where Carolyn Ames's funeral is?" she said.

"Yes ma'am," Sinkfield said.

The woman nodded. I thought she was a little younger than I was, around thirty-two or thirty-three, and she was even pretty in a soft, homey sort of way. She didn't look like a morning drinker. She looked like she should be home with an oven full of sugar cookies.

"Am I late?" she said, making sure that she pronounced the words carefully.

"You're right on time," Sinkfield said. "You a friend of Miss Ames?"

"Uh-huh, I was a friend of Carolyn's. I knew her a long time. Well, not a long time, I guess. Maybe six years. I was the senator's secretary. His private secretary. That's how I got to know Carolyn. My name's Gloria Peoples. What's yours?"

She was beginning to grow a little talkative so Sinkfield said, "My name's Sinkfield, ma'am, and maybe you'd better go on inside and find a seat. They're about ready to start."

"Is he in there?" she said.

"Who?"

"The senator."

"Yes, he's in there."

She nodded firmly. "Good."

She walked straight enough—straight enough for

a morning drinker anyhow. Sinkfield sighed. "There's at least one at every funeral," he said.

"What?"

"A drunk."

Inside we sat in the back row along with Sinkfield's partner, Jack Proctor, and the private investigator, Arthur Dain. The two front rows on both sides of the aisle were vacant except for the mourning parents—and Connie Mizelle. She sat with the senator on the left-hand side of the aisle. The mother sat alone on the right-hand side.

The services promised to be commendably brief, but halfway through the woman in the brown suit who claimed that she had been the senator's private secretary got up and started down the center aisle. She screamed as she went.

"Bobby! Goddamn you, Bobby, look at me!"

It took me a moment to realize that Bobby was former Senator Robert F. Ames. The services stopped and heads swiveled. All except the head of Robert F. Ames. Or Bobby.

"Why won't they let me see you, Bobby?" screamed the woman who said her name was Gloria Peoples. "I just wanta talk to you a minute! Just a goddamned minute!"

Sinkfield was up and moving down the aisle by then. But Connie Mizelle had moved even faster. She took the woman by the arm just as she yelled, "I only wanta talk to him a minute. They won't let me talk to him!"

Connie Mizelle put her lips up close to Gloria Peoples' right ear and whispered something. Even from where I sat I could see the Peoples woman grow pale. She slumped and then looked wildly around for a moment. After that she looked toward the front where the former senator sat. She got a good view of the back of his head.

Connie Mizelle said something else, not more than a few words. The Peoples woman nodded furiously, turned, and almost ran up the aisle, brushing past Sinkfield who turned and watched her go. By the time she passed me she was crying. Connie Mizelle returned to her seat beside the senator. Sinkfield came back and sat down next to me. The services were resumed.

"What do you figure all that was about?" Sinkfield said.

"I don't know," I said. "Why don't you ask Bobby?"

# 9

Most of the mourners had gone and I was standing on the church steps again wondering what my next brilliant move should be, when Ignatius Oltigbe stopped beside me, took a cigarette from his case, and tapped it on the back of his left hand.

After he lit it he blew out some smoke and said, "You're with Frank Size, aren't you?"

"That's right."

"Carolyn told me."

"Oh?"

"Yes, I was there when she called you the other day."

"That's interesting."

He smiled. "I was hoping you might think so. In fact, I was hoping that you would find it more than just interesting."

I looked at him more carefully. There was a hint of a smile around his mouth but it hadn't yet reached his eyes. It may have been too long a trip. "I take it we're talking about money."

"Well, yes, now that you mention it."

"I'll have to check with Size. How much money shall I tell him we're talking about?"

"Oh—say five thousand dollars."

"That's a lot of money."

"Not really. Not for what it will buy."

"And that's what?"

"Everything that Carolyn told you about."

"You've got it?"

"Let's say that I know where I can get it."

I nodded. "What's your rock-bottom price?"

He flicked his cigarette away. "I just quoted it. Five thousand dollars."

"As I said, I'll have to check with Size. It's his money."

Oltigbe smiled. "Good. Shall we meet for a drink later?"

"Okay. Where?"

"Somewhere quiet. Say the bar at the Washington Hotel. Fiveish?"

"Fiveish," I said. "But I won't be bringing the money."

"You mean Frank Size would like a peek at the goods first?"

"He's that way."

Oltigbe smiled again. His teeth seemed to get whiter and whiter. "I'll bring along a sample and if you're still interested, we can complete the transaction later on in the evening."

"All right."

"But do come by yourself, Mr. Lucas. No Frank Size and no—uh—cops."

"I can understand that. They might think you're up to something wicked, like withholding evidence."

"But I'm not really, am I? I'm offering it to you and I'm sure that Mr. Size will see that it eventually gets into their hands."

"Sure he will, but it'll cost them."

"Oh, really?" He looked interested. He probably always looked interested when the topic was money. "You don't mean he'll sell it to them?"

"That's right."

"For how much?"

"A dime," I said. "That's how much it'll cost them to read his column."

Frank Size looked grumpy. That was because we were talking about how much he would have to pay for information that he thought he should be able to steal.

"Well, I could always bang him over the head and take it away from him," I said.

Size brightened for a moment, but then lapsed back into grumpiness. "Nah," he said, "you're not the type."

"You're right. I'm not."

"Couldn't you jew him down a little?"

"I couldn't even gentile him down," I said.

"What d'you know about this guy?"

"Not much. He's half Nigerian, but he was born here so he's an American citizen. I think he must have grown up in England. He talks that way anyhow. Oh, yeah, he's also a paramount chief."

"What the hell's that?"

"I think it's sort of an honorary inherited title."

"Mean anything?"

"Well, it probably makes him rank a little higher than a Kentucky colonel. But not much."

"And he was the Ames girl's boyfriend, huh?"

"So I hear."

Size bit his lower lip. "Well, shit, five thousand bucks is a lotta money."

"That's what I told him."

"It'd better be worth it," Size said.

"I won't pay him if it's not."

"You think you've got that kind of judgment?"

"I'd better," I said. "It's what you're paying me for."

Frank Size chewed on his lower lip some more. Then he sighed and yelled, "Mabel!"

"What?" she yelled back.

"Come in here a minute."

After Mabel Singer came in she said, "What now?"

"Go down to the bank and get five thousand dollars."

"Out of the box?"

"Hell, yes, out of the box."

She looked at me. "What's he so pissed off about?"

"Spending money, I guess."

She nodded. "Uh-huh. It always makes him that way."

"How does Oltigbe want it?" Size said to me.

"He didn't say. Probably in twenties and tens. Old ones."

Size looked at Mabel Singer. "We got that much in tens and twenties?"

"I might have to throw in a few fifties."

"Okay." He looked at me. "You're gonna meet him at five?"

I nodded. "That's when I get a sample."

"All right. If it's any good, come by my place and you can pick up the money."

I rose. "Okay. I guess that's it."

"Where're you going now?"

"I thought I might go see the ex-senator's ex-secretary."

"You say she really threw a shit hissy at the funeral, huh?"

"Close to it."

"What do you think you might get out of her?"

"I don't know," I said. "Maybe just some cookies and milk."

When I left Frank Size's building I found a liquor store and bought a pint of J & B Scotch. My mother had tried to teach me that whenever I went calling I should take along a little gift. It didn't have to be expensive, she'd said, just thoughtful. I suspected that Gloria Peoples might think that a pint of Scotch was the most thoughtful gift in the world.

The phone book said she lived out in Virginia and her apartment was in one of those new high rises that are just past the Army and Navy Country Club on Shirley Highway. The lobby was guarded over by a woman in her sixties who failed to look up from her copy of *Cosmopolitan* when I pushed through the plate-glass door and crossed over to the bank of elevators. A tenants' directory said that G. Peoples lived in 914.

The elevator rose, playing me a tune. "Love and Marriage," I think. On the ninth floor I turned right and walked down a carpeted corridor until I came to 914. I pushed an ivory-colored plastic button and inside I could hear two-tone chimes ring. I waited thirty seconds or so and when nothing happened I pushed the button again. I had to wait another fifteen seconds before I heard Gloria Peoples say from behind the door, "Who is it?"

"Decatur Lucas."

"I don't know you. What d'you want?"

"I'd just like to talk to you, Miss Peoples."

"It's Mrs. Peoples and I don't wanna talk to anybody. Go way."

"I'd like to talk to you about Senator Ames."

"Go way, I said. I don't wanna talk to anybody. I'm sick."

I sighed. "Okay, but I'd just thought you'd like to know that your building's on fire."

The chain lock rattled as it was unhooked. A bolt

slid back. The door opened and Gloria Peoples poked her head out. "What d'you mean the building's on fire?"

I pushed the door open another foot, turned sideways, and slithered in past the woman. "Thanks for asking me in," I said.

She slammed the door. "Sure," she said. "Why the hell not? Make yourself at home. Have a drink."

"What're you drinking?" I said, glancing around the apartment.

"Vodka."

"I like Scotch."

"So do I, but I haven't got any left."

I took the pint off my hip and handed it to her. "Here. I brought you a present."

She took it and then looked at me more carefully. "I've seen you before," she said. "This morning. You were at the funeral."

"That's right."

"You got a name?"

"Decatur Lucas."

"Oh, yeah. You told me that. It's a funny name. What d'you do?"

"I'm a historian."

"Bullshit."

"I work for Frank Size."

"Oh. Him." I noticed that a lot of people said it just that way. I did too once.

"Uh-huh," I said. "Him."

"Water okay?" she said.

"Water's fine."

She nodded, crossed the living room and disappeared into the kitchen after she passed through the raised dining alcove. I assumed that the raised alcove allowed the building's owners to advertise the living room as being sunken.

She kept the place clean anyhow. The furniture

looked as though it had been selected for much larger quarters. The tweedy couch was a little too long and the diameter of the low, black glass coffee table was a little too wide. There were a couple of easy chairs too many in the room and they scarcely left space for the cherry-wood secretary desk whose glass-enclosed shelves were crammed with books.

I walked over and read some of the titles: *Psychology and You*, *What Freud Meant*, *I'm OK—You're OK*, *Abnormal Psychology*, *Games People Play*, and *Be Glad You're Neurotic*. The rest of the books were mostly novels except for a copy of *The Executive Secretary's Handbook* and several poetry anthologies. I decided that they were the books of a woman who spent a lot of time alone and didn't much like it.

On the walls were some framed prints, mostly of Paris scenes, except for a large black and white print of Picasso's Don Quixote and Sancho Panza. I thought that if she would get rid of a couple of the chairs, buy another coffee table, and shift the rest of the furniture around, she would have a rather attractive living room. I liked to rearrange furniture mentally. It passed the time while waiting to see people who didn't particularly want to see me. During the past twelve years there had been a lot of them and I'd got to rearrange a great deal of furniture.

Gloria Peoples came back carrying two glasses. She handed me one of them.

"Well, you might as well sit down someplace," she said.

I chose the couch. She picked out one of the easy chairs and sank into it, tucking her right foot underneath her rear. Many women sat down that way and I could never figure out why. She was no longer wearing the brown suit. She had on a green housecoat that was buttoned up to her neck. She must have washed her face, because the lipstick was gone. The eyes that had been hidden behind the dark glasses were brown and enormous and a little sad, the way that most large brown eyes look. Their whites were a trifle bloodshot. Her nose glistened at its tip. Her mouth, now that the lipstick was gone, looked somehow childish and as if it pouted easily.

"Well, what d'you wanta talk about?" she said.

"As I said, Senator Ames."

"I don't wanta talk about him."

"Okay," I said, "we'll talk about something else."

That surprised her. "I thought you wanted to talk about him."

"Not if you don't want to. Let's talk about you for a while."

That was better. That was her favorite topic. It's almost everybody's favorite topic.

"You used to work for him, didn't you?" I said. "You used to be his private secretary."

"Yes, I used to be his private secretary."

"For how long?"

"I don't know. It was quite a while."

"A little more than five years, wasn't it?"

"Yes, I guess it must have been that. Five years."

"Ever since he came to Washington?"

"That's right. He hired me in Indianapolis. It was just after my husband passed—" She broke it off. "Died," she said firmly. "It was just after my husband died." I wondered which one of her psychology books had told her to say it that way.

"When did you stop being his private secretary, when he resigned?"

"It was before that."

"When?"

She looked away from me and smiled. It was a curiously gentle smile and it didn't at all go with the half-hard way she talked. I decided that it was her cookies-and-milk smile.

"You haven't met my star boarder yet, have you?" she said and I followed her glance. A large dark blue Abyssinian cat had appeared in the doorway and after settling back on his haunches and giving himself a couple of swipes with his tongue, he surveyed the room to see whether there was anybody who needed chucking out.

"Guess what I call him?" she said.

"Heathcliff."

"Silly, why would I call him that?"

"You asked me to guess."

"Well, I call him Lucky."

"That's a nice name."

"He's not very. Lucky, I mean. I had him fixed."

"He's probably happier."

"He hasn't got any claws either. Not any front ones. That's so he won't scratch the furniture."

"At least he's not blind."

"He doesn't need any claws really. The only reason he'd need any would be to climb a tree if a dog got after him, but I don't ever let him outside."

"I'm sure he understands."

"I don't know. Maybe I shouldn't have had him declawed. Maybe I should've let him use the furniture as one big scratching post. But he's the first cat I ever owned. He gave him to me. If I ever get another one, he's gonna stay the way God made him."

"Did he give him to you when you were still his private secretary?"

"Yeah. I was still his secretary then."

"Why'd you stop being his secretary?"

"I guess he got tired of me. Who wants a thirty-two-year-old bag around for a secretary? One day he called me in and told me I wasn't gonna be his secretary anymore, that I was gonna be Cuke's secretary."

"Whose?"

"Mr. Cumbers. Bill Cumbers. He was the administrative assistant. Everybody called him Cuke. You know, Cuke Cumbers. He didn't like it much though."

"Did the senator say why you were no longer going to be his secretary?"

"He said Cuke needed a secretary. The one he had got married and quit."

"When was this?"

"I don't know. About six months ago, I guess. Maybe seven."

"That was about the time that he started fucking Connie Mizelle, wasn't it?" Well, I thought, that's the first zinger, honey, and it's got a nasty hop. Let's see how you field it.

Gloria Peoples dropped her eyes. "I don't know what you're talking about. I don't like talk like that."

"He dropped you for her, didn't he?"

"I don't wanta talk about it."

"Why did you make the big scene today at the funeral, because Connie Mizelle won't let you see him?"

Lucky, the cat, wandered over to his mistress. She bent down and picked him up. He sat in her lap, kneading her breasts with his clawless paws. I could hear him purr across the room.

"I didn't want to bother him," she said, as if talking to the cat. "I didn't want to cause any trouble. But when Carolyn died I thought he needed me. He always used to come to me when he was in trouble. I'd take care of him. He used to come over here sometimes at night, around seven or eight, if he could get away that early. I'd fix him dinner and maybe we'd have a drink and maybe we wouldn't. And he'd sit in that chair over there and we'd watch television or maybe he'd tell me about something that went on that day. Sometimes we'd have popcorn. He could eat a whole, big bowl of popcorn all by himself. He liked it buttered. He'd talk his problems out here. He liked to do that. And that's all there was to it. We never went anywhere. He'd never take me anywhere. We'd just sit here and talk or watch TV. We did that for five and a half years and I never felt so goddamned married in my life."

"How did it end?"

She shrugged. "How does anything end? It just does, that's all. It was right after he met her. I know that."

"Connie Mizelle?"

She nodded. "It was right after that. He just called me in and said that Cuke needed a secretary and I was going to be it. I said why and he said because that's the way it was going to be. I said I didn't think it was fair and he said that if I didn't think it was fair, maybe I should resign. But I didn't. I just stayed on till he resigned."

"Where do you work now?"

"The Department of Agriculture. When I work. They're gonna fire me if I don't start showing up."

"What about his wife?"

"Louise? What about her?"

"Did she know about you and him?"

She shrugged again. "She does now, I guess. She was at the funeral. She saw me make a fool out of myself. But she never knew about he and I. Him and me. I don't even think she ever suspected anything. He never took me anyplace—except to bed. I was just someone he could come over and roll in the hay and eat popcorn with. Then he'd go home. Know what he used to call me?"

"What?"

"'My little sanctuary.' That's not much of a pet name, is it?"

"I don't know. Maybe he thought it was."

She took another deep swallow of her drink. "Nah, he didn't go in for pet names much or for any other kind of affection. Not him. Not with me anyhow. Maybe he does with her, with that Mizelle bitch. But not with me. I think he might have called me honey two times in five and a half years. Sometimes I just wanted him to put his arms around me and hug me. That's all. Just hug me. I'd have done anything in the world for him if he'd just done that. That's all I wanted."

Don't feel bad, sweetheart, I thought, that's all anybody wants whether they know it or not. At least you know it.

"What was he like after he met Connie Mizelle?"

"Whaddya mean, what was he like?"

"Did he change? Did he talk differently? Did he start hitting the bottle?"

She shook her head. "He just got sort of quiet. I didn't see him much except in the office. He started dressing different. He used to dress real conservative, but he went out and bought a whole new wardrobe. Bright colors. Big wide lapels. You know."

"What else?"

"It was only a month after he met her that he resigned when Frank Size printed that story. He started taking her everywhere right from the first. He didn't keep her out of sight like he did me. He took her everywhere—Paul Young's, the Monocle, Camille's. Sometimes he used to make me call up and make the reservations. It was just like he was trying to show her off."

"Did you ever see him with Colonel Bagger or a man called Cutter?"

"Cutter and Bagger," she said. "They're the ones who got him in all that trouble. I saw 'em one time. It was on a Saturday. I had to pick up his ticket at United. He was going out to California to make a speech. I had to pick up his ticket and then go over to a liquor store on Pennsylvania Avenue and cash him a check. That's why I had to come in that Saturday."

"How much was the check for?"

She took another swallow of her drink, almost finishing it. "I don't know," she said. "A hundred dollars, I think. Just enough for cab fares and tips and so forth."

"How'd you pay for his airline ticket?"

"Credit card. We had the forms in the office. He'd sign them and I'd take them down and United would make them out."

"So he hadn't forgotten his ticket?" I said.

"I gave it to him myself. What kind of a question is that?"

"I don't know," I said. "A dumb one, I guess."

"You gonna print all this—about me and him?"

"I don't think so."

"Well, I don't care if you do or not."

"You're still in love with him, aren't you?"

She didn't answer me. She finished her drink instead. "You don't take any notes or anything. You just sit there and listen. You're a pretty good listener, aren't you?"

"I try to be."

"I can tell. I'm a pretty good one, too. I used to listen to him all the time. You wanta know something?"

"What?"

"That silly son of a bitch used to think he could even be president. He used to talk to me about it." She paused. "Oh, I don't guess he was really talking to me. He was talking to himself."

"When was this?"

"Oh, years ago. When we first started—well, whatever it was we did together."

"When he first got elected senator?"

"Right after that. He had it all figured out. He'd

use his wife's money. She's got millions, you know, and he'd use that and his looks and being a Democrat from a pretty big Midwest state and—well, he really thought he could make it by the time he was fifty-six. And you know what I'd ask him?"

"What?"

"I'd ask him what he was gonna do about me when he was president." She laughed, but there was no humor in it. "He said we'd work something out. And then I used to sit around and have these fantasies about being driven into the White House at night in a big black limousine all dressed up in a mink and—" She stopped and her mouth opened slightly. Then it opened wider and turned down at the ends and it made her face look a little like the way that the Greeks thought tragedy should look. Her shoulders began to shake. She dropped her glass and the first wail came from somewhere deep inside her and the tears started running down her cheeks and into her open mouth. She pushed the cat to the floor. The wails began in earnest.

It was as good a time as any, I thought, so I said, "What did Connie Mizelle say to you at the funeral today?"

There was another loud wail and she said, choking it out, "She—she told me that if—if I tried to see him again she'd have me locked up in jail and let the lesbians get me. She—she scared me. She—she's bad!"

"Aw, Jesus," I said and went over to her and helped her up. I put my arms around her and stroked the back of her head. She still trembled violently, but the wails stopped She was only sobbing now.

"Ieelwevverseeimgin!" she said, at least the sobs made it sound that way.

"What?"

"I—I'll never see him again!"

I comforted her with some more pats and stroked

her hair. The sobs began to die away. She lifted her face up to me. She wants me to kiss her, I thought. Not me particularly. Almost anyone would do—anyone who was a little taller and a little stronger and who could tell her that everything was going to be just fine. So I kissed her and for a moment it was like kissing my sister. The youngest one. But then her lips parted and her tongue went to work and I could either bite it or kiss her back. So I kissed her back and then came up for air and gave her another pat and a meaningless phrase of comfort.

"Let's sit over here," I said, took her hand, and led her to the couch. "Which way's your bathroom?" She pointed.

I came back with a face cloth and a towel. "Here," I said, and she obediently turned her face up so that I could wash and dry it. "Would you like another drink?" I said.

She shook her head. "What're you asking me all these questions for?"

"I'm trying to find out what happened to him."

"He didn't take any fifty thousand dollars like Size said he did."

"No?"

"No."

"Why do you say that?"

"I just know he didn't. He wouldn't do anything like that."

"Then what happened to him?"

"I don't know. Everything was all right until he met her."

"Connie Mizelle?"

"It's all her fault. Every bit of it." She looked at me. There was a slight, but serious frown on her face. "Would you like to go to bed with me?" she said. "You can if you want to."

"Let's think about it," I said and patted her knee. "When you're feeling better."

She'd already forgotten that she'd asked. "When you find out what really happened, it's going to be something bad, isn't it? It's going to be something bad and they're going to arrest him and lock him up in jail for a real long time, aren't they?"

"I don't know," I said. "Offhand I can't think of many ex-United States senators who've spent much time in jail."

# 10

Ten years from now there may not be any hotels left in downtown Washington. The Willard's long closed. The AFL-CIO bought the hotel that was next door to its headquarters and tore it down. The Annapolis folded. The Salvation Army took over the Hamilton. On Capitol Hill the Dodge is gone and so is the Congressional and the Continental. And for a while there was even talk of tearing down the Washington Hotel and transforming its ground into something useful such as a parking lot. The Washington is located just across the street from the U.S. Treasury Building and now that I think of it, the ground the Treasury stands on wouldn't make a bad parking lot either.

But the Washington Hotel bestirred itself. It refurbished its rooms. It put in some new elevators and opened a new French restaurant that's not bad. It also has a bar that at five o'clock in the afternoon is quiet—or dead—depending upon what you expect from a bar.

Ignatius Oltigbe was only a few minutes late. I was on time as always. I have a thing about promptness that almost amounts to a fetish. It also makes me spend a lot of time waiting for others.

"Terribly sorry," Oltigbe said as he slid into a chair at the small table I'd chosen.

"I just got here myself," I said, which is what I always say to people who are late, even if they're twenty-nine minutes late. If they're thirty minutes late, I'm not there.

"What're we drinking?" Oltigbe said.

"Scotch and water."

"Good," he said and after the waiter brought us our drinks Oltigbe picked up the black attaché case that he had brought with him and put it on a chair. I decided to ignore it for a while.

After he said cheers and we each took a swallow I said, "How'd you get to know the senator's daughter?"

"Carolyn? Well, I met her at a party. I was staying with some people here who had done a lot for Biafran relief—you remember Biafra, don't you?"

"I think they're calling it Eastern Nigeria again."

"Yes, well, Carolyn had been active in some college movement or other that had supported the Biafran cause and these people invited her and that's how we met."

"And you started going together after that?"

"It was a bit more than going together."

"All right," I said. "Living together."

Oltigbe nodded. "She was quite impressed that I'd fought for the Biafrans."

"Did you?"

"Rather. You see I'm an Ibo. Or half Ibo anyway. We Ibos are a dreadfully clever people."

"So I've heard."

"Of course, I didn't fight very long. Only as long

as they could pay me and it was quite good pay while it lasted."

"How much?"

"A thousand a week. Dollars, of course."

"What were they paying for?"

Oltigbe grinned. "They were paying for a former first lieutenant in the Eighty-second Airborne. That's what I was from 1963 to sixty-five. I just missed Vietnam, thank God."

"What do you do when you're not soldiering?"

Oltigbe gave me a wide, white grin. "I live off women. I am rather pretty, you know."

"Uh-huh."

"Actually, being a veteran of the Biafran campaign was most pleasant for a while. People would invite me to stay with them, both here and in England. It was something like being a veteran of the Spanish Civil War, I suppose. One becomes sort of a professional house guest. At least one does until the cause loses its popularity and one's hosts become puzzled as to why they thought to invite you in the first place."

"That's what happened to you?"

He nodded. "The party that I met Carolyn at was the tag end of it all. So I moved in with her about six months ago. She could afford me and we had quite some jolly times together."

"What are your plans now?"

"I think I shall go back to London for a while. I have friends in London."

"You were born in Los Angeles, weren't you?"

"My father was a student at UCLA. He was one of the few Nigerian students studying here in thirty-nine when the war broke out. I was born in forty-four. I never knew my mother."

"Did she die?"

"You mean in childbirth?"

"Yes."

"No, she was a strapping girl, I'm told. You see, I'm a bit of a bastard. But still in all, an American bastard."

"But you were brought up in England."

"Oh, yes. My father took me there right after the war when transport became available. I went to school there. Not a very good school, but it was a public school, if you know what I mean."

"I think so."

"And at eighteen I opted for American citizenship. I could have waited until I was twenty-one, but I wanted to come to the States and joining the army seemed the easiest way. I had the embassy in London in a frightful dither for a time."

"And now you're going back. To London."

Oltigbe drained his drink. "Providing I get the wherewithal."

"The five thousand bucks."

"Quite."

"Okay. What have you got to sell?"

Oltigbe looked around the bar. There were only a handful of people in it and none of them was paying any attention to us. He opened his attaché case and took out a small tape recorder. He plugged in a plastic earphone and handed it to me. I attached it to my left ear.

"This is only a sample, old man, but I assure you that the merchandise is most authentic and quite worth every penny of five thousand dollars. In fact, if I had—" He stopped. "Just listen."

He pressed a button and there was nothing for a moment and then there was the sound of a phone ringing—not of the bell itself, but of the sound that it makes over the receiver when you're calling someone else. It rang four times. Then a man's voice said hello. The voice sounded familiar. It should have. It was mine.

"Mr. Lucas?" It was Carolyn Ames's voice.

"Yes." My voice.

"Frank Size's office gave me your number."

"How can I help you?"

I listened for a while longer until it was apparent that the tape contained my entire conversation with Carolyn Ames. I took the earphone off and Oltigbe switched off the tape recorder.

"That's not anything I don't already know," I said.

"Quite," he said. "But all of that information she mentioned in her conversation with you—I have duplicates of it."

"Not the originals?"

"I'm afraid not. Only duplicates. Duplicate tapes and Xeroxed copies."

"And you know what it is?"

"Indeed I do know what it is and I also know that it's worth far, far more than five thousand dollars."

"Then why so cheap?"

"I didn't like the way that Carolyn died. It was, from what I heard, quite horrible, wouldn't you say?"

"Yes," I said. "It was horrible."

"She entrusted this material to me for safekeeping. She gave it to me right after she rang you. She'd made a duplicate tape of her conversation with you. We were really quite close, you know."

"What did you do with it?"

"With the tapes and things?"

"Yes."

"I put it in this case and locked it in the boot of my car."

"Was that the last time you saw Carolyn?"

"Really, cock, I've told the police all of this. I had a luncheon engagement that day—the day that you were to meet her. So I left her about noon. It was the last time I saw her."

"There's one thing I don't get," I said. "You're willing to sell this material to me—or to Size—for five thousand even though you say it's worth more. That I don't get."

"You mean I'm not the sort of chap to turn down a neat profit."

"That's right," I said. "You're not that sort of chap at all."

Oltigbe sighed. "Put the earphone back on," he said.

I did what he suggested. He punched the tape recorder again and the reel began to spin. There were a few moments of silence and then a man's voice said hello. It sounded like Oltigbe's voice.

"Mr. Oltigbe?" It was a man's voice coming over a phone. But it had a rasping, mechanical sound to it. Whoever was speaking was using a distorter and a good one.

"Speaking," Oltigbe said.

"Listen carefully. This is no joke. If you don't want the same thing to happen to you that happened to Carolyn Ames, bring the material that she gave you to the phone booth at Wisconsin and Q at twelve o'clock tonight. That's Wisconsin and Q at midnight. Leave it there and drive away. Don't contact the police. This is no joke. Don't bet your life that it is."

There was a click and then a dial tone. I took the earphone off and handed it to Oltigbe. He put it and the tape recorder back into his briefcase.

"You tape all your phone conversations?" I said.

"I have done ever since Carolyn died."

"Why?"

"I have a very suspicious nature, Mr. Lucas. I'd decided to sell this information, but I wasn't quite sure who was going to be my customer. Others might be interested, but the negotiations would probably take too long. And I don't think I have too much time."

"How do I know that that last tape wasn't faked?"

"You don't."

"When're you going to London?"

"Tomorrow morning. I have an eight o'clock flight out of New York. I'm driving there tonight."

There was a silence for a while and then I said, "Okay. Where do you want to pick up your money?"

"Your place?"

"All right. What time?"

He smiled. "Why don't we make it midnight?"

"Why not?" I said.

# 11

Ignatius Oltigbe was late again. Fifteen minutes late this time and I was pacing up and down my living room and peering out through my bay window at Fourth Street. For company I had Foolish, the cat. Sarah had gone to bed.

Frank Size had quizzed me for nearly an hour before he would hand over the five thousand in cash. It was packed in a shoebox and carefully tied with cord that made a loop that formed a nice little handle. Mabel Singer's touch, I decided. Frank Size wouldn't have bothered.

When he handed over the money I thought he was going to cry. But he hadn't although his voice had sounded a little choked when he said, "For God's sake don't lose it someplace."

"I never lost five thousand dollars in my life," I told him. Then I drove home and got there too late to make the meat loaf so we settled for hamburgers, which Sarah despises, and then we'd had a mild fight about something or other and she had gone upstairs around ten-thirty. We fought a lot, usually about nothing.

At twelve-eighteen I took another look through my bay window. Across the street most of my neighbors had turned out their lights and had gone to bed. The street lamp that was directly in front of my house spread its cold, garish yellow over some parked cars. The morning glories that Sarah had planted around the lamppost thought it was time to rise and had opened their faces up to the light. Sarah worried about the morning glories. She thought they might become neurotic.

At twelve twenty-one a car came down Fourth Street which is one-way. It drove slowly as if looking for a place to park. I thought that it looked like a Datsun 240-Z, Japan's answer to the Porsche. There was a space just down from my house on the other side of the street near the edge of the street lamp's glow. After some backing and filling, the Datsun got parked. The left-hand door opened and somebody got out. I couldn't see who because of the dark, but I assumed it was Ignatius Oltigbe. A Datsun 240-Z would be his kind of a car.

A gray Volkswagen went past my house, slowed, and stopped almost parallel to the parked Datsun. Oltigbe walked into the main circle of light. He was dressed in a sport jacket with an open shirt and dark slacks. He carried an attaché case in his right hand. He moved hesitantly, as if searching for the right address. I switched on my porch light. He started walking toward it.

He was halfway across the street, nearly in the center of the pool of light, when he stopped and turned—as if someone had called his name. He took a couple of steps toward the parked Volkswagen. Then he took a quick step backward. But it was too late. The first bullet slammed into him, probably into his right shoulder, and he dropped the attaché case. The second bullet must have plowed into his stomach because he doubled over clutching his middle. There was a third shot. It came while he was falling and caught him in the head or the neck, I couldn't tell which, but it seemed to hammer him down into the asphalt where he lay without moving.

A crouched-over figure raced from the Volkswagen, snatched up the attaché case, and scuttled back to the car. Gears clashed and chattered until whoever was driving the Volks remembered to throw out the clutch. Then the car roared off, its engine whining into the night the way that Volkswagens do, all noise and not much action, but still fast enough to keep me from running out and getting the license number, which I wasn't about to do anyway.

I tried to remember what the crouched-over figure had looked like. Whether it had been tall or short or just medium. It could have been any of them. Whoever it was it had been wearing black—black slacks, black sweater, and a black hat of some kind. There had been something over the face, too, but I wasn't sure what, except that it had been black. Or dark blue. The crouched-over figure could have been a man or a woman or a rather large dwarf. I couldn't tell. Whoever it was had been a superb shot. Or lucky.

I didn't rush out into the street. I took my time. At the sound of the first shot I had ducked down behind the window seat of the bay window, just keeping my head poked up high enough to see what was going on. When I was sure that the Volkswagen wasn't coming back I got up.

The shots had banged out into the quiet night. Lights were still coming on in the houses across the street. I held out my right hand and saw that it was shaking.

"What's going on?"

• I turned. It was Sarah standing on the landing of the stairs with a sleepy Martin Rutherford Hill in her arms.

"Somebody got shot," I said.

"The man you were waiting for?"

"I think so. Put the kid back to bed and call nine-one-one."

"What'll I tell 'em?"

"Just what I told you."

Sarah nodded and started back up the stairs. She stopped and turned. "You're not going out there?"

"I think it's over."

"Make sure."

"Don't worry; I will."

I looked out of the bay window again. There were some more lights on across the street. I turned to the front door and opened it cautiously. I caught a movement across the street. A neighbor was doing the same thing—opening his front door cautiously.

Foolish, the cat, swept by my legs and darted outside. "Go on and get shot," I told him. He disappeared into the darkness.

I went through the front door and down the seven steps to the sidewalk, around a car, and out into the street where Ignatius Oltigbe lay dead. I knew he was dead because nothing but death can make a man look so awkward. The street lamp beamed down on him. Another small circle of light, even brighter, suddenly appeared on his face. His eyes were open and glazed and looked a little crossed. I turned. The new light came from the flashlight of my black neighbor from across the street. "My godalmighty," he said, "he's sure as shit dead, ain't he?"

"He sure as shit is," I said. "You call the cops?"

"My old lady did."

"So'd mine."

My neighbor moved his flashlight around. There

was a lot of blood on Oltigbe's cream-colored shirt. His dark bronze hair seemed soaked with it.

"You know him?" my neighbor said.

"I think so."

"He's in front of your house."

"He's in front of yours, too."

"Huh. Sounded like a shotgun to me."

"Did it?"

"Sounded like a sawed-off."

"You know what a sawed-off sounds like?"

My neighbor seemed to think about that for a moment. "Yeah," he said. "I know what a sawed-off sounds like."

More neighbors began to appear. Mrs. Hatcher from next door came out in a green flannel bathrobe and scuffed slippers, carrying a coffee cup. She took a large gulp from it after she saw the body. I could smell the gin. "Jesus," she said, "is he dead?"

"He's dead," said my neighbor with the flashlight. "Sawed-off got him. Prid near cut him clean in two." He moved the beam of the flashlight up and down Oltigbe's body so that we could all see better.

"I'm gonna be sick," Mrs. Hatcher said. Instead, she drained her cup of gin.

We heard the sirens then. A Metropolitan Police Department squad car came roaring up Fourth from E Street going the wrong way. Another made the turn at D and came screaming down from the opposite direction. They hadn't had far to come. The First District substation was just around the corner on E Street. They slammed to a stop and the uniformed cops tumbled out and shouldered their way through the crowd. They used their own flashlights to look at the body.

The oldest cop took charge. He was tall and lean and competent-looking and all of twenty-five. "All right, folks, just move back a little. Now is there anybody here who saw this happen?"

"I heard it," said my neighbor with the flashlight, "but I didn't exactly see it."

The tall young cop sighted. "Okay, what's your name?"

"Henry. Charles Henry. I live right over there." He pointed at his house.

"Okay, Mr. Henry, just what did you hear?"

"I heard some shots. Sounded like a shotgun. Sounded like a sawed-off."

The tall young cop looked up from his notebook with interest. "How do you know what a sawed-off sounds like?"

Henry looked as if he'd like to bite his tongue off. "On TV," he said lamely. "I've heard 'em on TV."

The young cop went back to his notebook. He wasn't quite so interested. "Yeah, sure," he said. "Now just how many sawed-off shotgun shots do you think you heard?"

"Two," Henry said and looked around defiantly. "Just two."

"There was three," somebody else said. "I heard three."

"So'd I," said another neighbor.

I decided it was time to put in my oar. "There were three," I said.

"What makes you so sure?" the young cop asked.

"Because," I said, "I saw it happen."

# 12

---

I didn't tell Lt. David Sinkfield about the $5,000 or about the packet of information that Ignatius Oltigbe claimed that he'd had for sale. Instead I lied a little and told him that Oltigbe and I had had a drink the day before at my suggestion and that we had talked about Carolyn Ames and her father and that Oltigbe had said that he had some information that might or might not interest me which he would drop off at my house on his way up to New York.

We were sitting in Sinkfield's office again. He shared it with his partner, Jack Proctor. It was what you might expect. Not much. There were the beat-up desks and the hard-seated chairs and the bile-green walls and the scuffed-up floor. A bulletin board with some old wanted notices and some reward offers was there for those who needed something to look at. The place also smelled. It smelled of old sweat and old smoke and old fear.

"You could've called me," Sinkfield said. There was a measure of reproach in his tone. "You could've called me and we could've talked it over and maybe I'd've thought it was a good idea to be there when Oltigbe dropped by your place and maybe things would've turned out different."

"You should've called him," Proctor said. "Oltigbe wasn't supposed to leave town. We weren't through with him yet. Not by a damn sight."

"You sure he was going to London?" Sinkfield said.

"That's what he told me."

"Yeah, well, we did some checking. He had a reservation on Air India all right, but he hadn't paid for his ticket."

I shrugged. "I guess he'd've paid for it when he got there. At Kennedy."

"With what—the thirty-two bucks he had in his pocket?"

"Credit card," I said. "Who pays cash?"

"He didn't have any credit cards."

"Maybe he was going to sell his car. Those two-forty-Z's cost forty-five hundred. He could've got two thousand for it easily."

"If it had been his," Proctor said.

"Whose was it?" I said.

"Carolyn Ames's," Proctor said. "It was in her name. He just drove it. Nobody'd gotten around to take the keys away from him yet."

"You know what I figure?" Sinkfield said.

"What?" I said.

"I figure Oltigbe was gonna put the touch on you. I figure he was gonna trade off this information he said he had for enough bread to get to London. What's that? Two hundred and fifty or three hundred for a one-way ticket?"

"About that," Proctor said.

"I don't keep that kind of money around my house," I said. "You keep that kind of money around your house and you get burgled. At least you do in my neighborhood."

"Yeah," Sinkfield said. "We checked."

"You checked what?"

"Your bank account. The last check you cashed was for seventy-five bucks three days ago. But that doesn't mean anything. You could've gotten it from Frank Size. What's two or three hundred bucks to him? A couple of dinners at Sans Souci."

"He hangs out at Paul Young's," I said, "and he doesn't like to pick up the tab."

"You know something, Lucas?" Sinkfield said.

"What?" I said.

"You've been a witness to two homicides now and you haven't been able to tell us shit about either of them."

"I told you what I saw."

"I'm talking about motive."

"I didn't see any motive."

"Hah. The Ames girl calls you up and tells you she's got a pile of stuff that'll clear her father. She wants to give it to you, but before she can, she gets blown up. Then her boyfriend says he's got a couple of tidbits for you, too, although he doesn't say what, but before he can drop 'em off somebody shoots him three times with a thirty-eight. Hits him three times from about twenty-five feet away while sitting in a car on a dark street. Some shooting."

"Find yourself a pistol expert who can also put together an exploding briefcase and you've got yourself your murderer," I said.

"You know anything about pistol shooting?" Sinkfield said.

"Not much."

"I've known dudes in this town that've gone after a guy from three feet away with a forty-five and they've emptied the clip and they've missed every goddamn time. Not just hit him in the hand or leg or maybe the big toe, but they clean missed him. And then I know one bimbo who decided her boyfriend was cheatin' on her so she takes out his thirty-eight with a one-inch barrel and chases him out into the street. It's the first time she's ever had one in her hand but that don't matter. She hits him five times in the back while he's running, weaving and ducking at least thirty feet away from her and with the sixth blast she takes off the top of his head. So I don't much go around looking for pistol shooters anymore."

"How about an explosives expert?" I said.

"Shit," Proctor said.

"I agree," Sinkfield said. "Christ, all you have to do is pay a quarter for a copy of the *Quicksilver Times*, or whatever the freaks are putting out now, and turn to their recipe page and there it is—all you need to know about how to build your own homemade bomb."

"So you're ruling out experts, huh?" I said.

Sinkfield sighed. "No, I'm not ruling them out. I'm just keeping it all in perspective."

"You got anybody in mind?"

"You know something, Lucas?"

"What?"

"I wanta cooperate with you and Frank Size. I really do. Hell, I wouldn't mind having real nice things said about me in eight hundred newspapers. What cop wouldn't? But fairy tales I don't need."

"I haven't told you any fairy tales."

"You haven't, huh?"

"No."

He sighed again. "You just keep on with your snoopin'. Nobody's gonna stop you. You just keep on with it. I hear you're pretty good. But don't tell me anything about what you find. Or if you do tell me, shave it down real nice so it won't mean diddely fuck. Shave it down just like you did the Oltigbe stuff. And keep on snoopin' and pokin' around and maybe you'll turn something. But don't tell me about it. Make sure you don't tell me about it. Make sure nobody knows about it except you and just one other person, the person you're snoopin' around after. And then go out and start your car one morning and bingo, up it goes in one big boom and you with it and I've got another homicide dropped in my lap."

I got up. "I'll keep all that in mind. Anything else?"

Sinkfield shrugged. "Who you gonna light on next?"

"I was thinking of the senator himself."

"Good luck. You'll need it."

"Why?"

"To get to him you're gonna have to go through Connie Mizelle."

"Did you?"

"I'm a cop, not a reporter."

"That's right," I said. "I keep forgetting."

Everybody must have heard of the Watergate co-operative apartments by now. A U.S. attorney general's wife once used the phone there a lot. The Democratic National Committee headquartered there until it got burgled and moved to cheaper quarters although the former didn't have much to do with the latter. The rich live there. The very rich and the half rich and some not so rich. One grifter I know who lives there is not so rich. In fact, he can barely make his car payments. But he drives a $12,000 Mercedes coupé and he runs up tabs in all the better saloons and everybody in town is falling all over each other to give him credit—even though he's a slow pay—because he lives at the Watergate. In the basement. He scraped up the down payment for a $17,000 efficiency and what does it matter if the windows are about nine inches high and offer a view of nothing but ankles and sidewalk? It's still the Watergate. And that's all he puts on the engraved stationery that he still owes Copenhaver's for: his name, The Watergate, and Washington, D.C. No zip code. Zip codes are common.

Former Senator Robert F. Ames and Connie Mizelle lived in a top-floor apartment in Watergate East. A penthouse, I suppose. It had a view of the Potomac and the Kennedy Center and Virginia across the river. By slow cab it was about seven and a half minutes from the White House. I looked it up later downtown and found that the senator had paid $135,000 for it, which isn't bad although you can get a nice little six-room house in Georgetown with warped floors, a leaky roof, and a bit of history for about the same price.

I had had a little trouble getting in to see the senator. Sinkfield had been right. I had had to go through Connie Mizelle and she hadn't been too anxious to let me talk to Ames. I was used to that. When I had been with government few of the people that I went calling on really wanted to talk to me. But they did because if they didn't talk to me, they might find themselves talking to a Senate committee. Now that I was no longer with government I had to depend on the power of Frank Size's name. It had about the same effect as a subpoena from a Senate committee. People talked. People saw me and talked to me because they thought that if they did, Size might print what they said about themselves instead of the stuff that he might dig up from God knows where else.

I made a mental note of the living room that Connie Mizelle and I were sitting in. Frank Size liked details. He especially liked brand names. He operated on the theory that if he wrote about someone who was suspected of dipping into the till, the story would gain immeasurable credibility if he also wrote that the suspect did the dipping while wearing a four-button blue Oxxford suit, a pale gray Custom Shop shirt with no breast pocket, a maroon Countess Mara tie, and green Jockey shorts. I think I agreed with him. Authentic detail can always be used to beef up unsubstantiated theory. I remember once that I beamed for a week when I accidentally discovered that Captain Bonneville was left-handed. Of such minor discoveries are historians made.

It was a big living room, probably fifteen by sixty-five, and one side of it was all glass that looked out on a balcony that contained some lounging chairs and a glass and wrought-iron breakfast table. If you got bored with looking at the river or the Kennedy Center from the balcony, you could always count the planes that landed at National Airport.

Opposite the glass wall was a fireplace whose gray stonework ran up to the ceiling. Twin white couches flanked the fireplace and in between them was a gnarled and twisted piece of polished driftwood that served as the base for an inch-thick chunk of glass that had been cut into a shape that vaguely resembled a kidney. I decided that it was the decorator's idea of a coffee table.

There were some big lamps here and there and some easy chairs and against one wall was a spindly legged chess table whose top formed a board made out of inlaid wood. The chess pieces were Oriental and carved out of ivory and looked very old.

There were also some oil paintings on the walls, done by what I suppose the decorator called "contemporary European artists." They were mostly street scenes of cities that I didn't recognize. But they were genuine oils on genuine canvas and that may have been all that the decorator had in mind.

Against the other wall with a door that looked as if it led to the dining room and the kitchen was a baby grand piano, a Steinway, and its lid was propped open and some sheet music was on its rack. By squinting my eyes, I could make out the music's title. It read, "Show Tunes from the Thirties."

"Does Senator Ames play?" I asked Connie Mizelle who was sitting on the couch across from me.

"He sings; I play," she said.

"You must have some cozy evenings."

"They're quiet evenings, Mr. Lucas. We intend to keep them that way."

I couldn't help staring at her. I suppose I was looking for flaws, but I still couldn't find any. She hadn't exactly got dressed up to receive me. She wore faded blue jeans and a white blouse and blue sneakers. It was the comfortable, eminently practical uniform that millions of women wore, but not the way that Connie Mizelle wore it. On most of them it looked like jeans and a shirt. On her it looked like a couple of million dollars. The jeans looked as if they'd been applied in coats and the shirt was a little too tight and a little too thin and she wasn't wearing a brassiere, not that she needed one, and I found the view to be almost completely distracting.

I thought I had a fairly normal sex life. Sarah and I made love almost every day. My fantasies, I thought, were not much more bizarre than most. As a rule, pornography failed to turn me on because I insisted on some kind of a story. And there were days when I went for an hour or more without even thinking about sex, which in our time is a pretty hard thing to do. But all I had to do was be in the same room with Connie Mizelle and I got an erection.

"The only reason that the senator has agreed to see you, Mr. Lucas," she said, "is because he doesn't want Frank Size to print any more lies about him. Or his family."

"Size printed the facts as he had them," I said.

"Facts can be used to form a lie."

"Frank Size isn't interested in printing lies," I said.

"If that's all he did, he wouldn't be in eight hundred and fifty-odd newspapers. But he's in a race seven days a week and unless he wins that race at least a couple of times each week, he's not going to be in those newspapers, and he likes living in his house on Normanstone Drive and he likes to drive his Bentley and fly first-class and all that good stuff, and so sometimes he gets a little overeager."

"In other words, he lies."

I shook my head. "Never intentionally. And never with malice. If he prints a lie, it's because somebody has lied to him and he hasn't been able to verify the story—to check it out. So he's faced with a choice and the choice involves risk. Either he can go with what he has—and be first—or he can do some more checking and be second or third. The news business doesn't pay for place and show. Size has been in the business a long time, ever since he was seventeen. He's developed a kind of a sixth sense or intuition about news. He likes to call it judgment, but it's not. It's hunch mostly. Most great reporters have it. And some historians. And maybe even some detectives. I don't know why."

"Do you have it, Mr. Lucas?" she said.

"Some," I said, "but not enough to ever make me great so that's why I never rely on it completely. Mine's not good enough to rely on the way that Size relies on his. He can trust his because it's right about ninety-nine percent of the time."

"And how often is your intuition or hunch right?" she said.

"I never thought about it. Probably ninety-seven or even ninety-eight percent. Just enough to make me good, but not enough to make me great."

"And you'd like to be great at—uh—whatever it is that you do?"

"Not any more," I said. "Greatness demands ambition and ambition calls for hard work and hard work is something that I don't much care for."

If she had gone on listening like that, with her head cocked slightly to one side, her lips slightly parted as if she were tasting my every word and finding them all delicious, I might have gone on talking for a couple of hours, telling her stories about my childhood and even a couple of fairly dark secrets that I'd never told anyone else before.

But she didn't. She lit a cigarette instead and said, "I'm sorry the senator's a little late, but he's tied up on a long-distance call with his mother. She's an old lady and Carolyn's death upset her tremendously."

"How old is she?"

"Seventy-five. She lives in Indianapolis."

"That's where he was born, isn't it?"

"The senator? Yes."

"You were born in Los Angeles, weren't you?"

She smiled. "Hollywood. May twenty-first, 1946."

"Happy birthday," I said.

She looked a little surprised and then she said, "Why it is, isn't it? I didn't even think about it. Thank you."

"You went to school in Los Angeles?"

"Are you interviewing me, Mr. Lucas?"

I shrugged. "You're part of the story. Maybe even a very important part."

"All right," she said and put her knees together and rested her clasped hands on them and threw back her head and began to recite in the singsong voice of a child: "I was born in Los Angeles of very, very middle-class parents and Daddy died when I was ten and Mommy had to go to work as a secretary and I went to Hollywood High and studied real hard and won a scholarship to Mills where I didn't study very hard, but had lots of fun, and then I went to work and held several jobs and one of them brought me to

Washington where I now live on top of the Watergate."

"On top of the world, aren't you?" I said.

She dropped her pose. "I like it," she said in a hard tone that I hadn't heard before. "But that's my life story, Mr. Lucas. It's not very exciting and it's not very glamorous but it's a long way from Gower Street."

"In Hollywood?"

"That's right; in Hollywood."

"What did your father do?" I said.

"He was an engineer. He worked for a firm of consulting engineers. They were very hot when it came to bridges, I understand. They helped design a lot of them all over the world."

"And he died when you were ten?"

"Of a heart attack. My mother was a secretary before she got married so she went to work for the same firm. She knew a lot about bridges, I guess, because she told me that's all Daddy ever talked about. I don't remember too well."

"What was the name of the firm?"

"Collinson and Kearney. On Beverly Boulevard. The phone number's CRestview 4-8905. Or it used to be. I had to call it every afternoon at three forty-five to let Mother know that I'd got home from school okay."

"Why did you tell Gloria Peoples that you'd put her in jail and let the lesbians get her?"

It wasn't much of a zinger, but it was the only one I had. Connie Mizelle knocked it out of the park. She laughed. It was a bright golden laugh that seemed to match her hair. "You mean the little lush mouse?"

"I mean Gloria Peoples, the senator's ex-secretary. Is that what you call her, lush mouse?"

"You've been talking to her, haven't you?"

"Yes, I've talked to her."

"Was she sober?"

"Fairly so."

"It's a wonder. She keeps calling up at all hours of the day and night wanting to talk to the senator. We keep having the number changed, but she manages to get it somehow."

"It's not hard to in this town," I said.

"Yes, well, the reason I said what I did to little Miss Peoples at the funeral is that I wanted to shut her up. That seemed to be a good way to do it and it was."

"You say she has this thing about lesbians?"

"So it seems. She had a rather bad experience when she was thirteen or so. A friend of her mother's, I believe."

"She told you about it?"

Connie Mizelle laughed again. "Hardly. She told the senator. Pillow talk, I would think. He told me."

"Then you know about his affair with her?"

"Of course," she said, stubbing out her cigarette. "He keeps no secrets from me." She looked at me. "None at all."

"How did you get along with his daughter—with Carolyn?"

"We weren't friends, but we got along. After she realized how the senator and I felt about each other, I think she even tried to like me, but I'm not sure that she succeeded. But she tried. She was very mature for her age."

"How do you and the senator feel about each other?"

"Really, Mr. Lucas, isn't that a rather callow question?"

"Maybe," I said, "but it's still a question."

She seemed to look past me, over my shoulder. There was a faint smile on her face. "All right," she said, "I'll answer it. We're in love. We're deeply, completely in love."

"That's right," a man's voice said from behind me. "We are."

I turned. It was Senator Ames and he seemed to have aged ten years since I had last seen him three days before.

# 13

He also seemed to move less quickly and to stand just a little less straight. It may have been my imagination, but I thought there were some new lines in his face. I wasn't imagining the dark rings under his eyes, however. The rings made the eyes look as if they had sunk deeply into the skull and if they had glowed before, they burned now. Or seemed to.

"Darling, this is Mr. Lucas," Connie Mizelle said. "You're with Frank Size, aren't you?"

"Yes," I said.

He held out his hand and I shook it. I don't think he really wanted to. He did it out of habit. It was a political handshake and it meant nothing at all.

"Sit over here by me," Connie Mizelle said, patting the seat beside her. Ames nodded and sat down carefully, the way a very old man sits down when he's afraid that there's something that might break.

"We've just been talking about poor Gloria," she said.

I thought there was a flicker of something in Ames's

eyes. Interest, perhaps. Or even pain. Whatever it was, it died quickly.

"Is she all right?" he said. "At the funeral she—well—"

"She's drinking again," Connie Mizelle said. "Or so Mr. Lucas says. He talked to her yesterday."

Ames turned to look at her. When he spoke, his tone was hesitant and uncertain. "Shouldn't we try to do something for her? I don't know quite what we could do, but—"

"I'll take care of it," she said, giving his arm a pat.

He nodded. "Yes. Do something for her, if you can."

"Mr. Lucas wants to ask some questions," she said. "He's very good at it."

"Are you very good at it, Mr. Lucas?" he said.

"It's my job."

"I thought I'd answered all the questions that anyone could conceivably ask. I didn't think there were any more."

"Before your daughter died, Senator, she called me. She said she had information that would—well, exonerate you. Do you have any idea what this information could have been?"

"Exonerate me?" he said. "I don't think I need any exoneration. I haven't been charged with anything, have I?" He looked at Connie Mizelle. "Have I?" he said again.

"Of course not, darling."

"You resigned from the Senate," I said. "You resigned under what's usually called a cloud. Some say you took a fifty-thousand-dollar bribe. You say you didn't. If you didn't, that's news and that's what Frank Size prints."

"Strange," he said. "Once it was news that I supposedly took a bribe. It was never proved. It never will be. But that doesn't matter. News seems to feed upon itself. Now you say it will be news if I didn't take the bribe. Sometimes I find your profession a little weird, Mr. Lucas."

"So do I. Did you take the bribe?"

"No."

"What about the two thousand dollars that was traced to your account?"

"I borrowed the money from Colonel Bagger. It was a foolish mistake on my part."

"Why'd you borrow the money?"

"I'd inadvertently left my wallet and airline ticket at home in Maryland. I was due to make a speech that evening in Los Angeles. It was a Saturday and the banks were closed. So I borrowed the two thousand dollars to pay for my ticket and incidental expenses."

"But you canceled the trip?"

"Yes. At the very last moment. I was to speak at a labor union's annual convention, but they were having an internal fight so one of the union's representatives called and advised me not to come. The delegates weren't in any mood to listen to speeches."

"Your former secretary tells a different story," I said. "She says that you didn't forget your ticket. She says that she handed it to you that day herself. She also says that she cashed a hundred-dollar check for you at a liquor store. She says, in effect, that you had your credit cards and that you didn't need that two thousand."

Ames looked at Connie Mizelle who gave him a small, almost imperceptible nod. It could have been a nod of encouragement. Or permission. I wasn't sure which.

The senator sighed. "You were at my daughter's funeral, I understand."

"Yes."

"You saw how my former secretary behaved. I think

that she must be a rather ill person. I'm sorry that she is. But in her present state I don't think that she's a responsible person. Not for what she does—nor for what she says."

"You're saying then that she's lying?"

"Yes."

I shook my head. "She's not lying, Senator. You are. I checked with United. Their records show that you were issued a ticket to Los Angeles that Saturday on your American Express card. I had Frank Size check your bank account. You may not like it, but Size can do things like that. It shows that you cashed a check for one hundred dollars that same Saturday at the Apex liquor store on Pennsylvania Avenue. Those are facts. It's also a fact that you took at least two thousand dollars in cash from Colonel Wade Maury Bagger. You deposited it to your account. Bagger had fifty thousand on him that day. That's how much he was prepared to pay you for making that speech. But Bagger himself says you only asked for a two-thousand-dollar loan. You say you needed the loan to cover your expenses for a trip to Los Angeles. But you didn't need it for that. So why did you take it and deposit it to your account? It doesn't make any sense."

Ames looked once more at Connie Mizelle. There seemed to be a look of utter helplessness on his face. She patted his arm again.

"You don't have to answer that, darling," she said. She looked at me. "Perhaps it was just a mistake, Mr. Lucas. An error in judgment. Would you accept that?"

"No," I said. "I won't accept that. Not when it wrecked his career. Not when it forced him to quit the Senate with everybody thinking that he'd had his hand out for a fifty-thousand-dollar bribe. No, I won't accept it."

"I'm afraid you'll have to," Ames said, staring at the carpet. His voice was very low, almost a whisper.

"It was a mistake in judgment. I think I've paid for that mistake." He looked up at me. "Don't you?"

Look, Senator," I said. "I'm not trying to hang you twice. Honestly, I'm not. But you made a speech on the floor of the Senate that you shouldn't have made. You were offered fifty thousand dollars to make it; you turned that down. But you made the speech— and it looks as if you made it for peanuts, for only two thousand dollars. Why is all I'm asking. There must be some reason—maybe even a good one—the kind that would explain the whole thing. If there is, Size'll print it."

Once again he looked at Connie Mizelle. This time the almost imperceptible movement of her head was a slight, negative shake. He looked at me and when he spoke his voice was hard and firm and deep. "I refuse to discuss it any further," he said.

I knew that tone. I'd heard it often enough before. It came when you had backed them into a corner and there weren't any more lies that they could tell, not any good ones anyhow, so they did what they should have done in the first place. They shut up.

"All right, you don't have to answer my questions. But it seems strange that you'd keep silent if your answers would help the police find your daughter's murderer."

He was staring at the carpet again and his voice was back to a whisper. "I have told the police everything that I possibly can."

"Your daughter said she had information that would clear you. She was going to give it to me. Before she could, somebody killed her. The only possible motive for her death was that somebody didn't want that information to surface. Now who would that somebody be, Senator?"

"I have no idea," he whispered to the carpet.

"He's already told the police all of this, Mr. Lucas,"

Connie Mizelle said. "Can't you see that it pains him to talk about Carolyn?"

"All right," I said. "Let's talk about something not quite so painful. Let's talk about Ignatius Oltigbe."

The senator raised his head. In the past ten minutes he seemed to have aged another five years. I remember thinking that if I didn't leave soon, he might hit a hundred. "Ignatius," he said. "He's dead, too."

"He was shot to death in front of my house—for the same reason that your daughter was killed."

"In front of your house?" he said. "They didn't tell us that, did they?" He was looking at Connie Mizelle now.

"No," she said. "They didn't."

"Who told you, Lieutenant Sinkfield?"

"Yes, Sinkfield. He called quite late last night. About two in the morning, in fact. We were still up. We had been playing bridge with Cuke and his wife. We don't see many people anymore and it was rather pleasant. They had just left when Lieutenant Sinkfield called. I was sorry to hear about Ignatius. I never really approved of him although he was amusing, I suppose. Carolyn was quite fond of him though, wasn't she?"

"Very," Connie Mizelle said.

"Maybe Cuke would like to play bridge again tonight?" Ames said.

"I don't think so, darling," she said and then looked at me, adding, "Cuke is Bill Cumbers. He was the senator's administrative assistant."

"Did you wish to ask me something about Ignatius, Mr. Lucas?" the senator said.

"No," I said and got up. "I seem to have run out of questions."

The senator didn't get up. He was looking off somewhere. At the piano, perhaps. "After I left the Senate there really wasn't much to do and my former friends didn't seem to want to have anything to do with me. I can't blame them really. But Ignatius used to drop by sometimes and we'd have a drink or two and he'd tell me stories about Biafra. Lies mostly, no doubt, but still amusing. The man was what used to be called a rascal, I suppose, but he had a lot of charm and Carolyn was very fond of him."

A tear ran down the senator's cheek. The right one. I don't think he knew it. He looked at me and said, "The poor fellow didn't have any money so I'm taking care of his funeral expenses. I'm going to have him buried next to Carolyn. I think that would be all right, don't you, Mr. Lucas?"

"I think it would be just fine, Senator," I said.

# 14

As the elevator went down my depression rose. Waste always bothers me and ex-Senator Robert F. Ames was total waste. He wasn't the first man to wreck it all because of a stunning figure and a beautiful face. But few men had done it so stupidly. I decided that nobody could be that dumb—not unless he had help.

There weren't any cabs, of course. That went with my foul mood. Sarah had the car so I said some nasty things about her to myself and then decided that perhaps a drink might help. Maybe even several of them. I looked at my watch. It was not quite eleven. The Watergate had a restaurant and a bar but it probably wouldn't be open yet—just to spite me, of course.

"Would you like a lift, Mr. Lucas?" It was a man's voice. It came from behind me. I turned. It was Arthur Dain, the establishment's own private investigator. Confidential inquiries discreetly handled. Wandering husbands found. Evidence preserved by photography. No fee for consultation. Walk in. At least he was somebody to snarl at.

"No I don't want a lift, I want a drink."

He smiled as if he found that perfectly understandable. "I know a nice quiet place," he said. "Mind if I join you?"

"Is this just a coincidence," I said, "or do you keep the love nest up there under twenty-four-hour surveillance?"

He smiled again. "My car's right over here," he said. "And it's no coincidence. I was looking for you."

"How'd you know where to look?"

"Lieutenant Sinkfield told me."

"All right," I said. "Let's get that drink."

Dain drove a Cadillac, the small one, but it was still nice enough not to embarrass his clients if he had to park it under the porte cochere. He didn't drive very well. He drove like a man who had never really been much interested in cars.

The bar he picked out was on Pennsylvania Avenue about eight or nine blocks west of the White House. It was located in an old town house and it had the reputation of being a haunt for the town's singles. It was called The Riparian Rights which, I suppose, was as good a name for a bar as any. We took a booth and gave our order to the long-haired waiter. I ordered a martini. Dain asked for an imported beer. We were the only customers in the place.

I took a large swallow of my drink without bothering to mention Dain's health. It didn't taste quite right, so I took another swallow. Dain hadn't touched his beer yet. He was watching me. I beckoned to the waiter. When he came over, I said, "Bring me another one of these and have you got any Lucky Strikes?"

"In the machine," he said.

"Okay. Bring me a pack, would you, please?"

I finished the martini while I waited. Dain continued to leave his beer untasted. "You really wanted that drink, didn't you?"

"That's right."

"You seem a little upset by something."

"Does it show?"

"Yeah," he said. "It shows."

"Waste," I said. "Waste bothers me."

The waiter brought my second drink and the cigarettes. I opened the pack and lit one before I could change my mind. It was my first cigarette in more than two years and after the first drag I wondered why I'd ever quit.

"You're talking about the senator, I take it," he said.

"Yes. The senator."

"How did he look to you?"

"Bad," I said. "Very bad. He was crying a little when I left."

"Oh? What about?"

"About a guy who got killed in front of my house last night."

"Oltigbe?"

"That's the only one I know of."

"He was rather fond of Oltigbe."

"When did you talk to him?"

"To the senator? Never. I just keep tabs on him."

"For his wife?"

Dain decided to find out what his beer tasted like. He took a swallow. A small one. I shoved the package of Lucky Strikes at him. He shook his head. "I don't smoke."

"Neither did I until two minutes ago."

Dain looked interested. "How long had you been off?"

"Two years."

"That's a long time. Why now?"

"I feel bad," I said. "Whenever I feel bad I do

something that's self-indulgent. Like eating a whole box of candy. Or having a number of drinks. I'm weak."

"Hah," Dain said because he must have thought that I was making a joke. I don't think he was sure though. He didn't look like a man who had much humor. He looked like a man for whom life was a terribly serious proposition.

"When's she getting the divorce?" I said.

"Who?"

"Your client. Mrs. Ames. The senator's wife."

Dain took another swallow of his beer. He seemed to like the second one better. "She's not," he said.

"Why not? Does she enjoy humiliation?"

"No, she doesn't like it. She hates it, in fact."

"Then why doesn't she get rid of him? He's not worth much to anyone the way he is."

"He's worth a couple of million now, unless you think that's not much."

"I wasn't talking about that," I said

"I know," he said. "What'd he look like to you?"

"You asked me that."

"You said he looked bad. That he was crying a little. What else?"

I thought about it for a moment. "He looks like a guy who's going all the way down and knows it and doesn't much care anymore. He looks like a guy who's run out of hope and who just keeps on going because it's a habit, but one that he wouldn't mind giving up too much."

"Suicidal?"

"Could be, but I don't know that much about suicides. I thought they usually had to be either depressed or bitter. He's neither. He's in a kind of a mild shock that he comes out of and then sinks back into every five minutes or so. He seems totally dependent on Connie Mizelle. She probably even tells him when to go to the bathroom."

"What did you think of her?" Dain said. He sounded curious.

"She gave me a hard-on."

"Besides that."

"Tough, smart and dangerous."

"How do you mean dangerous?"

"I could see how she could make a guy do almost anything she wanted him to do."

"You sound a little afraid of her."

"Maybe," I said. "You ever talk to her?"

"A couple of times," he said. "She won't let me near the senator."

"How do you keep tabs on him then?"

"By talking to people like you—people who've seen him. I spent half an hour with his former AA this morning. A man called Cumbers."

"What did he say?"

"That the senator's bridge game has fallen off. He also said almost the same thing that you did. Except he put it a little differently. He said that the senator seems to have lost his talent for decision. He can't make up his mind about anything without checking with her first."

I shrugged. "Maybe it's lucky for him that she's around."

"His wife doesn't think so," Dain said.

"What does she think?"

"She thinks that he's under a spell."

I stared at him. He looked down at his glass of beer as though he were slightly embarrassed.

"You mean a real spell?" I said. "With witches and warlocks and all?"

"No, nothing like that. She just thinks that Connie Mizelle exercises some kind of strange influence over him."

"Ask her if she's ever heard of sex," I said.

"You think that's all there is to it?"

"I don't know," I said. "I'm not fifty-two years old and I haven't been through a series of pretty severe emotional crises. I don't know what it would be like to go through them and find that I had Connie Mizelle around to lean on. Maybe I'd get to like it. I don't think it would be too hard. A lot of guys have given up more than the senator has for a hell of a lot less."

"What do you know about her?" he said.

"You interested in a deal?"

"Maybe."

"I'll tell you what I've got in exchange for an appointment with your client."

Dain frowned. For some reason, it made him look more 1950-ish than ever. "How do I know that you've got anything I can use?"

"You don't."

He thought about that for a while—maybe an entire minute. Then he said, "When do you want to see Mrs. Ames?"

"What about this afternoon?"

"She doesn't need any publicity."

"I'm not selling publicity. I'm doing a report on her husband. If she wants to make sure that I get the whole report, she'll see me. Otherwise I might have to write around her. And that's not much good. At least not for her."

Dain nodded. "I'll be back in a minute," he said. He rose and walked to the front end of the bar where the pay phone was. He talked into it for almost five minutes. He must have had to do some convincing. When he came back he said, "She'll see you at three-thirty this afternoon. You know where it is?"

"No."

"I'll draw you a map. I'll draw it while you're telling me what you know."

So I told him everything I knew. Or almost everything. While I talked he used a ball-point pen to draw a map on a napkin. Every once in a while he would look up at me with those smart cool green eyes of his, as if to tell me that he was still listening although he didn't quite know why. It made me want to talk more. I decided that it was a listening technique that he had developed in the FBI. Or the CIA. He still looked like a banker, a cautious one, and he made me feel like I was applying for a loan that I had no business having. I felt that I was long on talk but short on collateral.

When I finally stopped talking, Dain kept on drawing the map. It had all sorts of little lines and arrows and even a carefully drawn compass that showed north. Then he pursed his lips, the way a banker does when he's decided to say no, and said, "That's not much, Mr. Lucas."

"It's more than you had before."

"Is it?" he said and raised a graying eyebrow.

"What have you got that I haven't?"

He shook his head the way a regretful banker might shake his. "We've made our deal," he said. "If you come up with anything else you'd like to trade, come see me."

"You've got something that I might be interested in?"

"I may," he said. "I just may."

I took a five out of my wallet and put it on the table. "At least let me pay for the drinks," I said.

On Dain sarcasm was a waste. He said, "If you insist," and handed me the map. I looked at it and it seemed to be rather well drawn. It also must have been the only thing that he was giving away that day.

When I got home Sarah took one sniff and said, "My, we've been drinking this morning, haven't we?"

"Smoking, too," I said.

"What happened?"

"I had a bad morning."

"What else?"

"I had to listen to a lot of lies."

She put her hand on my arm. "The kid's asleep. We can go up and crawl into bed and you can tell me about it."

"You think that'll cure almost anything, don't you?"

"Don't you?"

"Damn near," I said and grinned at her.

She grinned back. "Have we got time?"

"Not now, but we will tonight. Or maybe early this evening."

"Okay, if you won't have your way with me, how about some lunch?"

"What do you suggest?"

"What have you been drinking?"

"Martinis."

She nodded. "Peanut butter and jelly sandwiches. They'll soak up the gin."

After the sandwiches, which weren't half bad, I went over to the wall phone, picked it up, and looked at my watch. It was twelve-thirty. In Los Angeles it was half past nine. I punched the L.A. area code, 213, and then I punched the CRestview number that Connie Mizelle had mentioned earlier that morning. I was sure I remembered it. I had repeated it to myself often enough. CRestview 4-8905—the number she said she had called every afternoon at three forty-five to let her mother know that she had got home from school safely.

There was the usual buzzing and beeping and then the phone began to ring. It was picked up on the fourth ring and a man's voice said, "Stacey's."

"Stacey's what?" I said.

"Stacey's Bar, chum, and if you're thirsty we don't open till ten."

"How long've you had this number?"

"Ever since I opened the joint up twenty years ago. You just lonely, chum, or do you really want something?"

"Are you Stacey?"

"I'm Stacey."

"I'm just lonely," I said and hung up.

# 15

The map that Arthur Dain had drawn directed me out Highway 50 past Annapolis, across the Chesapeake Bay Bridge, and south down to Easton. At Easton I drove west on Route 33 that went through the center of a long finger of land that curved down into the bay. I was in Talbot County and Talbot County has more millionaires per capita than any other county in Maryland and that's saying something because there are a swarm of millionaires in Maryland and a lot of them live on the Chesapeake Bay.

I turned off Route 33 and took a narrow winding road that went down toward the water. The estates that I passed all seemed to have names, some of them cute ones such as "Old Woman's Folly" and "Why Not?" I kept looking for one called "Dunrovin," but I didn't spot it.

The estate of Mrs. Robert F. Ames was called "French Creek." A pebbled steel plate with raised lettering said so. The plate was imbedded in one of the twin stone pillars that formed an entrance to the place. There was also a big iron gate, but it was open. It looked as if it were always open.

I turned through the gate and drove up a long curving crushed blue-stone drive. The drive went up between two rows of English elms with whitewashed trunks. At the top of the slight rise was the house. I approved of it. Almost anyone would. It had been built of long narrow slabs of gray stone. Its roof was made out of real copper shingles that the salt air had turned a dark, dull green, but which would last forever. It was a big, sprawling one-storied house that angled this way and that as if trying to provide each room with a fine view of the bay.

Beyond the house with its four-car garage was a stone stable and a white-fenced paddock. Next to the stable was a long, low row of kennels. The house itself was surrounded by what seemed to be a couple of acres or so of well-rolled lawn. There were also some big old pines for shade and some shrubs for decoration and beyond these, and back of the house, was the pasture which sloped down to the marsh land that edged the bay.

I parked the Pinto, got out, and crossed a slab of dull red concrete to the front door. It was an old door, wide and tall, and the worn, carved panels on it told some kind of a story—about one of the Crusades from the look of them.

I pushed the bell and waited. I didn't have to wait long. The door was opened by the lithe, olive-complexioned young man who had helped Mrs. Ames from the car at her daughter's funeral. He still wore the same dark gray suit that wasn't quite a uniform. I don't really know that it was the same suit. He might have had seven of them. I decided that he must be the combination butler-chauffeur-valet, someone to call on if you needed a car driven, a horse saddled, a drink served, or a shotgun loaded. There aren't too many personal manservants left in the United States, but of those that are, a lot of them can be found on the rich, quiet estates that spread along the shores of Maryland's Chesapeake Bay.

He had a polite, still face, not quite pretty, and he let his black eyes study me for a moment. He didn't seem overly impressed, so before he could say we don't want any, I said, "Mrs. Ames is expecting me."

"Mr. Lucas?"

"That's right."

"This way, please."

I followed him down a wide hall whose walnut paneling, thick brown carpet, heavy furniture, and somber oils won my quick approval. It was exactly how I thought money should be spent, provided that one had a great deal of it. It was all good, solid stuff, the kind that would last forever.

The young man in the dark gray suit opened a door, stood to one side, and said, "Mr. Lucas is here, Mrs. Ames."

I went into a large, rectangular room. One wall was built out of nothing but floor-to-ceiling Thermopane. It looked out over a spectacular swath of the bay whose May afternoon blueness was dotted with a fair wind's whitecaps. Anything else in the room would have to fight the bay for attention, but the fireplace that dominated the other long wall did so easily. Raised a foot or so above the floor, it was tall enough for a six-footer to walk into without stooping and deep enough and long enough for a small pony to turn around in a couple of times. Besides that it looked old, very old, and I decided that she must have picked up the fireplace at the same castle where she had bought her front door. There was even a fire in the thing. Three five-foot-long logs, almost as big around as telephone poles, burned merrily away on large, old brass andirons, staving off the chill that crept in from the bay's blue water even on a May afternoon.

The room itself was furnished with low, comfortable chairs and couches upholstered in warm autumn colors and arranged so that, depending upon the mood, one could stare out over the bay or gaze dreamily into the fireplace. In one corner was a grand piano, a Knabe, that was positioned just right for being gathered around on a chill winter night, a glass in one's hand, a song of Princeton perhaps on one's lips, and the real world locked out and far away.

She stood in front of the fireplace and watched me cross the room. When I was halfway across it, she said, "Hello, Mr. Lucas. I'm Louise Ames."

I put her down as being forty-five, but that was only because I knew that she had had a twenty-two-year-old daughter. She looked younger—young enough and trim enough to wear the tight-fitting tan slacks that revealed a firm, well-rounded rear and a flat stomach that she didn't seem to be holding in. She also wore a yellow sweater, probably cashmere, and she filled that out nicely, too.

She was still a handsome woman, almost pretty, in fact, with short, waving auburn hair that was graying at its ends; a heart-shaped face with a delicate chin; dark brown eyes, ringed by shadow or sadness; well-tanned skin, not at all leathery; a good, straight nose; and a mouth that looked as if it had forgotten how to smile.

"Thanks for letting me come on such short notice," I said.

She cocked her head a little to one side and studied me for a moment, much as she might study a bad painting done by a good friend.

"Well, at least you don't much look like a liar," she said after a long moment.

"Is that what I'm supposed to be?"

"You do work for a Frank Size."

"That's right."

"I would assume then that he employs liars—excellent ones, of course. You just don't look like one."

"I'm still learning the trade," I said.

She almost smiled, but apparently thought better of it. "Sit down, Mr. Lucas. You'll find that chair over there quite comfortable."

I took the chair that she indicated. She continued to stand in front of the fireplace. "Would you like a drink? I'm going to have one."

"A drink would be fine," I said.

"Scotch?"

"Scotch would be good."

She moved a step or two to her left. I assumed that she stepped on a button, for a moment later the olive-complexioned young man entered carrying a silver tray that held a decanter, a soda syphon, a silver pitcher of water, a silver bucket of ice, and two glasses. They must have rehearsed it.

He served me first. After I mixed my drink, Louise Ames mixed hers and the young man disappeared—back to his post in the scullery, I assumed. The senator's wife raised her glass a little and said, "To happy marriages, Mr. Lucas. Are you married?"

"Not anymore," I said.

"Did you fight a lot?"

"No, not really."

She nodded. "I suppose that's a sure sign of a marriage going to hell—when it's no longer even worth yelling about."

"Yes," I said, thinking of Sarah. It wasn't quite a marriage, but there was still plenty of yelling going on.

"You want to talk to me about my husband, don't you?"

"About him and other things—or persons."

"Who for instance?"

"Arthur Dain," I said. "Why'd you hire him?"

She took a swallow of her drink. "To look after my investment," she said.

"What investment?"

"Do you know what my husband did when I married him?"

"He was teaching."

"He was an instructor in government at Indiana University and with his politics and his luck, he might have made associate professor by the time he was fifty. Instead, he became a United States senator at forty-six and I bought it for him every step of the way from state representative to state senator to lieutenant governor because that's what he said he wanted. It cost me more than two million dollars all told to buy his way into the Senate. That's a considerable investment, Mr. Lucas, and now it's gone sour and that's why I hired Arthur Dain. To find out why."

"Is that all?"

"Is that all what?"

"Is that all you want him to find out?"

"You've talked to her, I understand."

"To whom?"

"To the Mizelle woman."

I nodded. "Yes, I've talked to her."

"If it hadn't been for her, my husband would still be a United States senator and my daughter would still be alive. Now she has him under her spell." She looked at me. "That's right, Mr. Lucas, I said spell. There's no other word to describe it."

"I suggested one to Dain," I said.

"What?"

"Sex."

She laughed. She still didn't smile, but she managed to laugh. She threw her head back and let it come out—a derisive, scornful noise totally lacking in humor. It was an ugly sound, even cruel.

"Sex, you say."

"That's right."

"Well, she fairly drips it, doesn't she?"

"Some women do," I said, "but not exactly like she does."

She stared at me for another long moment. "You might," she said.

"I might what?"

"You might give it all up for something like her—home, marriage, children, career—whatever you had. You might say to hell with it all, that's what I want and that's what I'm going to have. That's what I've got to have. You might do that. Any normal man might. But not Bobby."

"The senator?"

"That's right. Senator Bobby."

"Why?"

"You know something?"

"What?"

"I think I'll tell you why."

"All right."

"You won't print it though. Not even Frank Size would print it."

"Why not?"

"Because it's about Senator Bobby's sex life. Or perhaps I should say his lack of it. Are you still interested?"

"I'm interested."

She laughed again. It was as cruel as before, maybe even more so. "I'll bet you are. Aren't you going to take any notes?"

"I don't take notes."

"And you can remember everything that somebody tells you?"

I nodded. "It's a trick," I said, "but not much of one."

"Well, let's see where I should begin. What about at the beginning?"

"That's a good place."

"Well, our sex life was normal at first. Very normal. Perhaps I should say too normal. I don't think he'd had much experience before we got married. Some, of course, but not much. Well, after Carolyn was born things went on much as before. Two or three times a week and gradually it became less and less until by the time he was forty and I was thirty-three we were making love twice a month at the most."

"Then what happened?" I said.

"Our birthdays are on the same date. October the thirteenth. You know what I gave him on his fortieth birthday?"

"A million dollars," I said.

"That's right. A million dollars. He was a state senator then. He'd already decided to make politics his career. I agreed. The academic life never really appealed to me. So we planned it together at first. What moves he would make—everything. You know what that silly son of a bitch thought?"

"What?"

"That someday he could even be president. And you know what was even worse?"

"No."

"I believed him. My money and his looks. A winning combination, right?" She took another swallow of her drink, this time a big one. I decided that it wasn't her first drink of the day. But then it wasn't mine either. If one wanted to sit around and lap Scotch all afternoon, it was a fine place to do it in.

"Where were we?" she said.

"On his fortieth birthday."

"That's right. I gave him a million dollars. Guess what he gave me?"

"I have no idea."

"An apron. That's right. An apron—a gingham one with little lace flounces on it. And you know where he wanted me to wear it?"

"In bed," I said.

"That's right. In bed. He said it excited him. So is Frank Size going to print that?"

"Did you wear it?" I said.

"Wear it? Hell, no, I didn't wear it."

"Then I don't guess Frank Size will print it. It's not much of a story. There's one congressman that I know about who's got a whole closetful of clothes. The only trouble is that they're women's clothes. His. It turns him on to wear them. His wife goes along with it all. In fact, I understand that they're pretty happy."

She looked down at her drink. "Size wouldn't print it anyhow, even if I did wear it, would he?"

"No."

"But that's not the point."

"What is?"

"We gave up on sex then. At least together. He found whores who didn't mind wearing his aprons and I found—well, you've seen what I found."

"What's his name?"

"This one? This one's name is Jonas. Jonas Jones and he knows all the tricks there are."

"You know something, Mrs. Ames?"

"What?"

"You talk too much. I don't mind listening, but you really talk too much."

She shrugged. "It's probably this," she said, giving her glass a swirl. "I'm drinking too much, too. But I have a point to make. You want me to make it or not?"

"Go ahead."

"Well, he had his whores who'd wear his aprons for him and then he found what he'd wanted all along—a sweet little ball of fluff who'd mother him and cluck over him and treat him like the child he is and who didn't at all mind wearing an apron to bed. God knows what cute little games they played. Doctor, probably."

"You're talking about his former secretary, aren't you? Gloria Peoples."

She nodded. "You were at my daughter's funeral, weren't you? Arthur Dain says you were there. Then you must have seen little Gloria. And heard her. Dear sweet mousy homey little Gloria. That went on for five years. More really, and he didn't even think I suspected. Well, she just proved my point."

"Which is what?"

"That sex isn't the hold that Connie Mizelle has on my husband. It's hard to define, but I'm more like the Mizelle woman than I am like poor little Gloria. But he prefers Gloria. And when he got tired of her, he'd have moved on to another one who was even more like—well, hell, why not say it? More like Mommy."

"You think that's it?"

She finished her drink. "I know it is. Arthur Dain isn't the first private detective I've hired. I've got some interesting tapes. Maybe you'd like to come out some rainy afternoon and listen to them. Do you think that might—as they say—turn you on?"

"I don't think so."

"Let's have another drink."

"All right."

She had a little trouble finding the button under the rug this time, but she found it, and once again Jonas Jones appeared with the tray. As he bent down toward me his back was to Louise Ames. He barely moved his lips and he said it just loudly enough for me to hear: "That's private stock, friend."

"Yours?" I said.

He waited until I had mixed my drink. Then he straightened up and in a normal tone said, "That's right, sir. Thank you very much."

After Jones had gone, she said, "He wasn't a bad senator, you know. He might even have become a great one. He has a good mind. Or at least he had one."

"What do you think happened?" I said.

"Her. That's what happened."

"I mean before that."

She put her drink down on the raised hearth, picked up a package of cigarettes, shook one out, and lit it. "You want one?" she said, offering me the pack. I'd almost forgotten that I was smoking again. "No thanks," I said, "I'll stick to these." I lit a Lucky Strike, my seventh for the day.

"Before that," she said. "Well, before that we had a little talk. About four years ago. That was when he still had his notions about becoming president and I had my fantasies about being first lady. I'd have liked that, you know."

"Sure."

"Well, we had this little talk. It was ever so polite and ever so formal. We decided that while a divorce wouldn't wreck his career, it certainly wouldn't help it. So we decided that I would buy a place far enough from Washington so that it would be impossible for him to commute. That way he could take an apartment in town without creating much comment. He did. He took an apartment at the Shoreham and I bought French Creek. After that we went our separate ways— he with little Gloria and I with, well, with my dogs and my horses and my own personal stud service. We did a minimum amount of entertaining out here, and in Washington we attended those functions together which were impossible to get out of. There weren't too many really. Politics is still a man's world."

"What did your daughter think of the arrangement?"

Louise Ames tossed her cigarette into the fireplace. Her back was to me. "Carolyn sympathized with her father. I don't think Carolyn ever really liked me." She turned back to face me again. "Her father doted on her. I suppose she and I were jealous of each other." She smiled for the first time, a bitter, rueful smile. "People really fuck up their lives, don't they, Mr. Lucas?"

"Some of us work at it," I said. "Then he made that speech, didn't he?"

She nodded. "Ah, yes, that speech. That speech for which he supposedly was to have taken fifty thousand dollars. Then it was two thousand dollars and then there was all that talk about a Senate investigation and then he resigned." She paused and then said, almost to herself, "She made him do it. Connie Mizelle."

"Why?"

"It was her job."

"You mean for the Bagger Organization?"

"That was whom she worked for. She may even have had another employer."

"Who?"

"There're at least a dozen men in Indiana who wouldn't mind being United States senator."

"You mean you think one of them set him up?"

She was just tight enough to try to look sly and cunning. She didn't make it. "I have my own theories."

"You stick with them," I said.

"You don't like them?"

"I think they're lousy. You say your husband's

smart—intelligent. Yet he makes one speech and ruins his career. There's no possible way that a political rival could get him to do that—not if he's half as smart as you say he is. For a while I thought it might be sex. Or maybe even love. I've seen Connie Mizelle. She could make almost any man walk out his front door and never come back. She might make me do it, if she got really interested. But she wouldn't get interested in me because I'm small time. But from what you say your husband doesn't swing that way. He's got a bend. For him sex is frilly aprons and soft, cooing sounds, and hot buttered popcorn in front of the TV set. You say it's all tied up with Mommy, but I'm not so sure about that either. Maybe he was just looking for something that not even eighteen million dollars would buy him. A happy home life for instance, and if that took a frilly apron or two maybe you should have tied one on and hopped into bed with him. Maybe he'd still have been senator with a shot at the White House. But that's all wiped out now and he did it all by himself. What I'm trying to find out is why, and I'm not getting anywhere."

"You know you look really quite attractive when you let yourself go like that," she said. "Your eyes get rather dangerous-looking."

"Ah, Christ, lady," I said and got up.

She moved over to me. She stood very close, far closer than she needed to. Her left hand, the one that wasn't holding the drink, smoothed down a lapel that didn't need any smoothing. "The little Mizelle bitch," she said sweetly. "She made him do it."

"Is that what Dain says?"

"Arthur Dain is very expensive," she said. "Do you know how much he charges?"

"Five hundred a day, I hear."

"So the information he's given me about her is rather costly, isn't it?"

"And you're not going to tell me what it is, if it is anything."

"I might," she said, her fingers just touching the hair above my collar, her face less than six inches away. "I might," she said again, "when we get to know each other better."

I'm not all that attractive. I'm six-foot-three and I weigh 161 pounds, because if I don't weigh exactly that it all goes to my gut, and my posture is odd because I list a little to port, but not much, and Sarah once told me that I have a face like an unfriendly spaniel. A smart, unfriendly spaniel, she'd added. So women don't throw themselves at me or send me little somethings from Camalier & Buckley or pick me up in dark cozy bars. But once in a while it has happened. A lonely housewife who might or might not have known something about how her husband had gone about cooking the government books would let her housecoat gape open and let it stay that way. Her husband wouldn't mind because he was probably in Buenos Aires by then. I knew all the signs anyway and I knew that unless I made a dash for it I was going to have eighteen million dollars' worth of slightly bored, slightly liquored-up housewife all over me. For a second I debated whether it would be worth it to find out what she knew, if she knew anything. I decided that it wouldn't. I'm still not sure what would have happened if I had decided differently. Maybe a couple of people would still be alive. But then again, maybe they wouldn't.

I didn't have to brush her off though. Somebody else did that. The voice that said, "Will there be anything else, Mrs. Ames?" It was Jonas Jones standing near the door that I thought must have led to the scullery. I looked at him over her shoulder. His black eyes were snapping at me. His face was a bit drawn and white, but he kept it all out of his tone. It was still polite. A little icy perhaps, but polite.

She didn't jump back or start. She let her hand slide down my chest, slowly, and then she turned. "Mr. Lucas was just leaving, Jonas. Would you see him out?"

"Yes, Mrs. Ames."

He crossed the room and stood by the other door that led to the wide hall. "We should talk again sometime," she said to me. "Sometime soon."

"All right," I said. "Let's."

"It might save you a lot of bother," she said. "And it also might be rather interesting. For both of us."

"It might," I said.

"I'll call you."

"You do that," I said, turned, and walked toward the door that Jonas Jones held open.

He followed me down the hall, passed me on the left, and opened the big, old carved door for me.

I stopped and stared at him for a moment. "You like your job here?" I said.

"It's better than Miami Beach, friend," he said. "Not so much competition."

"You want to keep it?"

He nodded. "I plan to."

"Then you'd better start doing your homework," I said.

# 16

I rented a green Chevrolet Impala from Hertz at Los Angeles International Airport, checked into a motel on Western Avenue not too far from Wilshire, hung up my suit, bounced my rear up and down on the bed a couple of times, mixed a drink from the pint of Scotch I'd brought from Washington, picked up the phone, and called Frank Size.

It was about one o'clock in Washington and Size was headed out for lunch. "I'm in the Gamine Motel," I said.

He asked what the number was and after I told him, he said, "I've turned this town upside down, but I couldn't find much. He's been out there a lot, but who hasn't? The first time was in 1929 when he was nine years old. That same year he also went to the Grand Canyon as well as Yellowstone Park, Yosemite, San Francisco, and Flathead Lake. That's in Montana."

"Sounds like quite a trip," I said.

"They drove it," Size said. "In a 1928 Essex Super Six, if that's of any interest."

"His family?"

His mother, his father, and his seven-year-old sister. Martha. She died of polio in 1935."

"No help," I said. "When else was he out here?"

"About two or three dozen times after that," Size said. "Christ, everybody goes to California. I haven't been able to find out much about his trips out there before he was senator, but when he was, he went out there fifteen times. About three times a year."

"To Los Angeles?"

"He went all over. Sometimes to Los Angeles. Sometimes to San Francisco. A couple of times to Sacramento. Once to San Diego. He had a friend in La Jolla. He stayed there a couple of times."

"Girlfriend?" I said.

"His roommate in college."

"That might be something," I said. "What's his name?"

"His name's John Svendson, but he won't be of any help to you. He died four years ago. Ames went out for the funeral."

"Okay," I said, "what about before he was senator?"

"Mabel got on the phone to his mother this morning. She lives in Indianapolis. That's how we found out about the Essex Super Six. She's an old lady and she talked for almost an hour—most of it about that trip they took. She didn't remember any other time he was out there except during the war. He shipped out of San Francisco."

"He was a pilot, wasn't he?"

"Navy pilot. Or rather a marine pilot. A hot one. He came out a captain."

"When?"

"According to the Pentagon he was discharged on August fourteenth, 1945."

"That was V-J Day, wasn't it?"

"That's right."

"Where'd he get discharged?"

"His mother said it was in Los Angeles and that he couldn't get home for two days because they kept bumping him off flights and the cake she'd baked for him went stale."

"Well, if he was a marine that means he got discharged at Camp Pendleton. That's outside of L.A. You got anything else?"

"We wrecked our whole morning here getting you all that."

"It's not much," I said.

"It's what there is."

"Well, I guess I'll take it from there," I said.

"Take it where?" Frank Size said.

"I'm not sure."

"That's what I was afraid of," he said and hung up.

The firm of Collinson and Kearney, consulting engineers, was on the second floor of a court-shaped three-story building on Beverly Boulevard. I walked up a flight of stairs and down the open-air corridor that looked down on the court. There was no bell to ring so I went in without knocking. A woman was seated behind a plain gray metal desk. She was working on the crossword puzzle in the *Times*. There were a few uncomfortable-looking chairs, the kind that are usually found in dentists' offices, some photographs on the walls of various suspension bridges, none of which I recognized, and a woven hemp rug on the floor.

The woman was probably just a shade this side of sixty. She had brittle orange hair and a brittle orange mouth. There were also two round spots of orange on either cheek. She looked up at me through bifocal glasses—the kind that swept up at the outer ends and were popular fifteen or twenty years ago.

"You're wasting your time if you're selling something," she said in a cold tone. "Mr. Kearney only comes in on Tuesdays and Thursdays."

"What if I wanted to build a bridge on Friday?" I said.

"Hah-hah-hah," she said, as if reading it.

"Business not too good?" I said.

She went back to her crossword puzzle. "Business is lousy," she said.

"Maybe if Mr. Collinson and Mr. Kearney would stay in the office more, things would pick up."

She put down her ball-point pen and spread her hands flat on the desk top. The orange nails matched the rest of her makeup. Her eyes, I noticed, were a robin's-egg blue. Orange didn't do much for them.

"Mr. Collinson," she said, "has been dead for fifteen years. Mr. Kearney is seventy-seven and the only reason he comes in is to get away from his wife. His wife, I might add, is a bitch. As for building bridges, we do not build bridges. We design them. Or to be more accurate, we tell people how to design them, and we haven't told anyone how to design a bridge in nine years."

"I guess things are a little slack," I said.

"What're you really after?" she said, folding her hands and resting her chin on them. "You can tell me some lies. I don't mind. I'm bored stiff."

"You worked here long?"

"Thirty-one years come June."

"I'm interested in some people who used to work here."

She smiled. "Oh, good, gossip. Who? I've known everybody."

"A man named Mizelle. And later his wife. Mizelle was an engineer, I understand."

"You with the credit bureau?"

I shook my head.

"Cop?"

I shook my head again. "Sorry," I said. "I'm sort of a reporter."

"Not for TV though?" She sounded a little disappointed.

"No. I work for Frank Size."

As usual, the trumpets blared, the drums rolled, and the drawbridge came down. It nearly always happened when I mentioned Frank Size's name to those who are starved for attention. There seem to be a lot of them. They are not only eager to talk, they are also anxious to tell you more than they really know. In fact, they'll often say things that they've never said to anyone else, either because they've been ashamed to or because they were afraid. But the shame and the fear seem to vanish when there is a chance of seeing their name in print—or their face on TV. Sometimes I think it's because they feel it's their last chance at immortality. I don't really know though.

The woman with the orange hair said, "My name's Phoebe Mays."

"I'm Decatur Lucas."

"Aren't you going to write it down?"

"What?"

"My name."

They like to see you take notes, too. Perhaps it gives them time to think up better lies.

"We don't do that anymore," I said. "It's old-fashioned."

"How in the world do you remember anything?" she said. "I can't remember a thing unless I write it down."

"I have a small tape recorder in my hip pocket," I

said. I shot my left cuff and gave her a glimpse of my wristwatch. "The watch is actually a thirty-three-pan cycle multiphasic microphone with directional sensors. You know, the kind that the astronauts used."

She nodded. "I remember hearing about those. On TV."

Sure you did, I thought. I don't know why I bothered to lie to her. Maybe it was because she seemed so bored. And so lonely. At least I would give her something to talk about for a week. If she had anyone to talk to.

"What about Mizelle?" I said. "Did he work here around fifty-six or fifty-seven?"

"Maybe," she said. "What's he done?"

"I don't know that he's done anything," I said. "He may be dead for all I know."

She sniffed. "Drank himself to death probably."

"He did work here though—as an engineer."

"Engineer!" She made it sound like a mild curse. "He was a draftsman and he only lasted four weeks. Mr. Collinson fired him himself. It was one of the last things he did before he took sick."

I nodded. "What about Mizelle's wife? She ever work here?"

She sniffed again. "What wife? Billy Mizelle was never married. He was out every night to all hours and showing up here late smelling like a gin bottle and telling the most godawful lies except you couldn't help laughing with him because he was so—well— so happy about it all. About everything."

"When did he work here?" I said.

"From May fifteenth, 1956, until June fifteenth, 1956."

"How do you remember so well?"

She used her right hand to pat a stiff orange curl into place. "Billy Mizelle is somebody you remember," she said, smiling a little.

"It is Miss Mays, isn't it?" I said.

"That's right. Miss Mays. Not Mrs. Mays or Ms. Mays—or however those dikes pronounce it."

"You say he drank a lot?"

"Everybody drank a lot then. Billy just drank more than most. He wasn't a lush, he just liked a good time."

"Was he a pretty good draftsman?"

"In the afternoon he was good. Very good and very fast. He wasn't worth a damn in the morning though."

"What do you think about drinking?" I said.

She raised her plucked eyebrows. They were dark brown. "You mean in general?"

"In particular," I said. "I was thinking particularly about the pint of J and B that I've got in my left hip pocket."

"Right next to the tape recorder, huh?"

I grinned. "That's right."

"Wait'll I get the glasses."

She took two green plastic glasses from a desk drawer and set them up. I poured a generous jolt into both of them. "How about a little spring water?" she said.

"Fine."

There was a cooler in the corner, the old-fashioned kind with a big upside-down bottle that gurgled when she added water to the two glasses. She handed me mine, then raised hers a little, and said, "To old broads."

"You're not that old," I said.

She drank and then gave her hair another pat. I thought that it must have felt a little like rusted iron. "I get by," she said.

I grinned again. "Got a fella?"

She actually blushed. "There's this old coot that squires me around some. He's got one foot in the grave, and they've had to drag him kicking and screaming into old age. He drives a dune buggy. Of course, he's got another car, but he likes to come by and pick me up in his dune buggy."

"Sounds like fun."

"I know how it sounds," she said. "It sounds goddamned ridiculous, but it's better than shuffleboard. You ever see them?"

"Who?"

"Our senior citizens. You oughta see 'em sitting around MacArthur Park waiting to die. At least old Fred's not like that."

"Fred's your fella, huh?"

She nodded. "You know where he is this afternoon?"

I shook my head.

"Taking a flying lesson. Of course, they'll never let him solo, but he likes to get up there with an instructor and fool around."

"You know something?" I said.

"What?"

"I bet I know why you remember Billy Mizelle so well."

"Why?"

"I bet he made a play for you, didn't he? Maybe that's why he got fired. Your boss didn't like it. Mr. Collinson, I mean."

Her face softened a little. It may have been the liquor, but I like to think that it was memory. "I was too old for Billy."

"You weren't too old for him. You couldn't have been more than thirty-two or thirty-three then," I said, shaving my true estimate by eight or nine years.

"I was thirty-eight," she said, probably shaving it herself by a couple of years. "He was just barely thirty. A wild man. A real wild man."

"Whatever happened to him?"

She shrugged. "What happens to the Billys of the

world? They grow old, but never up, I guess. He'd be forty-seven by now, wouldn't he?" She shook her head. "I just can't see Billy being forty-seven."

"He wasn't married though?"

"Not him," she said. "Milk was too cheap. You know the old joke, don't you?"

"You mean why buy a cow?"

She nodded. "Why buy a cow when milk is so cheap? He used to say that a lot. He would."

"He ever mention any family?" I said. "A brother or a sister?"

"He had a brother, Frankie," she said. "A year or two older. He came by here once to borrow twenty from Billy. Billy didn't have it, of course, so he borrowed it from me and gave it to his brother. I never got it back. I don't guess I really expected to."

"What did Frankie do?"

"He was a musician. Played the piano around town. Sang a little. You know the kind. Pretty as silk with real curly hair and a what-the-hell smile and the cocktail lounge'd turn the lights down real low and he'd croon 'Stardust' right at the old broads who were working on their fourth martini and all the old broads would want to take him home until they found out that he'd already been spoken for. By the bartender."

"Was he like that?"

"Frankie, you mean?"

"Uh-huh."

"Frankie was double-gaited, I think. You know, AC-DC. Any more Scotch in that pint?"

"Plenty," I said. She held out her glass and I poured in another overly generous measure. I poured a little less into my own glass. She filled them up with water from the cooler. When she sat back down, she looked at me with her robin's-egg blue eyes. They seemed to glisten a bit more than they had.

"Billy's not in trouble, is he?"

I shook my head. "No. I don't think so."

"What's somebody like Frank Size looking for him then?"

"It's a long story, Miss Mays. I'm really looking for somebody who might have known a little girl named Connie Mizelle. Or maybe Constance. She would have been around ten or eleven back in fifty-seven and fifty-six. I thought Billy might be her father."

Phoebe Mays smiled and shook her head. "No way," she said. "And Frankie couldn't have been her father either."

"Why?"

"Back in the mid-fifties was back in the stone age. It was way before the Pill. Well, both Frankie and Billy had something that made them awfully popular with the ladies."

"What'd they have?"

"When they were thirteen and fifteen they both had the mumps."

# 17

Phoebe Mays wanted me to hang around and meet Freddie, her fella, who was due back from his flying lesson any moment. She said we all might go for a ride in his dune buggy, but I said I had a previous appointment that I couldn't break.

"If you do find him, say hello for me, will you?" she said.

"You mean Billy Mizelle?"

"Uh-huh. Billy."

"Want me to ask him to drop by and see you, if I run across him?"

She thought about that for a moment. "He'd be about forty-seven now, wouldn't he?" she said.

"About that."

She shook her head. "Probably bald by now. Maybe even fat."

"Maybe not," I said.

"No, just tell him I said hello. That's all. Just hello."

"Phoebe says hello," I said.

She smiled, a little sadly, I thought. "That's right. Phoebe says hello."

I went out of there and down the steps and just as I was getting into my car, a Volkswagen dune buggy with a flimsy striped top and big fat rear tires roared in and more or less screeched to a stop. A sprightly old party swung his bare tanned legs over the side and got out. He wore plaid shorts, a red, short-sleeved shirt, and a white, clipped moustache and somehow it all fitted together with his Prince Valiant haircut. He started toward the stairs at a brisk stride and as he passed me, I said, "How's it going, Fred?"

He stopped, flashed me a white grin, and said, "Couldn't be better, son. I know you?"

"I think we've got a mutual friend."

"Phoebe?"

I nodded.

"Some dish, huh?" he said and gave me a huge wink.

"Lot of woman," I said.

He grinned, winked again, turned and went up the stairs two at a time. It made me feel tired just watching him.

I drove out of the courtyard and made only a couple of wrong turns until I got on the Hollywood Freeway that headed downtown. I parked in a lot as close to Temple and Broadway as I could get and put what was left of the Scotch away in the glove compartment. The parking-lot attendant saw me do it and said, "Tsk-tsk. They got a law against that."

"I've got a cold," I said.

"Jesus, that's too bad. So do I."

"Help yourself."

"You kiddin'?" he said.

"Not at all. Just watch the fenders. It's rented."

"Well, thanks, buddy, I just might take a nip."

"For your cold."

"That's right," he said, "for my cold."

I took the ticket he handed me and started walking toward Los Angeles' New Hall of Records that was about five years old that year and located right downtown in the Civic Center at 227 North Broadway.

Inside the building I found a directory that said that I should be looking for Room 10. Room 10 was on the ground floor and inside it, behind a long counter, was a cute little blond who didn't seem at all upset about being a civil servant. In fact, she even seemed proud of the fact that she knew all there was to know about her job. Her job was birth certificates.

After I got through telling her how important I was, she said, "You know, I read his column sometimes."

"Good."

"He always seems mad about something. Is he?"

"Usually."

"I'd hate to stay mad all the time."

"So would I."

"What can I do for you?"

"I'd like to check out a girl called Connie Mizelle. Or maybe Constance. I'll spell Mizelle for you."

After I did, she said, "Born in Los Angeles?"

"Right."

"Do you know when? If you've got the date, it's quicker."

"May twenty-first, 1946," I said.

"It'll take a minute."

It took three, actually. She came back with a letter-size form. "Birth certificates are a matter of public record," she said in the singsong tone of someone who has said the same thing over and over. "I can't give you a copy of it, but I can tell you what information it contains."

"Fine," I said. "What was the child's full name?"

She looked down at the form. "Constance Jean Mizelle."

"The father?"

"Francis N-M-N Mizelle."

"What's N-M-N—no middle name?"

"Right."

"What was his occupation?"

"That's number thirteen," she said. "Usual occupation, musician."

"What about the mother's occupation?" I said.

"That's number eight. It says hostess."

"What else does it say?"

"Well, there're twenty-seven items here. Length of residence, birthplace of mother, father's race, usual residence of father, mother's maiden name, name of hospital, street address, children born to this mother—"

"That one," I said.

"Number twenty-one," she said. "Children born to this mother, two. How many alive, two. How many dead, none. How many miscarriages, none."

"What was the other child," I said, "a girl or a boy?"

"A boy."

"And the mother's maiden name was what?"

"Gwendolyn Ruth Simms," the little blond said. "We don't get many Gwendolyns now. It's sort of nice and old-fashioned, isn't it?"

"Sort of," I said. "Is this filing system of yours set up so that I could get the name of the brother?"

"Same mother and father?"

"I don't know," I said. "I don't think so though."

"You know the brother's name?"

"No."

"His birth date?"

I shook my head.

"What about the mother's name? I mean not her maiden name, but her married name?"

"Nope."

She shook her head regretfully. She didn't like it.

She was falling down on her job. "We're just not set up that way to do it by mother's maiden name alone. Gosh, I'm sorry."

"Don't worry about it," I said. "Can we try one more?"

"Sure," she said with a bright smile.

"This one I've only got the year for and the name."

"That's okay."

"The year's 1944 and I'll spell the name for you." So I spelled the name of Ignatius Oltigbe for her and this time, because I didn't have the date of birth, it took her a little longer. About five minutes. I'm still not sure why I asked for Oltigbe's birth certificate. Maybe it was because he had been shot dead in front of my house and I thought that somebody owed him a little immortality, even if it were nothing more than making sure that he had been born. Or perhaps it was just curiosity about how a Nigerian chief gets born in Los Angeles in the middle of World War Two. Sometimes I kid myself and try to believe that it was a brilliant hunch, the kind that great historians have when they make a tremendously important discovery. The only trouble with those tremendously important discoveries is that they happen because one dull Saturday in London or Boston or San Francisco somebody gets bored and decides to clean out an attic.

When the little blond came back she was wearing a small, tight smile of reproval. "You knew all along, didn't you?" she said.

"Knew what?"

"Okay," she said, "we'll just play some more games." She looked down at the form on the counter. I tried to read it upside down, but her voice distracted me. "Ignatius Oltigbe, born December nineteenth, 1944. Father's name, Obafemi Oltigbe. Race, Negro. Nationality, Ethiopian."

"Well, that was close."

"Was he really an Ethiopian?"

"Nigerian," I said.

"Well, they're both in Africa, aren't they? I think that's what they called all Africans back in 1944 — Ethiopians, I mean."

"I suppose."

"Father's usual occupation," she said, "student."

"What about the mother?" I said.

"You already know that," she said.

"Know what?"

"It's the same as the other."

"Are you sure?"

"It has to be," she said, "unless two girls with the maiden name of Gwendolyn Ruth Simms both lived at the same address on Gower Street."

# 18

The parking-lot attendant gave me a strange look when I handed him my ticket and paid the fee. I decided that it must have been because the smile on my face looked a trifle silly. It was my historian's smile, the one I wear when I learn something vitally important such as the fact that Captain Bonneville had gray eyes, not blue as most historians believed. Now there was a tremendous discovery.

I felt the same way about my discovery that Connie Mizelle and Ignatius Oltigbe had the same mother. If I had been merely a great detective, I would have called it a vital clue. But since at that moment I thought of myself as a great historian, I decided to label it brilliant research—the kind that uncovers the missing fragment of fact that provides an entirely new perspective on a bygone era. Connie Mizelle was Ignatius Oltigbe's half sister. Of course. Now it all fitted.

Except that it didn't. By the time I reached my car it was just another piece of information. It was a little more kinky than anything else I had turned up. But no more useful.

The parking lot was the kind of a place where they let you drive your own car out if it's not blocked. Mine wasn't so I sat behind the wheel and ran it all through my mind. I got nowhere except that there was more to it than the coincidence that both Connie Mizelle and her half brother had turned up in the life of Senator Robert F. Ames at about the same time, six or seven months ago. Connie Mizelle had fastened herself onto the senator. Her half brother had scored with the senator's daughter. Now the daughter was dead and so was Ignatius Oltigbe. That should mean something. Something terribly wicked probably. The word "cahoots" kept entering my mind and taking a little bow. A U.S. slang word from the French *cahute*, meaning hut or cabin. Captain Bonneville had used it in a letter to the Secretary of War. "I went cahoots with Nat Fisher." It meant partnership then; now it usually means conspiracy. Maybe Connie Mizelle had been in cahoots with her half brother. It was a theory and one I would ask her about the next time I saw her. I found that I was looking forward to seeing her. It was more than looking forward to seeing her. I was anxious to see her. Yearning really, if that's not too sloppy a word.

I drove out of the parking lot and after a couple of blocks, I understood why the lot attendant had given me the look that was more strained than strange, now that I thought about it. It was because of the cold piece of metal that touched me just below the ear lobe. I jumped a little. About a foot maybe.

"Just keep driving, mister man. Don't panic." The voice was either a high baritone or a low tenor and it should have belonged to a man, but it didn't. It belonged to a woman.

"Was that a gun you poked in my ear?" I said.

"It was a gun."

I reached up slowly and adjusted the rear-view mirror.

"Wanta see what I look like, huh?"

"That's the idea," I said.

"Take a good look, sonny," she said. I did. She had a wide, almost square face. No makeup. Her hair was short, shorter even than mine, and it was a carroty red. She was probably thirty-five or forty with a pug nose and a hard mouth. I decided that she must have been a hell of a tomboy at one time.

"Not too pretty, huh?" she said.

"You want me to lie to you?"

"The girls like it," she said. "A lot of them."

"You got a name, mister?" I said.

"You're a cutup, aren't you?"

"I'm just driving," I said, "but I'm not sure where."

"Just keep on going up here for a few blocks. Then you can turn right until we get on Wilshire. Then you take Wilshire all the way."

"All the way where?"

"To a nice quiet little spot I know."

"Then what?"

"Then we'll see."

"This isn't just the newest L.A. ripple in stickups, is it?"

"Don't you wish it was."

"I'd be glad to hand you my billfold and let you out at the next corner."

"Just keep driving."

I kept driving. It was almost three-thirty. Traffic was medium heavy. I took another look in the rear-view mirror. I couldn't see the gun. All I could see were her eyes. They were staring into mine. She had green eyes and there was nothing cool about them. They looked hot and angry.

"Who you working for?" I said.

"I don't know, Jack, and I don't really care."

"You do a lot of this kind of thing?"

"Don't get nervous on me. It'll be over soon."

"How much?" I said.

"How much what?"

"How much they paying you?"

"For you?"

"That's right."

"For you they're paying three big ones. You're sort of a budget special on account of I need the bread."

"I can come up with five thousand, if you're interested in a better offer."

"Where'd you get five thousand between here and the beach? You are a cheapster, aren't you? I've had guys offer me twenty thousand to let 'em off. The only trouble is they had to go someplace and get it. Fat chance."

"We could work it out," I said.

I watched her shake her head in the rear-view mirror. "No way," she said. "Besides, I got my rep to think of."

"Where'd you pick me up?" I said.

"At the airport. I got a good description and you're not hard to spot. You walk funny."

"I've been sick," I said.

"Yeah, well, you're not gonna have to worry about that much longer. Just don't start cryin' on me. A lot of guys start cryin' on me and that just makes me mad. You don't wanta make me mad, do you?"

"No," I said, "I don't want to make you mad."

"That's good," she said. "Now hang a right at the next corner."

We were moving west on Pico Boulevard. At the next corner was a stop light. The street she wanted me to turn right into was Wilton Place. I glanced around at the traffic. It was still medium heavy. It was probably always medium heavy in Los Angeles. I swung the car over into the right lane. I took my foot off the gas. The light at the corner turned red. Ahead of me were two cars. They had stopped for the light. I glanced at the outside rear-view mirror. There were at least three or four cars behind me. Cars were also moving up on the left side. I hit the gas pedal and speeded up. At the last moment, I slammed on the brakes before I hit the car in front of me. I snatched the keys from the ignition and threw them out the window. Then I opened the door and started to get out.

"Get back in here," she snapped.

I turned slowly in the seat, still backing out of the car, butt first. I could see the gun. She held it in her right hand. The hand was steady. The gun looked like a .38 revolver with a short barrel. I shook my head.

"If you're going to do it, honey, you're going to do it now," I said, and kept on slowly backing out of the front seat, still a little bent over. Behind me, some cars started honking. She looked back. Then she looked at me. I thought I could see her forefinger tighten on the trigger. But I wasn't sure. It was what I expected to see.

"You prick," she said, lifted up her sweater and shoved the gun into the waistband of her jeans. I straightened up outside the car. She scuttled across the seat and got out the right rear door. Some more horns honked. The light had turned green. She started jogging down the sidewalk. I noticed that she wore tennis shoes. She didn't look back. She just kept on jogging down the sidewalk in an easy, practiced way as if it were what she did every afternoon around three-thirty. Maybe it was.

A man in the car behind mine got out and came up to me. He was about forty with a drinker's cherry cheeks and nose.

"Well, that's one way to get rid of 'em," he said.

"Yeah," I said, "I suppose it is."

"Have a fight?"

"Something like that."

"I saw you throw your keys out. If I was married to something like that, I'd throw 'em out too."

"You see where they went?" I said.

"Over in this next lane, I think," he said. "I'll play traffic cop and you can go look."

He held up his right hand palm forward the way traffic policemen do and traffic stopped. That's one thing about Los Angeles. A pedestrian has a fighting chance. I started looking for the keys. I found them after a forty-five-second search. I had thrown them farther than I thought. I held them up so that the red-faced man could see that I had found them. He nodded and then started waving the traffic on. He seemed to be enjoying himself.

As I was getting into the car, he came up to me and said, "Now that you got rid of her maybe you'd better keep it that way."

"I think you're right," I said.

"She was a lot older than you, wasn't she?"

"A lot," I said. "That's what we were fighting about."

He slapped the sill of the car door with his palm. "You oughta get yourself one who's a little younger. And maybe it's none of my business, but maybe you oughta get one who's a little more girly, too."

I looked up at him as I started the engine. "What'll I do about the kids?"

He shook his head and started to say something else, something wise probably, but I drove off before I could hear what it was.

# 19

I didn't go far. I didn't go far because my right foot was tapping away on the accelerator and there was nothing I could do about it. My left foot was all right because I had it jammed up against the floorboard under the brake. It didn't shake, but it wanted to. My hands were all right, too, as long as I gripped the steering wheel. I went a couple of blocks, found a parking space, and pulled in. When I tried to turn the ignition off, I had to fumble for the keys twice.

It took another full minute to hit the lock on the glove compartment and get it open. The pint of Scotch was about two-thirds gone. I tipped it up and took a large swallow. It could have been water for all the good that it did. I lit a cigarette after a couple of tries. It tasted fine, the way that they do after you come out of a long movie. I sat there and smoked and sipped at the Scotch and thought about how close I had come to dying.

She could have pulled the trigger a couple of times, jumped out the rear door, and trotted away with nobody trying to stop her. Not in Los Angeles. Not in any town. But she was a professional—or said she was—and the odds were bad. She was easy to spot and she probably had a record, a long one. The odds had been in my favor—six to five maybe, but if I had driven to where she wanted to go, I would have died.

That is how I rationalized it as I sat there in the car and comforted myself with what was left of the Scotch. It all seemed extremely logical now. But when I had snatched the keys from the ignition and thrown them away, I had been acting not out of logic, but out of fear—fear of dying. If I had to die, I wanted to die at home in bed, not slumped over the wheel of some rented car.

I held my right hand out, fingers wide. It still shook a little, but now it was more of a fine tremor rather than the uncontrollable flutter of palsy. I decided that another drink might help. It couldn't do any harm. I tipped the bottle up. A woman walking down the sidewalk, dragging her groceries behind her in one of those folding metal two-wheeled carts, saw me and quickly averted her eyes, as if I had just done something obscene.

"Medicinal purposes only, lady," I said to myself and then was a little surprised to find that I had said it aloud. I put the Scotch away, started the car, and drove back downtown to the parking lot near the Civic Center.

I didn't get out of the car when the attendant came over. I don't think he much wanted to talk to me.

"How much did she pay you?" I said.

"You mean your wife?"

"Sure," I said. "My wife."

"Ten bucks. She said she wanted to surprise you."

"Tell me something."

"What?" he said. He was getting nervous now.

"Did she look like my wife?"

167

"How the hell should I know what your wife looks like?"

"Did she look like anybody's wife?"

He shrugged. "Guys get married to all sorts of broads. How should I know."

"What did she look like to you?"

"Well, hell, mister, she looked like a bull dike to me."

I tried to make my voice as hard as possible. "You're talking about my wife, pal."

It was a little after four by the time I found the place. It was on Normandie Avenue just north of Wilshire and it was low and long and built out of what looked to be used brick. It had a shake shingle roof with wide sloping eaves and some mullioned windows with opaque colored glass that was dark maroon and green and blue. A small red neon sign, so small that it was almost discreet, hung from the low roof just above the entrance and spelled out COCKTAILS. Old English letters, a foot high and carved out of wood that had been painted black, spelled out the name of the place, Stacey's.

There was a small, asphalt lot next to it so I parked the car and went inside. It was dark and cool and quiet. To the right was a curved bar with comfortably padded seats. Highbacked chairs that were upholstered in what looked like suede, but probably wasn't, were clustered around small low tables. There was a small console piano in one corner with a microphone on a flexible cable attached to it. Beyond the piano was the dining area which contained about a dozen or so tables. It looked like a nice, quiet place where you get a good drink and decent steak without it costing half the week's grocery bill.

There was nobody at the bar, but there was somebody behind it. He looked familiar. He was a tall, tanned man with a full head of dark wavy hair that was going nicely gray. He had an interesting face, not quite handsome, with strong features and a curiously gentle mouth that kept him from looking tough. There were a lot of laugh or squint lines around the corners of his gray eyes. He wore a white sport shirt that was open to his breastbone. He had quite a bit of hair on his chest and it was going gray, too. He looked up at me as I approached the bar, nodded, and then went back to whatever he had been doing, peeling the lemons, I assumed.

I knew where I had seen him then. It had been at least ten years ago and usually he had been wearing some kind of vaguely western garb and he had always been carrying some kind of an animal—a calf or a young fawn or a small bear cub. He would come walking out of the woods or from behind a boulder carrying the animal, which at first you thought might be sick or crippled. Then he would put it down and the camera would follow it as it raced off to join its mother and you saw that it wasn't sick or crippled after all. It was just lost. Then the camera would move in close for a tight shot of that rugged, not quite tough face with its strangely gentle smile and he would stick a cigarette between his lips and light it with a kitchen match and a voice over would tell you what a wonderfully mild, rich-bodied smoke that cigarette was.

I slid onto one of the bar stools. He put down the knife that he had been using to cut up the lemons, wiped his hands on a towel, and pushed a small napkin toward me along with a bowl of peanuts.

"And what are we having this afternoon to ease the pain?" he said. The voice went with his size. It was deep and mellow. He'd never spoken on those TV commercials, but I'd heard his voice once before— on the telephone when I'd called the number Connie Mizelle had rattled off.

"Scotch," I said. "And water. Make it a tall one."

"What kind of Scotch?"

"Dewar's."

He mixed the drink deftly, served it, and went back to his lemons.

"I'm looking for Stacey," I said.

He didn't look up. "Why?"

"Ask him a couple of questions."

He put down the knife, wiped his hands again, and leaned forward on the bar, bracing himself with both hands. On his left wrist he wore a wide leather strap with three small buckles. "I'm Stacey," he said. "Who're you?"

"My name's Lucas. I work for Frank Size."

He nodded at that. "The guy with the column."

"Uh-huh."

"You're a little far from home."

"A little."

"Now why should somebody like Frank Size be interested in somebody like me."

"He's interested in somebody you might know. Can I buy you a drink?"

He thought about that for a moment, glanced over his shoulder at a small electric clock, and said, "Why not. You buying or is Size buying?"

"Size."

"Then I'll try a touch of Chivas."

After he had mixed his drink and tasted it, he went back to bracing himself on the bar and I got to admire the muscles in his bare, solid forearms. They were covered with a mat of hair, too, but it wasn't graying.

"Well?" he said.

"Gwendolyn Ruth Simms," I said. "Also known as Gwen Mizelle."

He let a little silence build before he said, "That goes back a ways."

"How far?"

He thought about that. "Twenty years at least." He used his right hand to make a small gesture that managed to take in the entire establishment including the parking lot. It was an actor's gesture. "She came with the place when I bought it twenty years ago."

"She worked for you?"

He nodded. "I kept her on. She brought in some trade. She wasn't a bad-looking fox then."

"How long did she work for you?"

"Ten, maybe eleven years."

"What happened?"

"She moved on."

"Why?"

"When I bought this place it was a dump. And the people who drank in here weren't so hot either. Some fast-buck boys, some hustlers—they hung out here. When some john would come in from out of town and ask the bellhop where the action was, he'd tell 'em Stacey's. It was that kind of a place, if you know what I mean."

"Sure," I said.

"Well, I was still doing a little film work, but not much, because the industry had gone to hell, but then I landed this TV deal. Cigarette commercials."

"I remember," I said.

"A lousy cigarette, but swell commercials. So I made some loot out of that and I put it all back in here. Remodeled the whole place. Then I started getting some uptown trade and for a little while this was sort of the in place to go—you know, because they could come in here and see me working behind the bar and then go home and turn on the TV and watch me let a baby skunk loose or something. Well, I raised the prices and hired a decent cook and the hustlers and the fast-buck boys moved on. They didn't feel comfortable anymore. And Gwen went with 'em."

"This was what, nine or ten years ago?" I said.

He nodded. "About that."

"Did you know Gwen's kid?"

"Connie?" he said. "Sure, I knew Connie. She used to call up here every afternoon about four after she got out of school to find out if her mother had made it to work. Gwen started drinking a little there toward the last. Connie still in Washington?"

"She's in Washington," I said.

"She part of the story you're working on?"

"She seems to be."

Stacey took another sip of his Chivas Regal. "She came in here a couple of times after she graduated from that college up in Oakland."

"Mills?"

"Yeah, Mills. She walked in here and she could've had any guy in the house. Me included."

"She's something all right," I said.

"I tell you what she was," he said. "She was the best-looking head I ever saw in this town and this town's not noted for its dogs."

"You're right there," I said.

"Smart, too," he said. "Book smart and gutter smart. That's a hard combination to beat. She making out all right now?"

"Seems to be," I said. "What about her father? His name was Frank Mizelle, wasn't it?"

"Old Frank," Stacey said. "I haven't seen him in years either. I sort of expected to see him at Gwen's funeral, but he didn't show. Maybe he didn't know about it."

"She died about seven months ago, didn't she?"

He thought a moment. "About that. It was in late October. The guy she was living with came around and put the bite on me and so what the hell, I gave him a couple of bills."

"You go to the funeral?"

He nodded. "Yeah, I went. Me and the guy that

put the bite on me. He was a no-good bum. And maybe three other people. I didn't know 'em though."

"What'd she die of?"

"Booze mostly, I guess. They said it was pneumonia, but what the hell, they lie a lot."

"But Frank Mizelle didn't show?"

"Huh-uh. You know, he and Gwen were shacked up off and on for maybe twenty years—from a few years after World War Two till about seven or eight years ago. Hell, I think old Frank raised Connie—if anybody did. He taught her piano and knocked the shit out of her if she didn't go to school. Just between you and me, I think old Frank was getting a little of that."

"Connie, you mean?"

"Yeah. He was strict as hell with her."

"I hear he'd swing either way."

Stacey gave me a disgusted look. "Is that some kind of a crime?"

"Not in my book."

"Well, old Frank might have been double-gaited, but he still made out all right with the broads. You know, that's one thing he and Gwen never fought about. He went his way and Gwen went hers and maybe they'd fight like hell on Sunday morning, but it wouldn't be about who was screwing who."

"What did they fight about?"

"Connie, mostly—from what I heard. Old Frank couldn't do enough for Connie. Like I said, I think he was getting some after she was maybe twelve or thirteen. He made her dress right and he made her hit the books and he gave her enough money so that she wouldn't feel bad with those twits at Hollywood High. Like I said, I guess old Frank raised her, if anybody did. Gwen sure as shit didn't care what Connie did."

"You think Frank was really her father?"

Stacey shrugged his wide shoulders. "Who the hell knows? Gwen fucked everybody in town. It could have been Frank or a dozen other guys. Of course, old Frank told everybody who'd listen that he'd had the mumps when he was a kid and couldn't knock up anybody. He got a lot of ass that way, but I think he was lying."

"But you don't know if he's still around, huh?"

The big man gave his head a couple of negative shakes. "I don't think he's in town anyhow. He'd of showed at Gwen's funeral. He might be playing some joints up in Frisco. That's where he was from originally."

"Tell me something," I said.

"Sure. What?"

"How'd you know Connie was in Washington?"

Still braced against the bar, Stacey looked toward his right at the door that led to the street. "Well, you know something, that's a funny story."

"Why don't you fix us both another drink and you can tell me about it."

Stacey looked at me. "Frank Size still buying?"

"He's still buying."

Stacey made us two more drinks, tasted his, and then went back to leaning on the bar. "Well, like I said, it's a funny story. Not really funny, but sort of sad."

"Uh-huh," I said, just to show him that I was still interested.

"Well, about two weeks before Gwen died, this horrible-looking old broad comes in here. It was about this time of day. Not much action. Well, this old broad is really a mess. She's fat and she's got her lipstick on wrong and a lot of paint on her cheeks and she looks just like death warmed over. But there's something about her that looks familiar. So I take another look and who the hell do you think it is?"

"I don't know," I said, not wishing to ruin his story.

"It's Gwen herself. I mean she looks awful. Well, what the hell, we were pretty good friends once and she never put the touch on me for anything, so I buy her a drink—a double because she looks like she can use it. She brightens up a little after that, but she still looks terrible. I mean real bad. So I haven't got anything else to do and we talk a little about old times and finally she wants to know if I'll do her a favor. I figure she wants to put the bite on me for a twenty maybe and I say sure, I'll do you a favor, if I can."

Stacey bowed his head and shook it a little, as if in disbelief. "You know, Gwen was about my age. Forty-seven, maybe forty-eight. I try to keep in shape. I run a couple of miles every morning around noon and work out a little at home. But I don't hardly recognize Gwen. I mean she looks maybe sixty almost. And she's dressed all crummy and she's carrying this shopping bag with her the way old broads do and she's got a couple of teeth missing. I mean she's a mess. So I say, Gwen, what can I do for you? So she reaches into this shopping bag she's got and comes out with a package and a letter. She hands them to me and says, mail these for me in case something happens to me. So I say, in case something like what happens to you, and she says, in case I die, stupid. Well, hell, nobody wants to talk about dying so I kid her a little and buy her another drink and then she gets up and starts to go. But she stops and says, 'You know something, Stace?' So I say what, and she says, 'You know, I don't think I've been a very good person.' Then she turns around and goes out and that's the last I ever see of her—except at her funeral and then I didn't really see her because they didn't have the casket open."

"Huh," I said. "Who was the letter to?"

"The letter was to some guy in London, England. He had a funny name."

"Oltigbe?" I said. "Ignatius Oltigbe?"

"Yeah, I think that was it. What is that, French?"

"African," I said.

"No kidding," he said. "Well, Gwen knew all kinds."

"Who was the package to?"

"That was to Connie. It was addressed to her in Washington. That's how I knew she was there."

"What kind of package was it?" I said.

He used his hands to show me. "Oh, so big. You know. About the size of a cigar box."

"And you mailed them?" I said

"Sure. Right after that bum that Gwen was living with comes around and tells me she's dead and puts the bite on me for a couple of bills, I take 'em down to the post office and mail 'em. They already had the stamps on 'em and everything."

"How much did the package weigh? Do you remember?"

He shrugged again. "I don't know. About as much as a box of cigars would weigh."

"Or a book?" I said.

"Yeah, maybe. About a pound anyway." He looked at me. "Now what's the story on Connie? How come Size is interested in her?"

"He thinks she's news."

"Big news?"

"Maybe."

"How big?"

"It seems to reach all the way to the Senate."

"That sounds big. She in trouble?"

"Not yet."

"Money involved?"

"Could be."

"How much? I mean just a guess."

"It could run into the millions—maybe."

Stacey nodded his head in a self-satisfied way. "I always said so," he murmured, almost to himself.

"Said what?"

"I always said that with her brains and looks, someday Connie'd hit the big time."

# 20

I got out of Los Angeles fast. I didn't go back to the motel to pick up my suit and shaving stuff. Frank Size could buy me some more. I drove directly from Stacey's to Los Angeles International, handed over my keys to the Hertz people, and caught the first flight going east. It went to Chicago and I had an hour layover at O'Hare before I could get on the next plane that went somewhere near Washington. It was an American flight and it went to Friendship which is about halfway between Washington and Baltimore. I would have liked to fly into National Airport at Washington, but planes don't land there after midnight because they make too much noise. By midnight everybody in Washington has been in bed for an hour—at least everybody who has anything to say about when planes can take off and land.

I splurged on a taxi from Friendship and by the time I got home it was nearly four in the morning. Sarah awakened when I crept into the bedroom. She always did, no matter how quiet I tried to be.

"How was it?" she said

"Not bad."

"Can I get you something?"

"Not a thing. Any calls?"

"A lot of them."

"Who from?"

"You going to return them now?"

"No. Just curious."

"Well, there was Lieutenant Sinkfield. He called twice. And Mr. Arthur Dain called once. He's got a smooth voice. And then there was your fan club. There was the senator's wife, Mrs. Ames. And there was someone who sounded a little weepy and called herself Gloria Peoples. And finally there was Miss Connie Mizelle, the girl with the satin voice."

"You ought to see her body," I said.

"If it matches her voice, you're probably in love again."

"I'll get over it. What did you tell them?"

"That you were in Los Angeles, but I didn't know where, and if it were important, you could probably be reached through Frank Size's office. Now come to bed."

"I was thinking of putting on some pajamas."

"You're not going to need them," she said.

I sensed that there was somebody there. I opened my eyes just in time to see the hand, fingers stiff and extended, coming fast right for the base of my nose. I rolled my head to the left and the fingers caught me near the right ear. "Whang!" Martin Rutherford Hill said, instead of good morning.

"You're a killer, aren't you, kid?" I said and then tried to decide whether I had a hangover from all the booze I had drunk the day before. Not quite, it seemed, but almost.

"Deke!" said Martin Rutherford Hill.

"Hey, Sarah!" I yelled.

"What?" she yelled back from downstairs.

"The kid said a word."

"I'm bringing it," she yelled.

A few moments later she came in carrying a cup of coffee. I propped myself up in the bed and accepted it gratefully.

"You want a cigarette or are you going to quit again?"

"I'll quit next week. They're in my coat pocket."

She found them, put one in my mouth, and lit it for me.

"Thanks," I said. "The kid said a word."

"A real one?"

"He said my name. Deke. Say Deke again, Martin Rutherford."

"Deke," Martin Rutherford said promptly.

"See?"

She shook her head. "He's been saying that all week."

"Go way, kid," I said. "Come back when you can say Decatur."

"In about five years," Sarah said.

"What time is it?"

"A little past ten."

"You working today?"

She shook her head. "Not today."

"Get a sitter for the kid and we'll go out to dinner tonight."

"Gosh, Mr. Lucas, I'm aflutter. What's the occasion?"

"No occasion at all."

"Good," she said. "That's the best kind."

By ten-thirty I was showered, shaved and dressed and sitting at my desk in the other bedroom that had once been my office-study, but which I now shared with Martin Rutherford. The room faced the east and the sun streamed down upon my desk which faced away from the window. The room's third tenant, Foolish the cat, was curled up around the phone. I tried not to disturb him as I punched the number that Lieutenant Sinkfield had given Sarah.

He came on all business and no nonsense with a snappy "Lieutenant Sinkfield" that made him sound as though he was all set to lead the next charge in the morning war on crime.

After I told him who I was, I said, "You called twice. I thought it might be important."

"It seemed that way yesterday," he said. "Today it only looks kind of interesting."

"You guys ever eat lunch?" I said.

"Sure, we eat lunch. We eat at Scholl's Cafeteria a lot because it's cheap and they've got all those religious sayings around. We find 'em quite a comfort in our line of work."

"I was thinking of something a little fancier."

"I was hoping you were," he said.

"What about Duke Zeibert's?"

"That's fancy enough."

"When do you like to eat?" I said.

"I like to eat around noon, but then I'm sort of country."

"Noon's fine," I said. "By the way, you know anybody in Homicide out in L.A.?"

"I know somebody out there," he said in a careful tone that wasn't giving anything away.

"Yeah, well, I think somebody tried to kill me out there yesterday and I thought maybe your friends could find out who."

"You kidding?"

"No. I'm not kidding."

"You get a look at him?"

"It was a her," I said, "and I got a good look."

"Start talking," Sinkfield said. "I'm taping it, if it's okay with you."

"It's fine with me," I said.

At eleven-thirty that morning I slid my expense-account statement across Frank Size's desk. "First things first," I said. I slid it across to him upside-down. He frowned at it and then used the eraser of a yellow pencil to turn it around. I don't think that he wanted to touch it.

He read it and then looked up at me slowly. Disbelief was written across his face. There was disbelief in his eyes, too, but then they always held that. "One suit?" he said. "One electric razor? One toothbrush? One tube of Crest? One pair of Jockey shorts? One blue shirt? One hundred and eighty-three dollars and forty-five cents?" By the time he got to the forty-five cents his voice had reached the upper register of total disbelief.

"Do you want me to tell you about it," I said, "or do you want to see whether you can sing soprano?"

"Tell me about it," he said. "I haven't heard anything ridiculous all morning."

So I told him about it and he listened as he always listened, with complete absorption, making notes only of questions that he might want to ask when I had finished.

When I stopped talking, Frank Size used the pencil he had been holding to scrawl OK and his initials on my expense sheet. He pushed it across the desk toward me. "I don't think I would have stopped at Stacey's," he said. "I think I would have taken the first plane out—or gone for the cops."

"I had a lot of Scotch in me," I said.

He nodded. "What're you telling Sinkfield?"

"Just about everything, I think."

He nodded again. "Yeah. I think so. Then?"

"Then I call or see all those people who called me while I was gone. Maybe they might have something."

"We've already got enough for a bunch of columns," he said. "The way that Connie Mizelle and her half brother moved in on the senator and his daughter. That's a beauty."

"I think you could run for a week with what you've got."

"Except for one thing," Size said.

I nodded this time. "It doesn't hang together."

"No," he said. "It doesn't."

"A column or two might smoke it all out."

"Yeah, but I wouldn't have it then, would I?" he said.

"Not all to yourself."

"I want it all," he said.

"That's what I thought."

"You want to keep on it by yourself or do you want some help?"

"Who from?" I said.

"From me."

"Let's see what happens during the next couple of days. I've got the feeling something's going to bust open."

Size nodded. "So do I. That's why I want in."

"Well, hell, you're the boss."

"But what I want isn't always what's smart."

"If you know that, maybe that's why you're the boss."

"Yeah," he said. "Maybe it is."

I handed Mabel Singer my expense sheet and talked her into calling Duke Zeibert's and making a reservation for me at a table that wouldn't be right next to the kitchen door or jammed up so close to somebody else that Sinkfield and I would have to write notes to each other if we wanted to talk. It's not hard to rub shoulders with the sporty types who hang out at Duke Zeibert's. What's hard is not to.

But once again the name of Frank Size worked its wonders and when I got there a couple of minutes early (as always), I was given a choice table that was at least a foot away from its nearest neighbor. At Zeibert's, that's virtual isolation.

Sinkfield was on time or at worst, a minute or two late. He sank into his seat with a long sigh. "Bad morning?" I said.

"They're all bad," he said. "Let's have a drink."

A waiter came over and we ordered drinks. We also ordered lunch. Sinkfield asked for a steak and I chose trout. After the drinks came, Sinkfield took a swallow of his and said, "That was a pretty dumb thing you did yesterday. Or maybe it was pretty smart. I'm still not sure which."

"What?" I said.

"Jumping out of your car like that."

"Why dumb?" I said. "I'm still alive."

"It's a wonder."

"Did the L.A. cops know her?"

He nodded. "They think you ran into Big Bad Bea."

"Who's Big Bad Bea?"

"Big Bad Bea is Miss Beatrice Anne Wheat. They've never known her to kill anybody before, but she once did two years for working a guy over with a beer bottle. He damn near died. My friends out in L.A. say that she does a pretty fair stompin', too, or so they've heard. She gets paid for it, but they think she'd do it for kicks, if things got slow. They're interested in the fact that she pulled a gun on you though. They were wondering if you'd like to come out and maybe make a complaint. I told 'em I didn't think so."

"You're right," I said.

"They got three or four unsolved killings out there

that they think they just might tie her into. You say she pulled a thirty-eight on you?"

"It looked like a thirty-eight."

"That's what I told 'em. They think if they can catch her with it on her, they can put ballistics to work and maybe come up with something. I told 'em if they pulled her in they might do me a favor and try and find out who she was working for."

"That would be interesting," I said.

"You got any ideas?"

I shook my head.

"Aw, come on, Lucas."

"All right," I said. "I've got an idea. It's somebody who wants me either dead or scared off. That means it's probably the same person who blew up Carolyn Ames and shot Ignatius Oltigbe. It's somebody who knows their way around enough so that they can pick up the phone and call somebody like Big Bad Bea."

"You can hire all that," Sinkfield said. "Why would they want you dead? You got something you haven't told me about?"

"I don't know," I said. "About the only thing I found out in Los Angeles is that Connie Mizelle had a mother."

"Gwendolyn Ruth Simms," Sinkfield said. "Also known as Gwen Mizelle, common-law wife of Francis no-middle-initial Mizelle. She died October twenty-first."

"You checked, huh?"

"That's my job."

"Well, she had another kid. I mean Gwen Mizelle did."

"Oh?"

"Yeah. His name was Ignatius Oltigbe."

Sinkfield put down the piece of steak that was half-way to his mouth. He reached for a cigarette and lit it. His eyes were looking at something that seemed to be a long way off. After another drag on his cigarette, he crushed it out, reached for his fork and put the piece of steak in his mouth. He chewed it a few times and said, "It should fit, but it doesn't."

"I know what you mean," I said.

"They both showed up about the same time, didn't they? I mean the Mizelle girl and her half-spade half brother."

"Their mother sent them something after she died," I said. "A guy who owns a bar out there mailed them. A letter went to Oltigbe in London; a package about the size of a cigar box went to Connie Mizelle."

Sinkfield nodded and cut himself another piece of steak. He put it into his mouth and while still chewing it, he said, "What were you really after out there in L.A.?"

"Something that would tie Senator Ames in with Connie Mizelle."

"What were you thinking of, something dirty like Polaroid pictures of him and her and maybe another broad?"

"Maybe," I said. "She told me a couple of lies. They were sort of harmless ones though—such as her parents being respectable middle-class types. They weren't, but there's no crime in trying to dress up your past a little bit."

"She went to college out there on a scholarship," Sinkfield said. "I checked that out."

"She's pretty much what she says she is," I said and gave up on the trout because I'd made a mess of trying to debone it. "She went to Hollywood High and made good enough grades to win her a full scholarship to Mills and after that she worked at various jobs and wound up in Washington working for a lobbying outfit. But what she doesn't tell anybody is about growing up in Hollywood pretty much on her own and living with a piano player who maybe is and maybe isn't her father and him teaching her the piano along with maybe a few other tricks when she turned twelve or thirteen."

"It was like that, huh?" Sinkfield said.

"From what I could gather it was something like that. Whatever it was like, it wasn't easy. It might have been downright nasty."

"Did you turn up anything that would tie the senator in with her?"

"With Connie?"

"Yeah."

"No. Not a thing."

"What about the mother?"

"From what I heard the mother fucked everybody in town. Maybe she fucked the senator and like you said, took some pictures."

"And leaves 'em in her will to her two kids, huh?"

"Sure," I said. "Except that from what I learned about the mother, if those pictures had had any cash value, she'd have used them herself. If there were any pictures, which there probably weren't."

"How'd we get off on dirty pictures anyway?" Sinkfield said.

"You brought it up."

"Yeah, I guess I did."

"It's not much of a theory," I said.

"No, it sure as hell isn't."

"You want some dessert?"

"No, I don't want any dessert."

"How about some coffee?"

"I don't want any coffee either,"

"What do you want?"

"I wanta see Connie Mizelle," he said.

"What's stopping you?"

"Not a damn thing," he said. "Let's go."

# 21

We used Sinkfield's car to drive to the Watergate. It was an unmarked black Ford sedan, about two years old, and in urgent need of new shock absorbers. Sinkfield drove in a smooth, unhurried fashion that managed to make most of the lights.

"You said you had something to tell me," I reminded him.

"Oh, yeah, I did. I thought maybe it was a big, fat clue. You know, that's what us detectives like to work with—big, fat clues."

"What was your big, fat clue?" I said.

"I did some more checking on Oltigbe—when he was in the army with the Eighty-second Airborne. Guess what he used to teach a class in down at Fort Benning?"

"What?"

"Demolition. He was an expert. He could blow up damn near anything."

"Especially an attaché case, huh?"

"Yeah, especially an attaché case."

"Well, that's some clue all right," I said.

"You don't like it?"

"Do you?"

"Nah," he said. "I don't like it. Why should he blow up the senator's daughter? If he blows her up, he gets nothing. If he sticks around, maybe she'll marry him and he'll marry a million bucks."

"Maybe his half sister told him to blow her up," I said.

"Huh?"

"It's the latest Lucas theory. After years of separation, the half sister is reunited—or united, I guess—with her half brother. Out of the phone book they select themselves a couple of marks—Senator Ames and his daughter, Carolyn. Connie Mizelle moves in on the senator. Ignatius moves in on Carolyn who discovers the plot and threatens to expose the pair. They blow her up and maybe her information along with it. Then Connie Mizelle gets greedy. So she excuses herself from a bridge game on the pretense that she has to go pee. Instead, she streaks over to my house, shoots her half brother, and whisks back to the bridge game just in time to respond five hearts to her partner's conventional Blackwood bid of four no-trump. After bidding a small slam and making it, she serves coffee, carefully adding a minute dab of arsenic to the senator's."

"Ah, shit, Lucas," Sinkfield said.

"You got anything better?"

"No, but there's one thing."

"What?"

"I haven't got anything as bad."

Sinkfield used his badge to get us through the Watergate's Security. We had to wait for an elevator, but not long. In a high-priced cooperative such as the Watergate, it doesn't pay to skimp—especially on elevators. When the car arrived, a small bell dinged, its doors opened, and out stepped Washington's $100-an-hour private investigator, Mr. Arthur Dain, all dressed up in one of his Eisenhower-era suits.

"Well, we keep bumping into each other, don't we, Lieutenant?" he said, nodded at me and added, "Mr. Lucas," so that I wouldn't feel left out.

"You been up to the senator's?" Sinkfield said.

"That's right."

"That's a pretty strange place for you to be, isn't it?"

"Not really, Lieutenant. I sometimes serve as kind of a diplomatic courier between Mrs. Ames and her husband—although I usually don't get much farther than Miss Mizelle. Today, I had to deliver some bad news."

"Oh?" Sinkfield said. "What kind of bad news?"

"You recall the senator's secretary, Gloria Peoples?"

"The little lush at the funeral."

"Well, she's worse," Dain said. "She somehow got Mrs. Ames's telephone number and started calling her at all sorts of odd hours. Really ranting and apparently drunk out of her mind. Mrs. Ames was worried that she might hurt herself so she asked me to find out whether the senator would take the responsibility for having the Peoples woman committed someplace."

"Someplace like where?" I said.

"The Washington Hospital Center until she's dried out," Dain said.

"After that?" Sinkfield said.

Dain shrugged. "Some private sanitarium."

"They throw the keys away at some of those private sanitariums," Sinkfield said.

"The woman needs help," Dain said.

"Is the senator gonna give it?"

"He wasn't there, but Miss Mizelle said that I should go ahead and do whatever's necessary."

"She's taken over, huh?" Sinkfield said.

"We waited an hour for the senator to come back, but when he didn't, Miss Mizelle said that she would take full responsibility for the Peoples woman."

"Where's the senator?" I said.

Dain looked at his watch. "He went out for a walk about two hours ago. He hasn't come back yet."

"I wouldn't mind spending an hour with her by myself," Sinkfield said. "But I always gotta take somebody along like Lucas here."

"As his chaperone," I said.

Arthur Dain smiled just a little to show that he could recognize a joke when he heard one. It was a small, pained smile that went away quickly. "Mrs. Ames would like to see you, Mr. Lucas," he said.

"Is that what she called about yesterday?" I said.

"Yes."

"And is that what you called about?"

"That's right."

"All right, I suppose I'll go see her. When?"

"Are you going to be up there long?" Dain said.

I looked at Sinkfield. He shook his head. I said, "No, not long."

"Well, if you'd like," Dain said, "I can run you out to French Creek and back. I have to go out there anyway."

"Okay," I said. "Where'll I meet you?"

"Here in the lobby. I've spent a lot of time in this lobby."

Sinkfield looked around. "It's not a bad place to wait around in if somebody's paying you five hundred bucks a day to do the waiting."

Before Dain could say anything, I asked him, "What does Mrs. Ames want to see me about?"

"I don't know," he said.

"Did you ask?"

"I asked."

"What'd she say?"

"She told me that it was important," he said. "In fact, she told me that it was vitally important."

"Then I guess I'd better go see her."

"Yes," Dain said, "I think you should."

Both Sinkfield and I must have stared at Connie Mizelle when she opened the door. I don't know how long we stared, but it was probably several seconds. She wore a white dress of some double-knit material, but I don't think I would have stared any harder had she been naked. She had that kind of effect on me. She had the same kind of effect on Sinkfield. She must have had the same effect on most men.

"Well," she said, "both of you. How nice. Do come in."

We went in and watched Connie Mizelle sit down on one of the twin white couches that flanked the fireplace. She sat down gracefully, giving us a bit of a leg show. She made a small wave with her hand and said, "I think you'll both find that other couch comfortable."

We both sat down on the other couch. I waited for Sinkfield to begin, but he didn't. He kept staring at Connie Mizelle.

"Lieutenant?" she said.

"Yes."

"Do you always take a reporter around with you?"

Sinkfield looked at me. The look said that he wished that I would disappear. "Oh, I don't think of Lucas here as a reporter," he said.

"You don't?" she said.

"No, I sort of think of him as a historian."

"Not as a biographer—not as a kind of latter-day Jimmy Boswell?"

"Who's Jimmy Boswell?" Sinkfield said to me.

"He used to follow a guy named Johnson around a long time ago and take down everything he said. Johnson used to say all sorts of cute things."

Sinkfield shook his head. "No, I think of Lucas as a historian. Sort of a digger into the past. Like yesterday he was out in Los Angeles digging into the past. Your past, Miss Mizelle."

She looked at me. "And what did you find, Mr. Lucas—nothing too unsavory, I hope."

"No, I just turned up a few lies that you'd told me."

She laughed. "About my oh-so-middle-class background, you mean. Well, it wasn't very middle-class, was it? What do we call my kind of background? Certainly not a lower-class background. Not in this country. In this country I sometimes think one is either poverty-stricken, middle-class, or rich."

"What's wrong with being middle-class?" Sinkfield said.

"Nothing, Lieutenant," she said. "Just dull."

"Would you say your mother was middle-class?" he said.

"My mother?"

"Uh-huh. Your mother."

"What has my mother got to do with it?"

"Well, I was just curious what you thought about her," he said.

"I thought that she was my mother. She did as well as she could."

"And your father?"

"He taught me to play the piano," she said. "And a few other things."

"Do you know where Mr. Mizelle is?"

"No," she said. "He and my mother separated years ago. I don't know where he is now."

"Any brothers or sisters?"

"No," she said without hesitation. "None. Why all the questions about my family, Lieutenant?"

"You didn't know that Ignatius Oltigbe was your half brother?" Sinkfield said and I had to admire the way that he had led up to it. Connie Mizelle looked surprised. Her mouth opened and her eyebrows went up. Then she frowned. It's the way most people look when they are surprised—or want to seem to be.

"Ignatius?" she said with a lot of incredulity. "My half brother?"

"That's what his birth certificate says," Sinkfield said.

She thought about it for a moment and then she laughed. Her head went back and she laughed as if she had found something really funny. When she was through laughing she wiped her eyes quickly before I could see if there were any tears there and said, "You mean my mother went to bed with a black man back in what was it then, the early forties?"

"Apparently so," Sinkfield said.

"My mother hated blacks," Connie Mizelle said.

"She must not have hated Oltigbe's father."

"Maybe he raped her," she said.

"And then stuck around to give her his name." Sinkfield shook his head. "Like I said, she must not have hated all blacks."

"Oh, she just didn't hate jigs," Connie Mizelle said. "That's what she called them, jigs. She also hated the spics and the wops and the kikes. My mother had a lot of prejudices." She laughed again. "I can't quite get used to the idea. Of Ignatius being my half brother. If I'd known, I'd've gone to his funeral."

"Your mother never mentioned him to you?" Sinkfield said.

She shook her head vigorously and chuckled far down in her throat. "Never. I can just see my mother saying, 'And by the way, Connie, you've got a half-jig half brother over in England someplace.' She'd've died first."

"Remember a guy named Stacey?" Sinkfield said.

"Jim Stacey? Certainly I remember Jim. My mother used to work for him." She looked at me. "You've got quite a memory, haven't you, Mr. Lucas? That phone number I mentioned the other day—the one that I said I used to call to let my mother know that I was home from school okay—that was Stacey's number."

"So I found out."

"Did you see Stacey?"

I nodded. "I saw him."

"Still as cute as ever?"

"He's a dream," I said.

"This Stacey," Sinkfield said. "He knew you were in Washington. The reason he knew is that before your mother died, she gave him something to mail to you. She also gave him something to mail to Oltigbe in London. I was kind of curious about what it was that your mother mailed to you."

She smiled at Sinkfield. It was a sweet smile. "The family Bible, Lieutenant."

"The family Bible, huh?"

"That's right."

"You wouldn't still have it around here someplace?"

"I'm not much on Bibles, Lieutenant. Especially family Bibles belonging to my family. I never much liked my family and I didn't like its Bible. I threw it away."

"And that's all that your mother mailed you?" Sinkfield said.

"No, there was a letter with it. There was a lot of self-pity in the letter. Gwen was sorry that she hadn't been a better mother. Well, I'm sorry that Gwen wasn't a better mother, too. I could have used one."

"But she didn't mention Oltigbe?"

"No."

"Well, this is where it gets a little funny," Sinkfield said.

"How does it get funny?"

"That both Oltigbe and you would sort of descend on the Ames family at about the same time."

She thought about it for a moment. Then she smiled again. "I could see how somebody like you might think of it as being more of a conspiracy than a coincidence, Lieutenant, but I can only tell you this. I didn't know that Ignatius was my half brother—if he really was—until five minutes ago." She laughed a little again. "I'm sorry," she said. "It takes a little getting used to, I suppose."

"Yeah," Sinkfield said, "I can see how it might." He turned to me. "You got anything, Lucas?"

"Just one thing," I said. I looked at Connie Mizelle. "Do you happen to know somebody out in Los Angeles called Beatrice Anne Wheat? Also known as Big Bad Bea?"

She spaced the name. "Big—Bad—Bea? No. No, Mr. Lucas, I don't know anyone called Big Bad Bea. Should I?"

"No," I said, "I don't suppose you really should."

# 22

Arthur Dain still drove as if he were the only one on the street. He switched lanes frequently and never signaled. He tailgated. He would decide to pass cars and then change his mind when he drew abreast of them and hang there, thus preventing anyone else from passing. He jumped red lights and tried to beat the yellow ones. He was the kind of a driver that I invariably addressed as "you dumb son of a bitch."

Out on the highway it was a little better, but not much. He either drove too fast or too slowly. I put on the seat belt which is something I seldom do. I also fastened the chest strap.

"Have you been making any progress, Mr. Lucas?" Dain said.

"Some. And you?"

"We do our job," he said. "You were out in Los Angeles, weren't you?"

"That's right."

"I suppose you learned that Ignatius Oltigbe was Connie Mizelle's half brother?"

"How long have you known?"

"Several weeks."

"If you'd told me, you could have saved me a trip," I said. "You have anything else spicy?"

Dain reached into his breast pocket. "Mrs. Ames wanted me to give you this," he said. "It's a memorandum that I prepared for her, summarizing what I've been able to put together."

He handed me some folded sheets of onion skin. "Are we trading for something?" I said.

"That's for Mrs. Ames to decide, not me."

I unfolded the onion-skin sheets. There were two of them. Across the top in small black capital letters was Dain Security Services, Inc. Running diagonally across the page in one-inch, stenciled-like letters was the word SECRET. It was printed in red.

"That's a nice touch," I said.

"What?"

"Secret."

"The clients like it," he said.

"Can I keep it?"

"Yes," he said, "you can keep it."

The heading of the memorandum read, "The Mizelle Woman." The rest of it began the way most government memos begin, with "as you know." It read:

As you know, since learning that Connie Mizelle and Ignatius Oltigbe had the same mother, Gwendolyn Ruth Simms Mizelle, we have been endeavoring to establish a link that would prove that the pair acted in concert following the death of their mother. This we have been unable to do. We must therefore conclude that they acted independently.

These are the facts: Gwendolyn Ruth Simms Mizelle, the mother of both Connie Mizelle and Ignatius Oltigbe, died October 21st last year. She was 48 years old. She died of acute alcoholic poisoning. At the time of her death, she was living in Los Angeles with one John Paul Kearns, 54, unemployed.

At the time of her mother's death, Connie Mizelle was already working for the Bagger Organization here in Washington. She had been employed there for nearly a year. Prior to that she had been employed by the manager of a musical group whose tour collapsed in Washington. The Mizelle woman was stranded at the Hilton Hotel with virtually no funds and a hotel bill of $264. Within four days she had raised sufficient funds to pay her hotel bill and to move into a furnished apartment. Informants at the hotel say that she resorted to prostitution to supply herself with funds. The investigation that this organization conducted in San Francisco of the Mizelle woman during her attendance at Mills College for Women would tend to bear out the allegation that she engaged in prostitution. While attending Mills, she worked weekends in San Francisco as a "call girl" to supplement her scholarship income. The Mizelle woman, as far as can be determined, has never been arrested.

Five days after her mother's death, the Mizelle woman suggested to Colonel Wade Maury Bagger that Senator Ames be contacted to deliver the speech concerning the South Plains takeover. Colonel Bagger, according to him, informed the Mizelle woman that this would be an unwise move because Senator Ames would never agree. The Mizelle woman insisted that she could arrange for the senator to deliver the speech and that it would cost the Bagger Organization nothing or, at most, a few thousand dollars. According to Colonel Bagger, it was at a meeting in Senator Ames's office that the senator insisted on being paid $2,000 for delivering the speech. However, the senator, again according to Bagger, asked for the money to be paid in the form of a loan to finance a trip to California. Subsequent investigation by this organization revealed that the senator did not need the money that day to make the trip.

Ten days after his mother's death, Ignatius Oltigbe arrived in Washington from London, staying at the house of Mr. and Mrs. Edward B. Gist in Bethesda, Md. The Gists had been strong supporters of the Biafran Cause. As you know, Oltigbe served briefly in the Biafran army. It was through the Gists that Oltigbe met your daughter, Carolyn. A week after he met her he moved into her Georgetown apartment. He was already living with her when the senator made the speech about the South Plains takeover.

This organization feels that it is possible that the South Plains speech would have gone virtually unnoticed had not someone informed the columnist, Frank Size, about the possibility of a $50,000 bribe. Size was reluctant to say anything about his informant, but in exchange for information about a totally unrelated matter, he was willing to admit that his informant had been a woman. To the best of our knowledge, there were only two women who could have known about the senator's accepting either the $2,000 or the alleged $50,000. One was, of course, the Mizelle woman. The other was the senator's private secretary, Mrs. Gloria Peoples. Mrs. Peoples vehemently denies that she was Frank Size's informant and we tend to believe her. We must conclude, therefore, that it was the Mizelle woman. We must also conclude that the senator must be aware of this.

We have been unable to establish a link between the Mizelle woman and Ignatius Oltigbe, other than the accident of their births. They met after the senator began to share the same quarters at the Watergate with the Mizelle woman. Your daughter and Oltigbe were frequent visitors at the senator's apartment. It must be assumed that it was during these visits that your daughter, Carolyn, uncovered the information that she was prepared to give to Frank Size's employer, Decatur Lucas. It must also be assumed that Carolyn was killed because she had uncovered this information.

The method by which she was killed was a complicated one, requiring expert knowledge of explosives. It must also be assumed that only someone well known to Carolyn could have made the switch of the attaché cases. At this point it should be mentioned that Ignatius Oltigbe, by virtue of his service in the 82nd Airborne Division, was a demolition expert.

For a time, we entertained the theory that he could have acted in concert with his half sister, the Mizelle woman. However, his subsequent murder seems to eliminate this possibility. We must conclude that Ignatius Oltigbe was operating, for whatever purpose, entirely independent of the Mizelle woman. We must also conclude that whoever killed your daughter also killed Oltigbe.

We have without success tried to establish links with the senator's past and the Mizelle woman, her mother, her half brother, Oltigbe, and her father, Francis Mizelle, 50, whom we located in San Francisco. Mizelle denies, however, that he is Connie Mizelle's father. He claims that an attack of mumps when he was a teen-ager rendered him sterile. He carries with him a twenty-year-old letter from a Los Angeles doctor which attests to his claim. Francis Mizelle says that he has not seen nor heard from Connie Mizelle in ten years.

We deeply regret that we have been unable to determine what power it is that the Mizelle woman holds over the senator. Despite your own feelings, we must reiterate that the Mizelle woman's sexual nature is such that some men would find it extremely atttactive. It should also be noted that five days ago the senator changed his will making the Mizelle woman his sole beneficiary.

We will, if you insist, continue our investigation

of the Mizelle woman and also of the two homicides. But we must repeat what we have already informed you of verbally: we are now convinced that whatever hold the Mizelle woman has over your husband is of such a nature that it will never be revealed unless she or the senator chooses to do so.

It is, therefore, our considered recommendation that we be permitted to withdraw from the case.

"Well, that's quite a memo," I said, folding it up and putting it away in my breast pocket. "You've got a nice style."

Dain passed a car on the left and I closed my eyes. I had almost forgotten how badly he drove. "Anything in it that surprised you?"

"Well, I didn't know she was a hustler."

"She turned ten or twelve tricks at the Hilton to bail herself out," he said. "She charged a hundred dollars."

"Who told you?"

"The house detective."

"How'd he know?"

"I suppose because he was number one. For free."

"Oh."

"She worked out of the St. Francis in San Francisco when she was going to Mills."

"Maybe that's where the senator met her?" I said

Dain shook his head. "It doesn't work out like that. The timetables are all wrong."

"You really think that she's behind it all, huh?"

"The Mizelle woman?"

"That's right."

"Of course she is," he said. "The only trouble is that nobody's ever going to be able to prove it."

"Why not?"

"Because nobody's ever going to find out what it is she has on the senator."

"What do you think it is?" I said.

He shook his head. "I don't have the slightest idea. But it's something awfully bad and terribly nasty. It's something that would wreck his life more than it's wrecked right now. Look what's already happened to him. He was accused of bribery and resigned from the Senate. His daughter was murdered. He split up with his wife. He lost his girlfriend—the little Peoples woman. His daughter's boyfriend was murdered. All this happened because he did something once, or something was done to him, that he couldn't stand to have come out in the open."

"The daughter bothers me," I said.

"Why?"

"I can see him letting the rest of it slide by, but I can't see him letting his daughter get killed."

"He didn't let her get killed. She got herself killed."

"Because of him though," I said.

"That's right."

I shook my head. "I can't see it."

Dain looked at me. He looked at me far too long while driving a car at seventy miles per hour. "How old are you, Lucas?" he said.

"Thirty-five."

"I'm forty-six. I've been in this business since I was twenty-three. That's half my life and if there's one thing I've learned in twenty-three years it's that I haven't got the slightest idea of what people will do under pressure. About the only thing I've learned is that people under pressure will do damned near anything to save their own skins. You'll hear a lot of stories about guys who supposedly will lay down their lives for a friend. But if I wanted to keep my illusions, I wouldn't look into any of those stories too carefully."

"Wouldn't hold up, huh?"

"Not too well," Dain said.

"How long have you been on this case now?" I said.

"Couple of months."

"And you haven't spotted who she's working with— if she's working with anyone?"

He moved his head slowly from side to side. "She doesn't see anybody. She's too smart for that. There're no meetings at midnight at the Lincoln Memorial, if that's what you mean."

"What about the phone?" I said. "You must have tapped in on it by now."

"She keeps a lot of dimes in her purse," he said. "Whenever she wants to make a call, she uses one. There's also the United States mail. Once in a while, she writes a letter and then goes all the way down to the main post office to mail it."

"So you're bowing out?" I said.

"That's right."

"What's Mrs. Ames want to see me about?" I said.

"She said she wanted to see us both."

"About what?"

"About some information she came across."

"Did she give you a hint?"

"She gave me a hint. She said it would fascinate Frank Size and that it would keep me on the job."

"It must be pretty hot stuff," I said.

"To keep me on this job it's going to have to be."

# 23

It was a little past three when Dain turned his Cadillac into the drive that led up to the big, sprawling house with the dark green roof. Even with his erratic driving, we had made good time. It had taken us a little under two hours to drive from the Watergate to French Creek.

We got out of the car and Dain pushed the doorbell. While we waited I admired the carved panels on the big, old door. The figures in the carvings looked happy setting off for the Crusades. They looked unhappy coming back.

Dain got tired of waiting and pushed the doorbell again. When nothing happened after two or three minutes, he gave the large brass knob a twist. He looked surprised when it turned.

"Wait a minute," he said and stepped back from the door.

"What's the problem?" I said.

"Let's make sure somebody's home." He turned and moved off to his right. I followed. He stopped when he came to the four-car garage. The overhead door was up and the garage contained a black four-door Cadillac, a fairly new Camaro, and a Jeep station wagon.

"There's room for one more," I said.

Dain shook his head. "The senator took his with him. He's got an Olds."

Dain turned and went back along the red cement walk toward the front door. He twisted the brass knob again and pushed the door open. He went in and I followed.

"Mrs. Ames," he called. When no one answered he said, "Anybody home?" He didn't quite yell it.

"Maybe they're out with the dogs or the horses," I said.

"Maybe. We might as well wait for her in the living room."

We walked down the wide, well-furnished entrance hall and into the living room with its splendid fireplace and its equally splendid view of the Chesapeake Bay. About a half mile offshore a cabin cruiser was plowing lazily through the blue water.

The drinks tray was on the coffee table. There was a decanter of liquor, some ice, a syphon, and a glass. The bottle was about half full. The coffee table was in front of the long, low couch. Louise Ames sat on the couch. She wore a pair of pale blue panties and two red holes just above her bare left breast. Her mouth was open and so were her eyes. Her head was cocked at an odd angle. She was dead. She looked a little surprised about it.

"Jesus Christ," I said.

Dain didn't say anything. He crossed over to Jonas Jones, the slim young man who served the drinks and saddled the horses and drove the car and serviced the mistress. Jonas Jones didn't wear any clothes at all. He lay on the floor, face up, his mouth stretched back into a grimace as if it had hurt him to die. He had a couple of small red holes in his chest, too. A revolver lay near his right hand. It looked like a .38 caliber, the kind that has the short, stubby barrel. For the first time I noticed the blood. There seemed to be a lot of it.

"Come on," Dain said.

"Where?" I said.

"Where it probably started. The bedroom."

We went back to the entrance hall, turned right, and after opening a couple of doors found what apparently was the master bedroom. It had a large bed, the kind that is called king-sized. It was rumpled with the bedclothes spilling over onto the floor. There was a bureau and a vanity dresser and a chaise longue and a couple of paintings on the wall, both of them still lifes. Or lives. On the floor were two puddles of clothes, a man's and a woman's. The bedroom had a view of the bay. I noticed that the cabin cruiser was still out there chugging around, probably just for the hell of it.

"Well, shit," Dain said, turned and went back down the hall. I tagged after him like a well-trained poodle.

In the living room Dain went over to the couch and bent forward from his thick waist, apparently to get a better look at the late Mrs. Robert F. Ames. After he was through doing that he straightened up, moved over to the body of Jonas Jones, late of Miami Beach, knelt down, studied him for a moment, then rose and crossed over to the telephone. He picked it up, dialed 0, and waited for the operator to come on.

"This is an emergency," Dain said into the phone. "My name is Arthur Dain. I'm a private investigator and I want to report a murder and a suicide."

He kept on talking after that, but I stopped listening. Instead, I went over and took another look at Louise Ames. She still looked surprised that she was dead. Her left fist was clenched. I looked over my shoulder at Dain. He was still talking over the phone, his back to me. I opened Louise Ames's left fist. It had been wrapped around two keys. The keys looked as though they belonged to a door. A small piece of Scotch tape was stuck to the large end of one key, right below the hole. Underneath the Scotch tape was a tiny bit of paper just large enough to bear the number that was typed on it. The number was 712. I slipped both keys into my jacket pocket.

Dain remained on the phone. I went over to where Jonas Jones lay dead and stared down at him. He looked as if he were still in pain. His hands weren't clenched around anything so I counted the bullet holes in his chest again. There were still two of them.

Arthur Dain turned from the phone he had just hung up and said, "I got the sheriff's office. There's a deputy on the way."

"What do you mean suicide?" I said. "The guy shot himself twice."

Dain shrugged. "He did a sloppy job of it. A lot of suicides do. There was one woman I read about just a little while ago. She drove down to the funeral home, parked her car, went inside, paid for her funeral in advance, went back out, got into the car, and shot herself five times. She's still alive."

"Did you know him?"

"Who? Jones here?"

"Yeah."

"I met him."

"You ever talk to him?" I said.

"No."

"He was the hired stud and he liked what he saw in the mirror. He may even have been passionately in love with himself; most of them are. He might even have killed Louise Ames. But if he did, he'd have been four states away by now, not lying there getting blood all over the living-room rug."

Dain shrugged again. "You can tell the sheriff's deputy all about it," he said. "They like amateur theories."

"You don't buy it?"

"I buy what I see," Dain said. "I see what looks like it started out to be an afternoon roll in the hay. Maybe even a nooner. I see a half-empty bottle of booze. I see a dead woman with two shots in her chest and her panties still on so maybe they'd already done it when the fight started, or maybe they were just getting around to it, or maybe she'd just given him a head job. They've got tests that'll bring all that out. I see a guy lying on the floor with a gun about three and a half inches from his hand. It's a revolver so a paraffin test will work just fine. And they'll probably find his prints on the gun. The only thing wrong is that he shot himself twice, but suicides do crazy things because otherwise they wouldn't be suicides. One thing I know. The sheriff of Talbot County isn't going to try to psychoanalyze pretty boy here. To the sheriff he's just going to be another dead body and if he can wrap it up real neat with a murder and suicide label on it, then that's what he's going to do."

"You really think it was murder and suicide?"

"That's what I see," Dain said. "But they'll run their tests. They'll figure out the angle of entry and check for prints to see whether he pulled the trigger with his thumb or his forefinger. They'll take a look at the powder burns to see what the dispersal was. They'll run some tests to find out how much booze they had in them. If they were drunk enough, that'll give the sheriff just that much more reason to wrap it up as quickly as possible."

"Of course, there's a hell of a good motive for my double-murder theory."

"There's that," Dain said. "Somebody didn't want her to tell us what she was going to tell us."

"That would be Connie Mizelle, for one."

"She's got a pretty good alibi though," Dain said.

"What?"

"She was with me."

"That's pretty good," I said.

"You're leaving out somebody else who'd be a fairly good suspect," Dain said.

"No, I'm not," I said. "I'm just getting to him."

"The senator, huh?"

"Right. As you say, he seems to have something so godawful in his past that he'll put up with anything, even his daughter's death, just to keep the lid on it. Well, suppose his wife somehow found out what that something godawful was."

"How?" Dain said.

"Jesus, I don't know how she found out, but let's just say she did. Maybe she calls her not quite ex-husband and lets him know that she's going to tell all. He jumps in his Olds, drives out here, catches them in bed together, shoots them, and pleads the unwritten law."

"Aw, for Christ's sake, Lucas."

I shrugged. "Well, it's a theory, if not much of a one. You're sticking to murder and suicide, I take it."

"Maybe," Dain said. "But now that you bring it up, the senator did have a pretty good motive."

"What?"

"About eighteen million dollars. Now that her daughter's dead, the senator is his wife's sole beneficiary."

# 24

The deputy was the first to arrive. He was lanky and lean-jawed and had a pair of pale blue eyes that didn't look too bright. He asked us our names and wrote them down carefully and then went back to looking at the dead bodies. "That old boy sure was hung, wasn't he?" he said and then he didn't say much of anything else until the sheriff arrived.

The sheriff was around fifty and it didn't seem to be his first murder. He was a big man, taller than I and half again as wide, with a square simple face and small, smart brown eyes that didn't miss much, if anything. He had brought his technical crew with him and after he had looked things over and gone through the house, he took Dain and me into the kitchen.

I let Dain do most of the talking and he told it like a professional witness. I decided that he talked much better than he wrote. The sheriff listened to Dain and then to me. He listened patiently with just enough interest on his face to keep us both going. After we were through, he looked at Dain and said, "You think murder-suicide, huh?"

"Looks that way," Dain said.

"Be nice if it was."

"You don't think it is?"

"Didn't say that, Mr. Dain. That family's sure had a mess of trouble though, haven't they?" He didn't wait for an answer. "I'm surprised that you're not on the phone with a hot flash to Frank Size, Mr. Lucas."

"It's not his kind of news," I said.

"Might not be his," the sheriff said, "but it's sure gonna be somebody else's. When the word gets out on this the *Baltimore Sun*'s gonna be down here. The *Washington Post*. TV. Radio. Wouldn't be surprised if it didn't make the evening news shows—Walter Cronkite and that bunch. An ex-senator's wife and her—well, whatever he was—get themselves killed. Now that oughta be a pretty good story."

"It should be," I said because the sheriff was looking at me as though he wanted confirmation.

"Of course, if it's murder-suicide like Mr. Dain here says, then it's not gonna be so much of a story, is it? I mean it's still big news but it's only gonna last a day or two."

"So it's not going to be a murder-suicide?" I said.

"Well, not right off, Mr. Lucas. Not until after I conduct a thorough investigation and study the coroner's report and see what the technical boys come up with. I mean you just don't go jumping to conclusions when rich folks get themselves killed around here. The other rich folks might not like it."

"This isn't an election year, is it?" I said.

The sheriff grinned. "Naw, that was last year. I won right handsomely, if I do say so. Won so big it might even be called a mandate, if sheriffs are ever given mandates. Reckon I could have one for law and order though, couldn't I?"

"I don't see why not," I said.

"You want us for anything else today?" Dain said.

The sheriff thought about it. "No, I don't think so. I'd like you to come around tomorrow or maybe the next day though and give me a statement. By then I might have thought up some more questions to ask." He paused for a moment and let those smart brown eyes flick over both of us. "And by then you might've thought of something that you'd forgotten to tell me."

"We'll see you, Sheriff," Dain said.

"Just one more thing," the sheriff said. "Either of you know who's working on the murder of the Ames girl and her boyfriend in D.C.?"

"You mean out of Homicide?" I said.

"Yeah."

"A guy called Sinkfield," I said. "David Sinkfield. He's a lieutenant."

"The Ames girl's boyfriend was a nigger, wasn't he?"

"White mother, black father," I said.

"Think this Lieutenant Sinkfield would be interested if I called him up and told him what we've got over here?"

"I think he'd be eternally grateful," I said.

The ride back to Washington with Dain at the wheel was no better or worse than the ride out. We didn't talk much on the way back. But this time I almost welcomed the rotten way that he drove. It helped keep my mind off of the faintly surprised look that the dead face of Louise Ames had worn.

I glanced at Arthur Dain. He looked more like a banker than ever. He sat slumped and relaxed behind the wheel, his suit coat unbuttoned and his belly bulging out. His right arm was draped casually along the back of the seat. He guided the Cadillac at 75 miles per hour with two fingers of his left hand. I knew that if a tire blew, Dain would stomp on his power brakes and swing his power-steering wheel the wrong way and we would probably flip and roll seven times and if either of us were still alive, we wouldn't be able to get out of the car because the doors would be jammed and the power windows wouldn't work.

"You ever kill anybody?" I said.

He looked at me. Once more he kept his green eyes too long from the road. "What do you mean kill anybody?"

"With your driving," I said.

"I've never even had an accident."

"That's hard to believe."

"You don't like my driving?"

"I think it's lousy."

Dain didn't say anything for a moment. I thought he might be pouting. He put both hands back on the wheel. "I didn't learn to drive until I was twenty-five. Most people learn earlier."

"Why didn't you?"

"Because," he said evenly, "I couldn't afford a car until I was twenty-five."

"And now you drive a Cadillac," I said.

"The small one."

"You mind if I ask you a personal question? Frank Size likes me to ask personal questions."

"I don't really give a damn what Frank Size likes, but you can ask it. I don't know that I'll answer it though."

"How much money did you make off the Ames case?"

Dain was silent for a moment. Finally, he said, "I don't mind telling you. I took it on a flat monthly retainer, twenty thousand a month—in advance."

"That's about forty thousand dollars, right?"

"Right."

"You think Mrs. Ames got her money's worth?"

He looked at me again. I looked at the road, prepared to grab the wheel. "She will," he said, "by the time I'm through."

"I thought you were finished."

He shook his head. "I changed my mind."

"Why?"

"Two reasons," he said. "One is that I want to find out what's so godawful about the senator's past."

"What's the other reason?"

"The other reason is that I don't like to hand money back and I'm paid for through the end of the month."

We came into Washington on New York Avenue and I had Dain drop me off at Seventh Street. It was nearly six o'clock. There is a liquor store at Seventh and New York and I went in and bought a pint of Scotch—Black and White this time. I slipped the pint into my hip pocket and went out and flagged down a taxi and told the driver to take me to the Washington Hospital Center on Irving Street.

At the hospital's reception area they gave me a little map and I found Ward F-1 without too much difficulty. The ward had a locked double door. The doors had panes of thick glass. The glass was guarded on both sides by steel mesh. Through the glass and the steel mesh I could see a long hall. There were several people standing around, some in their street clothes and some in bathrobes and pajamas. There was a bell by the door so I rang it.

After a little while a nurse came to the door and opened it just a crack. She was a thin black woman with gold-framed glasses. "Yes," she said.

"I'd like to see Gloria Peoples."

"Who're you?"

"I'm her lawyer. My name's Decatur Lucas."

The nurse shook her head. "I don't know," she said.

"Mrs. Peoples is not feeling too well. Doctor say she's not supposed to have visitors."

"I've got some good news for her," I said. "Maybe that'll make her feel better."

The nurse was still reluctant. "It's past visiting hours."

"I won't stay long and it's rather important that I see her."

"Say you're her lawyer?"

"That's right."

"Well, okay, if you don't stay too long."

She opened the door and I went in. A tall blond young man of about twenty-four with his left forearm and most of his hand in a cast walked up to her and said, "I'm going now."

"You're not going anywhere, Freddie," the nurse said. "You just go on back to your room."

"No," he said. "I'm going now. My brother's coming for me."

"Well, if you can get through that door, you just go on."

The young man shook his head. "No," he said in a reasonable tone, "the door is locked. You'll have to open it for me."

"I told you I'm not going to open that door."

"Open the door!" the young man screamed.

The nurse sighed. "What do you wanta act up ugly like that for? Come on now." She took his right arm and turned him around. "Go watch TV," she said.

"My brother's coming for me," he said. "I must go through that door."

"I'll let you go through later," she said. "You go watch TV now."

The young man thought about that for a moment, nodded, and then moved off down the hall.

"What's wrong with him?" I said.

"He tried to cut his wrist. He cut it all right, but

like most of them who're really serious about it and don't just give themselves a little pink with the razor, he got his tendon. That's a messy job fishing that tendon back out."

"Is that all?"

"Oh, you mean the way he acts? He's just come out of shock treatment. They all act like that when they come out of shock treatment. They don't remember much for a while." She shook her head. "We got 'em all on this ward, all kinds of nuts." She pointed to one of the doors that lined the hall. "Mrs. Peoples is in there. Better knock 'fore you go in to make sure she's decent."

I knocked and a voice said come in. I went in and Gloria Peoples was sitting in a chair. She wore a cream-colored bathrobe and some kind of blue gown. On her feet were white fuzzy slippers. There was a hospital bed in the room, a dresser, a sink, and another chair, a straight-backed one without arms.

She sat hunched over, her head bowed. She looked up at me slowly. Her eyes were red from crying. So was the tip of her nose. Her hair was a mess.

"Hello, Gloria," I said. "How're you feeling?"

"I don't belong in here," she said. "This is the psycho ward. I'm not crazy."

"Who brought you here?"

She shook her head. "Two men. I don't know who they were. They came by my place this afternoon and said that they worked for Louise Ames."

"What time this afternoon?"

"About two. They came by about two and said Louise wanted me to have a rest. I didn't know what they were talking about. I didn't need a rest. I called Louise, but her phone didn't answer. They said that everything was arranged and that I could go to the hospital and rest. Well, I've been upset. I was tired. So I agreed to go with them and I wound up in here."

"They think you've been drinking too much," I said.

"Who said that?"

"Mrs. Ames said it. She said you'd been calling her at all hours and not making much sense."

Gloria Peoples shook her head furiously. "I didn't call her. She called me."

"What did she call you about?"

She shook her head again. "I don't think I want to talk about it."

"How much did you have to drink today, Gloria? And don't lie to me."

"I had a beer with my lunch. That's all."

"How about yesterday?"

She thought about that. "I had two martinis just before dinner. That's all. I haven't been drinking much lately. Not since I saw you that time. You brought me some Scotch then, didn't you?"

"That's right."

"I sure wish you'd brought some this time."

"Maybe I did," I said.

She brightened. Hope marched slowly across her face, turning the ends of her mouth up. "You're not kidding, are you?"

"No."

She looked around the room. "We need some glasses. Can you go out and get some glasses? Get something to mix it with, too."

"Where am I going to get any glasses?"

"Down at the nurses' station. They've got glasses down there and all kinds of fruit juices. Get some fruit juice."

"With Scotch?"

"Apple juice," she said. "I remember that they've got apple juice. That won't be bad with Scotch."

I looked at her and shook my head. "I don't know, Gloria. You're supposed to be in here to dry out."

"I told you I don't need to dry out. What I need right now is a drink."

"How bad do you need it?"

She looked away from me. "Bad enough."

"Tell me what you and Mrs. Ames talked about and you can have a drink," I said, feeling awfully noble just then. Not only was I noble, but I also relieved the suffering of the afflicted. I brought liquor to sad little women in hospitals so that they could get drunk and feel better. I was better than the Gray Ladies.

But Gloria Peoples wasn't having any of my proposition. She shook her head and pouted a little. Then she said, "You give me a drink *first*. Then maybe we'll talk."

I nodded. "Apple juice, huh?"

"Apple juice," she said.

I went down the corridor to the nurses' station. A plastic dishpan was filled with ice and bottles and cans of various juices. The thin nurse with the gold glasses watched as I poured apple juice into a couple of plastic cups.

"She said she wanted something to drink," I said.

The nurse nodded approvingly. "She oughta drink a lot of liquids."

"She looks pretty good to me," I said. "Better than I expected."

"Huh," the nurse said. "Should've seen her when they brought her in around two. She had a skinful. She's had a nice little nap since then."

"Really looped, huh?"

"Well, she'd sure been drinking something and it wasn't apple juice."

I carried the two cups of apple juice back to Gloria Peoples' room. She bit her lip when she saw them, rose, and reached out for them. Her hands shook.

"Stand over there by the door," she said.

I stood by the half-closed door.

"Don't let anybody in," she said, carried the cups over to the sink and poured out two-thirds of the apple juice from each cup. She turned to me. "Fill 'em both up," she said.

I took the pint from my pocket, twisted the cap off, and filled up both cups with Scotch. Gloria Peoples handed me one of the cups, spilling only a little. She used both of her hands to lift her own cup to her mouth. She took two deep swallows, sighed, sat back down, and fumbled in the pocket of her bathrobe. She brought out a package of Kents, shook one half-way out, and removed it from the pack with her lips.

"Got a match?" she said. "They won't let me have any matches. They got an electric lighter down there at the desk that I have to use."

I lit her cigarette and then one for myself. "Tell me about it, Gloria," I said.

The liquor had already gone to work. There was some color in her cheeks now. She handled her cigarette and her glass with more authority. She even held the cigarette and the glass in one hand so that she could give her hair a couple of pats that didn't do any good.

"Louise says I called her?" she said.

I nodded. "That's what I understand."

"Well, I didn't call her. I'd never call her. She called me."

"What'd she call you about, Gloria?"

"She wanted something."

I remained patient. The Good Samaritans of the world are always patient. "What did she want?"

"She thought if he could get in there, they'd find out what it was."

There was Job, of course. He might have given me a little competition in the patience game. But not much. "Who is he?"

That pet lap dog of hers. The muscle man. That creep she pays to fuck her."

"Jonas Jones," I said.

She took another deep swallow and then nodded. "That's him. Jonas Jones."

"And he was supposed to get in where?"

"To their place."

"Whose place?"

"Bobby's and that Mizelle bitch."

"And you had the keys, right?"

It took a little time, probably because of the alcohol and the tranquilizers that they had fed her, but it finally registered. "How did you know?" she said. "Nobody knew I had the keys."

"Louise Ames knew," I said.

"Well, that's different. She knew I always kept duplicate sets of his keys. He was always losing them."

"You were still working for the senator when he bought the apartment at the Watergate, weren't you?"

She shook her head. "I wasn't working for him then. I was working for Cuke. But I still kept duplicate sets of his keys and when he bought the Watergate place I made sure that there were a couple of extra sets. I guess I just kept on looking after him even when he didn't want me to anymore."

"What did you do, mail the keys to Louise Ames?"

She shook her head again. "No, Jonas came by and picked them up."

"Then what?"

She drained her drink. "I think I'll go get some more apple juice," she said.

"Here," I said, offering her my cup. "Take mine. I haven't touched it."

That cheered her up. She smiled at me gratefully. I was Doctor Wonderful who prescribed the best medicine in the world.

She took another large swallow. "Don't worry," she said. "I'm not going to get shit-faced."

"I know you're not," I said. "But what happened after you gave Jonas the keys?"

She shrugged. "I guess he snuck in there and found what she wanted him to find out. At least that's what she said."

"When?"

She thought about it. "Yesterday." She nodded vigorously. "Uh-huh, it was yesterday. That's when Louise called me and said all those awful things."

"What awful things?"

"About Bobby and me. She said she'd always known about us, right from the first, but she didn't care because his going to bed with me was just like him having a hobby. But she said Connie Mizelle was different. She said that Connie Mizelle had ruined Bobby and now she was going to ruin Connie Mizelle."

"How?" I said.

"That's what I asked her. How."

"What'd she say?"

"She just laughed and said I could read all about it in Frank Size's column."

"Then what?"

"Then nothing. Then she hung up and I had a couple of martinis. Well, maybe I had three. I was sort of upset." She started to cry. The tears started trickling down her cheeks. I was afraid that she was going to start bawling so I got up and moved over and patted her clumsily on the shoulder. "There, there," said good, gruff Doctor Lucas. "It's going to be all right," I said. I thought of saying "there, there" again, but I couldn't bring myself to do it. "What's the matter?"

She looked up at me. Her eyes were flooded with tears. Her nose was a bright pink. "Lucky," she said.

"Lucky?"

"My cat. I just went off and left him and now I don't know what he's going to eat or anything and he's never been alone before."

I found a handkerchief and mopped up some of the tears. "Come on," I said. "Have a drink. Don't worry about Lucky. I'll take care of him."

"You—you will?" she said and then buried her nose in the cup.

"I know a place out in Silver Spring. It's a real fancy place designed just for cats. I take mine there sometimes. He likes it. The cats've got their own TV and everything. I'll go by and pick up Lucky and take him out there."

The tears were stopping, but the hiccups were coming on. "He—he likes the weatherman."

"The weatherman?"

"On TV—he likes the weatherman. Channel nine. He always watches that."

"I'll tell the lady who runs the place."

She drained her glass. I estimated that she had drunk about six ounces of Scotch in fifteen or twenty minutes.

"Why don't you take a little nap now?" I said.

"Can you leave the rest of it?"

"The Scotch?"

"Uh-huh."

"If they find it, they'll take it away from you."

"We'll hide it," she said. "Give me my purse. I've got to give you my keys anyway. We'll hide it in my purse."

"That's a wonderful place," I said. "They'll never think of looking there. Not until after they look under your pillow."

"Well, where can we hide it?"

"Under the mattress."

She closed her eyes and frowned. "Under the mattress," she said. "Under the mattress. Under the mattress." She opened her eyes and looked at me brightly. "That's so I'll remember when I wake up."

I handed her her purse and tucked the pint away underneath the mattress. I was proud of myself. I had done some very good deeds that day. I had stolen from the dead. I had comforted the sick with strong drink. I was a peach.

"I think I'll take a little nap," Gloria Peoples said.

"That's a good idea."

She rose and walked steadily enough over to the bed and sat down. "Under the mattress," she said and nodded her head as if to confirm it.

"Under the mattress," I said.

"I looked at Frank Size's column this morning," she said, "but I didn't see anything about Bobby in it. Is it going to be in tomorrow?"

"I don't think so."

"When's it going to be in?" she said as she stretched out on the bed.

"I don't know, Gloria," I said. "Maybe never."

# 25

[              ]

Gloria Peoples' cat had hated the long car ride. It had yowled all the way from Virginia to Silver Spring, Maryland, despite Sarah's gentle reassurances. During the ride I had told Sarah the entire history of what I had come to think of as the Ames murder case. Sometimes I had had to shout a bit to make myself heard over Lucky, the cat, who hadn't seemed at all interested in my rather sordid tale.

Sarah and I were sitting now in one of the French restaurants in Georgetown that had opened up since the riots of 1968. Almost nobody goes downtown in Washington after dark. You can drive through the streets after ten or eleven o'clock and not see more than one or two persons a block and they look as though they're hurrying to get some place safe.

The food at the restaurant we were in was usually quite good although the service was a little wild with the waiters zipping around on roller skates. By the time our drinks were served and we had ordered I had finished my recitation. Sarah looked at me for several moments and then asked, "What ever happened to Captain Bonneville?"

"He's been delayed."

She shook her head. "If you stay with Frank Size, Bonneville won't be delayed, he'll be indefinitely postponed. When you're through with this one, and if somebody doesn't kill you, Size will come up with another story that he'll sic you on. There might not be as many dead bodies around, but you'll dive back into the slime pit and one of these days it won't wash off."

"You think I like it there, huh? In the slime pit, I mean."

"No, you don't like it there," she said. "But the people who swim in it fascinate you. They fascinate you because you think they're different from you, but they're not."

"You mean I'm like them?"

She smiled gently. I was extremely fond of that particular smile. "We're all like them, Deke. It's just that they've been confronted with a choice that we've never had to make. That's why most people stay honest. They've never had much of a chance to be anything else."

"You've joined the cynics," I said.

"No, I've learned from you. From watching you. When you were with government, were you ever offered bribes?"

I nodded. "A few times. I don't know, maybe more than a few. You can't always be sure when somebody's offering you a bribe."

"But you turned them down, didn't you."

"I never took any. I wouldn't say that I turned them down. Sometimes I just pretended that I didn't know what they were talking about."

"Why didn't you take them?"

I took a sip of my martini. It seemed just right.

Better than Scotch and apple juice. "Why didn't I take them? Moral outrage. A deeply offended sense of decency. Plus a strong fear that I'd get caught."

"One more," she said.

"One more what?"

"One more reason."

"Okay, what?"

"You didn't really need the money. What if you had a kid and the kid needed one of those kidney machines that cost about as much as you make a year and you were already up to your ears in debt and somebody said, 'Hey, Lucas, how'd you like to make a quick ten thousand for turning a blind eye?' What do you think you'd say to that? Remember, if you say no, the kid probably dies."

I grinned at her. "That's what I like about you, Sarah. You invent your own rules."

"And you're waffling."

"Okay, under those circumstances I don't know what I'd do. I might take the money; I might not. But I know one thing. If I didn't take it and the kid died, I wouldn't find any comfort in my honesty."

"Well, that's what I'm saying," she said. "People who can be corrupted always need money. In your case, you'd need the money to save your kid's life. In somebody else's case, they'd need a new cabin cruiser. And who's to say which need is greater? The guy who feels he needs the cabin cruiser or your need to save your child's life?"

"How'd we get off on this?" I said.

"We got off on this because I brought it up," Sarah said. "I brought it up because I think you're changing."

The waiter rolled up with the salad. After he left I forked a piece of it into my mouth. The dressing was superb.

"What do you mean I'm changing?" I said.

"You're beginning to bend the rules," she said. "You didn't used to do that. Two months ago you wouldn't have taken those keys from that dead woman's hand. You wouldn't have got that poor little Peoples woman drunk in a hospital. I think you're—well, I think you're obsessed."

"With what?"

"With the Mizelle woman."

"I barely know her," I said. "Eat your salad. It's good."

Sarah tried a bite. She nodded. "You're right; it is," she said and then switched back to the evening's prime topic: what's wrong with Decatur Lucas. "Okay, I'll buy that," she said. "You've only met her a couple of times. But you know her. You really know her. I can tell. You know her like you know Captain Bonneville and you never met him either. I think you know Connie Mizelle better than you know me."

"I don't know what she wants," I said.

Sarah laughed. It wasn't her pleasant one. "I don't know the woman at all but from what you've told me I know what she wants."

"What?"

"Revenge," Sarah said.

"That's a funny word."

"Why?" she said. "It belongs in the slime pit along with greed and hate and avarice and the rest of them. All old friends of yours. Or acquaintances."

"You're dishing out some interesting theories tonight," I said.

She took another bite of her salad and washed it down with some of the wine I'd ordered. She looked at me then and I thought I saw something in her eyes. Something soft. Maybe even tenderness. "You're going to chase it down, aren't you?" she said. "Down to the bitter, bloody goddamned end."

"That's right," I said.

"Why?"

"I suppose because I want to."

"Want to or have to?"

I shrugged. "It doesn't matter, does it?"

"And those keys you stole. What're you going to do with those keys?"

"I'm going to use them," I said.

She didn't say anything after that. In fact, she didn't say anything for the rest of the evening and we finished the meal in silence, the cold, dismal kind.

I decided that two-thirty in the morning was the right time to go aburglaring. Almost everyone is asleep by then. Security is at its slackest, even at the Watergate. The success of my brilliant scheme depended upon the cooperation of a deputy assistant Secretary of Agriculture for whom I had once done a minor favor. I had kept his name out of a report when I could just as well have included it. I also had let him know that I had kept it out and since then he had remained reasonably straight—like most of the other deputy assistant Secretaries of Agriculture.

He lived two floors beneath the penthouse apartment where dwelled ex-Senator Robert F. Ames and his great and good friend and constant companion, Connie Mizelle. I was in a pay phone on Virginia Avenue across the street from the Watergate when I dropped the dime and dialed the number. It rang five times before a sleepy voice answered with a mumbled hello.

"Hello, Hoyt," I said. "This is Deke Lucas. Sorry to bother you."

"Who?"

"Deke Lucas."

It took a while for that to sink in. Then he said, "You know what time it is?"

"Two-thirty," I said. "I'm awfully sorry, but I'm in

a bind. I was at this party and I must have lost my wallet and I don't have my car and I was wondering if you'd lend me five bucks so I could get home?"

"You wanta borrow five dollars?"

"That's right."

"Where are you?"

"Across the street."

"Well, come on up. I'm in five-nineteen."

"Appreciate it, Hoyt."

The guard on the security desk yawned and called upstairs to see whether I was expected. When he found out that I was, he nodded me toward the elevators. Inside the elevator, I punched number seven. I was whisked up to the seventh floor, got out, and waited for the elevator to start back down. When it was well on its way I hit the down button then raced toward the door with the big, red exit sign above it. I opened it, pressed back its lock, and then used the Scotch tape that I had bought at the all-night drugstore at 17th and K to tape the lock back in its hole. I closed the door gently and then ran back to the elevators just as the car I had rung for arrived. I got in and pressed the number five button. I got out on the fifth floor and wandered down the corridor until I found 519. I rang the bell. The door opened almost immediately and the man in the bathrobe and pajamas thrust a five-dollar bill at me.

"I'd invite you in, Deke," he said, "but my wife's not feeling too well."

"Many thanks, Hoyt. I'll get it back to you tomorrow."

"Just mail it, will you?"

"Sure."

The door closed and I waited a moment to make sure that it didn't reopen. I then went down the hall to the exit door, went through it, walked up two flights of stairs, removed the tape from the seventh-floor door, and moved down the hall to 712.

I took the keys that I had removed from the dead hand of Louise Ames and inserted them one at a time into the senator's door. I didn't worry about a chain. I had some heavy wire cutters hanging from my belt down inside my left pants leg. They were extremely uncomfortable.

I turned the keys carefully and then pushed the door. It opened. I pushed it another five inches and when nothing happened I pushed it open wide enough to go through it. I was in the entrance hall. A night light burned on a small table. I closed the door soundlessly.

I was wearing my burglar shoes, some crepe-soled desert boots, but I still tiptoed down the hall toward the living room. I stopped and listened, breathing through my mouth. That's the way all good burglars breathe. I had read that someplace. Or had seen it on TV. You could learn a lot about how to make a dishonest living by watching TV.

I listened for what must have been nearly a minute but I didn't hear anything. I took the rest of my burglar kit from my pocket. It was a small flashlight. I had bought it and the Scotch tape at the drugstore. The wire cutters I had borrowed from my neighbor across the street, the one who had claimed to know what sawed-off shotguns sounded like. I figured that if he knew that, he'd have a pair of wire cutters handy. He did.

I crossed the living room slowly, using the flashlight to keep from bumping into any furniture. I thought I knew the door that I was looking for. It was toward the far end of the room, near the piano. I opened the door and shined my flashlight around. It was the room I wanted. It was the study or den or library—depending upon what one considered fashionable.

I went in and left the door to the living room open. I thought I knew what I was looking for. I thought I knew because Connie Mizelle was such a good liar. And like all good liars, she used a lot of truth in the lies she told. It helped lend not only authenticity, but also a dash of verisimilitude. The only trouble was that she made the mistake of telling her lies to somebody with a trick memory like mine. If she hadn't rattled off that Los Angeles phone number, I would never have called Stacey's bar. And if she hadn't mentioned that her mother had mailed her a Bible, I would never have gone looking for it.

That's what I was after. A Bible. I assumed that a Bible was what Jonas Jones had found when he prowled the place. But I wasn't sure. It was merely a hunch—a historian's hunch. I shined the light around the room. There was a big desk, a large globe, some chairs and a wall of bookcases. Where better to hide a Bible than in a bookcase? I tried to make myself think like Connie Mizelle. Would I try to hide a Bible there if I were her? Yes, I would, and on the other hand, no, I wouldn't. I decided that I couldn't think like her. I decided that nobody could.

I played the light over the books. They all looked new with the dust jackets still on them. They seemed to be six months of indiscriminate selections from the Book-of-the-Month Club and the Literary Guild. They also looked unread.

On the very top shelf sandwiched between two novels that I had promised myself to read was what I thought I was looking for. A Bible. It was a black one about ten or eleven inches high and two and a half or three inches thick. It had a black shiny cover of limp leather and gilt letters that read *The Holy Bible*. It was so near the ceiling that I had to stand on my toes to reach it. I still don't know what I thought I would find in it. Maybe a true history of Connie Mizelle's family tree. I brought the Bible down and moved over to the desk.

I put the Bible on the desk and held the flashlight in my right hand. I opened the Bible. It was hollow. It was hollow and empty except for the gun and the newspaper clipping.

I had just started to read the newspaper clipping when I heard the sound. It was the sound of a door closing. It was a distant sound. I assumed that it had been the door to the corridor. Then I heard a woman's voice. It spoke in low, hushed tones, but I still recognized it. It belonged to Connie Mizelle. She even seemed to be laughing a little.

Then there was a man's voice that sounded like a low growl. Then her voice again, saying, "Can't you wait?" And then she laughed again, but not very loudly. Then there was a silence and after that a sigh and she said, "Over here, darling. Let's go over here on the couch."

Then a man's voice said something muffled, something that I couldn't make out. After that there was some grunting and some more sighing and the man's voice said, "Oh, goddamn, that's wonderful, that's great."

I was more than a little surprised because the voice belonged to Lt. David Sinkfield.

# 26

I got home by four. I got home by four because it wasn't until three-thirty that Sinkfield and Connie Mizelle had quit squirming around on the living-room couch. I had put the Bible back in the bookshelves and had crouched under the big desk listening to the sounds of their lovemaking. I think I may have been a little jealous of Sinkfield. A little jealous and awfully surprised.

Sarah let me sleep the next morning, but Martin Rutherford Hill didn't. At nine-thirty he banged me over the nose with his one-eyed teddy bear. He had chewed off the other eye and had swallowed it six months before.

After a while I went downstairs and Sarah poured me a silent cup of coffee. I sat there and sipped the coffee and thought. When I finished the first cup I got up and poured myself a second one.

"We didn't get the hollyhocks, did we?" I said.

"No," she said. "We haven't done a lot of things lately."

"Why don't you take the kid and go to the zoo today?"

She looked at me. "I don't want to go to the zoo. Neither does the kid. He hates the zoo."

"Take him someplace," I said.

"Why?"

"Another guy and I are going to do a little plotting," I said. "It would be better if you weren't around while we did it."

"What guy?" she said.

"Arthur Dain."

"That private investigator?"

"That's right."

"You found out something last night, didn't you?"

"I think so."

"Why don't you and Dain just turn it over to the cops?" she said.

I closed my eyes and tried to remember the sounds of lovemaking that I had heard earlier that morning. Much earlier. I shook my head and said, "Just take the kid and go someplace and tomorrow we'll go get the hollyhocks."

"Why tomorrow?"

"Because," I said, "it'll all be over by tomorrow."

I called Lieutenant Sinkfield and invited him over. He sounded sleepy. Then I called Dain. He sounded as though he had gone to bed at a decent hour. He sounded chipper. I told him what I had told Sinkfield, "I think I've got something that will wrap it up." They both agreed to come, but I made sure that they wouldn't arrive at the same time.

Sarah took Martin Rutherford Hill, loaded him into the Pinto, and drove off. When I asked her where she had decided to go, she said, "To the gypsies."

"Where?"

"To the gypsies. I don't know whether I'll join them or just sell them the kid."

I walked over to the Library of Congress. It was a nice day in Washington. The sun was out. Several young people who hang out at the library were on the lawn eating their lunches from brown paper bags. Some birds sang.

The clipping I had seen in the hollowed-out Bible in ex-Senator Ames's library had had no date. Nor had it borne the name of the newspaper that it had been torn from. I thought I knew both. But I had to make sure.

In the periodical and newspaper section, I asked for the back file on the *Los Angeles Times* that contained the papers published in August of 1945. Unlike the *New York Times,* the *Los Angeles Times* wasn't on microfilm. The papers for August, 1945, were held together by a wooden clamp. I turned to the August 15th edition. A big headline screamed that JAPAN SURRENDERS! It wasn't the story that I was looking for, but I read it anyway. It was interesting.

I leafed through the paper slowly. There were stories and pictures about how Los Angeles had gone wild on V-J Day and night. Back on page 31 was the story I was looking for. The headline read:

LIQUOR STORE ROBBED;
OWNER SLAIN BY PAIR

It really wasn't much of a story. At around eleven o'clock on the night of August 14, 1945, one Emanuel Perlmutter, forty-nine, the owner of the Quality Liquor Store on Van Ness Avenue in Hollywood, had been held up. Instead of handing over his money, Perlmutter had gone for the gun that he'd kept behind his counter. That was a mistake. He had been shot twice. The story didn't say whether it was the first or second bullet that had killed him. After shooting Perlmutter, the robbers had cleaned out the cash register. Witnesses said that they saw a man and a woman run from the store. The man had been wearing some kind of military uniform, but the witnesses disagreed on what kind. That was about all there was to the story, except that the killers had made off with about seventy-five dollars. According to his wife, Perlmutter never kept any more than that in his cash register. He had been robbed four times before in the last two years, police said.

I'm not quite sure how long I sat there at the table with the nearly thirty-year-old copy of the *Los Angeles Times* spread out before me. I sat there and wondered just how drunk Marine Captain Robert F. Ames had been when he and the mother of Connie Mizelle had gunned down Emanuel Perlmutter, forty-nine. And then I wondered how they had spent the money.

Arthur Dain was prompt. He arrived at my house on Southeast Fourth Street at one minute till two. He wore a dark blue suit with a faint red stripe, a white shirt with a starched collar, and a red-and-blue bow tie. It was the first time I had seen him wear a bow tie and I thought it made him look a little quaint.

He looked around my living room and nodded slightly, as if it were just about what he had expected—nothing much. Then he sat down in what I had come to think of as my chair and crossed his legs. His plain-toed black shoes glistened.

"You said you've got something," he said. "Something large."

I nodded. "Would you like some coffee?"

He shook his head.

"A drink?"

"No, I don't want a drink. What have you got?"

"I know what Connie Mizelle has on Senator Ames."

That stirred him. He uncrossed his legs. "What?" Dain said.

"On August fourteenth, 1945, V-J Day, Robert F. Ames, then a just discharged captain in the Marine Corps, and Connie Mizelle's mother, Gwendolyn Ruth Simms, held up a liquor store and shot and killed its owner, one Emanuel Perlmutter. Connie Mizelle's mother had an old friend out in Los Angeles mail the gun to her daughter after she died. I mean after the mother died. There was probably a letter from the mother explaining all about the gun. I haven't seen the letter; I have seen the gun."

"When?" Dain said.

"Last night. Or early this morning. I snuck into the senator's apartment."

Dain nodded. For some reason I thought it looked like a disbelieving nod. "That's a pretty hard place to sneak into."

"I had the keys," I said.

"Where'd you get them?"

"From Louise Ames's hand. Yesterday. When you weren't looking."

"Connie Mizelle was blackmailing him then," Dain said after a moment.

"Is blackmailing him," I said. "Not was."

"And living with him," Dain said.

"She's not through yet."

"You mean she isn't through blackmailing him?"

"That's right. Now that his wife's dead, the senator's an awfully rich man. And you told me that if he dies, Connie Mizelle will get everything. Everything would be about twenty million dollars, the way I figure it."

"That's about right," Dain said. "Twenty million." He was silent for a moment. Then he said, "That gun you saw. How do you know it's the same one that killed the liquor-store owner?"

"I don't," I said. "I'm just guessing. In fact, I'm just guessing about the entire thing. But it all fits. It all fits real fine."

"You tell the cops yet? Sinkfield?"

I sighed and shook my head. "No, there's a little problem there."

"What kind of problem?"

"While I was playing burglar this morning, Connie Mizelle came home."

"She see you?"

I shook my head. "No, she was too busy fucking Sinkfield on the living-room couch."

Dain grinned. "Well, I'll be damned."

"That's what I thought."

"That presents a problem, doesn't it?" Dain said.

"What about going to his partner?" I said.

"You mean Sinkfield's."

"That's right."

"He's a pretty good man."

"Maybe I should go call him now and get him over here," I said.

It wasn't a fast draw. Dain just reached inside his coat and brought out the gun the way he'd bring out a cigar. "I hope your girlfriend's not home," he said. "Or the kid."

I didn't move. "Come on," I said. "What's the gun for?"

"For killing people," he said. He glanced quickly around the room. "What's that door lead to, a closet?"

"A bath," I said. "A half bath."

"In there," he said.

"Don't try to make it look like a suicide again," I said. "It won't work."

Dain grinned. "You think you figured that out, huh?"

239

"It wasn't hard. Not after I found out from the Peoples woman that Jonas Jones had prowled the senator's flat with the same key I used. He must have found the same clipping. He told Louise Ames and she put it together. Then she told you, probably over the phone, and you went out there and killed them both and made it look like a suicide-murder. Then you came back to Washington and went up to see Connie Mizelle. She was going to be your alibi—if you needed one. And you were going to be hers."

Dain looked mildly curious. "What tipped you off?"

"The gun you just pulled on me. You want me to tell you the rest of it?"

"No," Dain said. "Just get in the bath over there. It'll cut down the noise a little."

I kept on talking. "You also killed the senator's daughter and Ignatius Oltigbe."

"Did I?"

"Sure. You killed Carolyn Ames because she must have overheard Connie talking to the senator. The girl was a snoop. She must have got something down on tape. Maybe she even taped some calls between you and Connie Mizelle. Anyway, she got enough to know that her father was being blackmailed by Connie Mizelle and you. So you killed her with that fancy exploding attaché case. Who did the switch, Connie?"

"I said into the bathroom, Lucas."

I didn't move. I kept sitting there on the couch. "You'd know all about explosives, wouldn't you, Dain? I mean anyone who'd spent that much time in the FBI and the CIA would know how to put together an exploding briefcase. You'd also have learned how to shoot a gun pretty well. Hitting Ignatius Oltigbe from twenty-five feet away on a dark street would be pie for you. Poor old Ignatius. His mother mailed him a letter and told him all about a United States senator who had once held up a liquor store and killed its owner. It was the least she could do for him. He might turn a few bucks out of it. But she didn't give him any proof. Maybe it was because he was half black and his mother had never really liked blacks too well, but still he was her son. The letter was his legacy. So Ignatius probably used his last pound to buy a ticket over here and who does he meet but the senator's daughter. That was a coincidence, but not much of a one. He would have met her sooner or later anyway. But Ignatius wasn't quite sure how he was going to use his information about the senator. He was still working on that when Carolyn Ames got killed. Ignatius didn't like that. He knew why she had died because she had given him duplicate copies of all the stuff she had. He must have looked at the stuff and decided that it was a bit rich for him. So he made up his mind to sell it to me for a quick five thousand and run. You tailed him over here to my house and shot him down in the street."

"If you want to die on that couch, it's fine with me," Dain said.

There was a sound on the stairs. It was the sound of something thudding down the steps. Dain looked. It was Foolish, the cat. He was bouncing down the steps, either on the way to his bowl of Purina Chow or his box of kitty litter. I threw the big ashtray at Dain. It struck him on the left shoulder.

I used the coffee table as a launching pad and sailed across the room. Dain saw me coming and stepped back quickly, too quickly for a man who was forty-five and wearing a pot gut. He swiped me across the face with the gun barrel while I was still in the air. I fell to the floor without touching him. I was on my hands and knees. Foolish brushed against my left arm. I looked up. Dain wore a slight smile on his face. The gun was pointed at my head. I stared at the gun and decided that although I very much didn't want to die, there was absolutely nothing that I could do about it.

The hard tough voice spoke then. It said, "Police, Dain. Freeze!"

Dain didn't freeze. He whirled and he got off one shot before the first bullet caught him somewhere in the stomach and the second one took away most of the right side of his face. He didn't drop his gun though. He went down on his knees and looked up the stairs. He tried to raise the gun and there was a third shot from the stairs that hit him in the throat just above the red-and-blue bow tie. He fell over on his left side and lay still.

Lt. David Sinkfield came slowly down the stairs followed by his partner, Jack Proctor. Sinkfield still carried a gun in his hand. So did Proctor. Sinkfield looked disgusted. "He didn't admit one damned thing," he said.

"Yes he did," I said.

"What?"

"He admitted that he wanted to kill me."

# 27

Sinkfield walked up to the security man at the Watergate and said, "We're going up to see Senator Ames and we'd kinda not like to be announced."

The man nodded. "Sure, Lieutenant," he said. "Sure."

In the elevator, Sinkfield said, "I know I'm making a mistake bringing you instead of Proctor."

"She's your girlfriend," I said.

"You didn't have to bring that up in front of Proctor."

"I don't know," I said. "He seemed to admire you for it."

"Yeah, well, you don't have to tell anybody else about it."

"Probably not."

We had left Proctor to take care of the dead Arthur Dain. We had left just as two police cars arrived with sirens screaming, thus bringing another touch of excitement into the ho-hummery of my neighbors' lives. Proctor had wanted to come along, but he hadn't argued about it. He had merely grinned at Sinkfield and said, "Maybe you'd better keep it in your pants this time, Dave."

"Yeah," Sinkfield had said, "maybe I'd better."

As we drove from my house to the Watergate apartments, Sinkfield said, "You know something?"

"What?"

"I wonder who approached who?"

"She approached Dain," I said.

"How do you know?"

"I don't. I mean I couldn't prove it, but I know."

"Just like you knew it was Dain who was partnered up with her."

"It had to be somebody."

"How'd you get on to him anyway? What'd he do, leave you some big, fat clues lying around?"

"He was too good for that," I said. "The only clue he left was his own competence. If anyone could have hired a Los Angeles dike to work me over, Dain could. If anyone could run up an exploding attaché case in his basement, it would be Dain. If anybody could set up a double murder to look like a murder-suicide and make it stick, it would be Dain. You ever talk to that sheriff over in Talbot County?"

"This morning," Sinkfield said. "He said all the tests check out perfectly—or as perfectly as those things ever check out. He said he could close it out as a murder-suicide. I talked to him after I talked to you so I told him to hold off."

"I wonder what Dain's cut was going to be?" I said.

"You mean before or after they got rid of the senator?"

"You think he was the next in line, huh?"

Sinkfield nodded. "Had to be."

"Maybe Dain was working on spec," I said. "Maybe he wasn't going to get his slice until they cut up the entire twenty million."

"Something tells me we're never going to know

for sure," Sinkfield said. "She's sure as shit not going to volunteer anything."

"How'd you get her to go to bed with you?" I said. "I mean I'm just curious."

Sinkfield took his eyes off the street long enough to give me a pitying look. "You ever take a good look at me?" he said.

"Yeah, I've taken a good look at you."

"You ever take a good look at her?"

"I've done that, too."

"Well, who do you think got who into bed?" He lit a cigarette from the butt of the one he was smoking and tossed the butt out the window. "Now I could tell you that I fucked her because I was trying to gain her confidence so I could make a break in the case, couldn't I? I mean I could tell you that."

"You could tell me that."

"But you wouldn't believe me."

"No. I don't think so."

"I don't blame you," he said. "So I'm gonna tell you the real reason. The real reason I fucked her is because she let me and I knew I'd never get a chance to fuck anything like that again if I live to be a hundred and if you could see my wife, maybe you'd understand what I'm talking about."

"The Mizelle girl can use it, you know," I said.

"How can she use it?"

"When it comes to trial."

Sinkfield gave me another pitying look. "You don't think this thing's ever gonna come to trial, do you?"

"Don't you?"

He shook his head. "Not in a million years," he said.

Connie Mizelle let us into the apartment. She opened the door, smiled at Sinkfield, nodded at me, and then let us follow her into the living room.

"The senator's quite broken up about his wife," she said. "It came as quite a shock to him."

"When's the funeral?" I said.

"Tomorrow. But it will be totally private."

"You'd better ask him to come in here," Sinkfield said.

"He's terribly upset."

"He's gonna be even more upset when he hears what I've gotta say."

Connie Mizelle was wearing a black sweater and black slacks, perhaps out of respect for the senator's dead wife. She looked sexy in black. She looked sexy in anything. To me Connie Mizelle was a sex object— the complete, perfect sex object. I didn't like her and her mind worried me because it was more clever than mine, but I could understand what Sinkfield felt about her. I could understand and I was jealous.

She was looking at Sinkfield curiously. "What do you have to say to him, Lieutenant?"

"Well, for one thing, Dain's dead. I shot him this morning."

She might have become a brilliant actress. Nothing moved in her face except her eyes. They blinked. "You mean Arthur Dain?"

Sinkfield nodded. "That's right. Arthur Dain, the private detective. You'd better go get the senator."

Connie Mizelle stared at Sinkfield for a moment. Then she said, "Yes, perhaps I'd better."

While she was gone I said, "What're you going to do?"

Sinkfield grinned briefly. It was a hard, cold grin. "Just watch," he said.

"All right. I'll watch."

The senator crept into the room like an old man. He wore a tweed jacket, a tieless shirt, and a pair of gray slacks. On his feet were bedroom slippers. His feet shuffled as he walked. Connie Mizelle walked beside him, her hand under his elbow.

"Hello, Senator," Sinkfield said.

Ames nodded at Sinkfield. "You wanted to see me?" he said.

"I'm sorry about your wife," Sinkfield said. "We caught the man who killed her. I shot him this morning. He's dead."

The ex-senator looked vaguely around the room. "I—I thought he committed suicide. They told me that he shot Louise and then committed suicide."

"No," Sinkfield said. "Another man killed your wife. His name was Dain. Arthur Dain. He was a private investigator who worked for your wife. He killed them both."

Ames found a chair and sank into it. He looked up at Sinkfield. "But she's still dead, isn't she? I mean Louise. She's still dead."

"Senator?" Sinkfield said.

"Yes."

"It's all over. I mean all of it. You don't have to pretend anymore. We know about Los Angeles in 1945. We know about the man you killed out there. Perlmutter."

The senator shifted his gaze from Sinkfield to Connie Mizelle. "I didn't think it would be like this," he said. "I never thought it would be like this."

"I wouldn't say anything more if I were you, darling," she said.

The senator shook his head. "They know. What difference does it make now?" He looked at me. "It'll be quite a story for Frank Size, won't it, Mr. Lucas? I got drunk when I was very young and killed a man. That's quite a story, isn't it?"

"That's not much of a story," I said. "That happens every day. The real story is what happened later. The real story is how you kept silent when your daughter was killed because she knew why you were being blackmailed. The story gets even better because you still said nothing after Ignatius Oltigbe was shot down in the street. Your silence cost the life of your wife and the fancy lad that tagged around after her. But the best part of the story is how Miss Mizelle here blackmailed you into it all. I'm curious, Senator. How does it feel living in the same apartment with your blackmailer?"

Ames looked up at Connie Mizelle. "I love her," he said. "That's how it feels, Mr. Lucas."

She smiled at Ames and then she turned that smile on Sinkfield. "Are you arresting the senator, Lieutenant?"

"That's right," Sinkfield said. "I'm arresting him."

"Then shouldn't you tell him about his rights? Isn't that what you're supposed to do, tell him about his rights?"

"He knows about his rights. You know about your rights, don't you, Senator?"

"I have the right to remain silent," Ames said. "I have the right to—" He looked at Sinkfield and sighed. "I know all about my rights. Let's get it over with."

"It'll take a little time," Sinkfield said. "I don't think you quite understand it yet." He nodded at Connie Mizelle. "She was in it with Dain. She put the pressure on you, and Dain did the killing. First your daughter, then her boyfriend, then your wife and the Jones guy. Dain killed them all. You changed your will making her your sole beneficiary. How'd she get you to do that?"

The senator shook his head. "You must be mistaken," he said. "It was my idea to change my will."

"Sure it was," Sinkfield said. "And maybe you would have lived another month or maybe even another year or two. When twenty million dollars is at stake, they weren't going to be in any hurry. They could afford to be patient."

Ames looked once more at Connie Mizelle. "He's not telling the truth, is he?"

"No, he's not telling the truth," she said.

Ames brightened. "No, I didn't think so. I killed a man, Lieutenant. A long time ago. Now I'm ready to face the consequences."

"That's wonderful," Sinkfield said. "That's really wonderful."

"Let him alone," Connie Mizelle said.

"Sure," Sinkfield said, turning away.

I watched as Connie Mizelle went over to the senator's chair and knelt by it. He looked at her and smiled. She ran her hand down the side of his face. He patted her hand. She drew his head down so that his ear was close to her mouth. I could see her whisper into his ear. Ames's face had been gray, almost the color of a wet sheet. Now it turned white. His mouth opened and he stared at Connie Mizelle. "No," he said. "It can't be. It just can't be."

"But it is," she said softly.

"You should've told me," he said, struggling up from the chair. "You shouldn't have kept it from me."

"That's the way it is," she said.

"Jesus God," he said. "Dear Jesus God." He turned to look at Sinkfield. "Will you excuse me for a moment, Lieutenant?" he said. "I need to get something in my study."

"Sure," Sinkfield said. "But we're going to have to take you downtown, Senator."

Ames nodded. "Yes. I know." He turned back to look at Connie Mizelle. He gazed at her for a long time and then he turned and walked slowly across the living room and into his study. He closed the door. The shot sounded a moment later. I was looking at Connie Mizelle. She smiled at the sound of the shot.

# 28

Sinkfield was the first one into the study. I followed him and Connie Mizelle followed me. Ames sat behind his desk. His head was back at an odd angle. He had shot himself through the roof of the mouth. He was a mess.

The Bible was on the desk, the hollowed-out Bible. It was open, but the gun it had contained was no longer in it. I walked around the desk. The gun was lying on the rug not far from Ames's lifeless right hand. The gun was a short-barreled thirty-two caliber. It was a Colt and it had a pearl handle. Imitation pearl, I thought.

Sinkfield walked over to Connie Mizelle. He bent down until his face was no more than a few inches from hers. "What'd you tell him?" he yelled. He fought for control of himself. I could see the muscles working in his jaw. He got his voice down until it was just a harsh grate. "What'd you tell him that'd make him come in here and do this? What'd you tell him?"

Connie Mizelle smiled at him. She reached out

and touched his face near his left ear. She ran her finger down his jaw and then tapped him lightly on his chin. "Be careful of your tone, Lieutenant-darling. You're talking to twenty million dollars now. Twenty million dollars doesn't like to be shouted at."

"What'd you tell him?" Sinkfield said, almost whispering the words.

"Don't you know?" I said.

He looked at me. "No, I don't know. I don't know what she could tell him that'd make him come in here and poke a gun in his mouth and pull the trigger. No, I don't understand that. He was all ready to go downtown on a murder charge. He'd admitted he killed that guy in Los Angeles. He sat there and took it when you told him that it was because of him that his wife got killed and his daughter. But that didn't bother him much. Maybe a little, but not much. But she whispers a couple of words in his ear and he hops up and comes in here and shoots himself. And you ask me don't I know why and I gotta admit that no, I don't know why."

"He could take all the rest," I said. "He could take all the rest because those people died so that he could keep out of jail. His daughter, his wife. They died because of him and it probably bothered him, but not enough to do anything about it. He could even live with the woman who was blackmailing him. Why not? With her looks it wouldn't be too hard. It wouldn't be too hard for me anyway. And it wouldn't be too hard for you, would it, Sinkfield?"

He shook his head slowly. "No," he said, his voice hoarse. "It wouldn't be too hard for me."

"What do you think I told him?" Connie Mizelle said. She was smiling at me. It was the same smile that she had worn when she had heard the shot.

"You told him the truth," I said. "And he couldn't

accept it so he killed himself. You told him that you were his daughter."

"Jesus!" Sinkfield said.

"See," I said. "It even bothers you, Sinkfield."

"Not as much as it bothered him."

"I'm not his daughter," Connie Mizelle said.

"Sure you are," I said. "You were born in May of 1946. That's nine months after his fling with your mother in August of forty-five."

"My mother," she said evenly, "could have fucked sixty guys during August of that year."

"Could have, but didn't."

"How do you know?"

I shrugged. "I don't."

"Frank Mizelle was my father."

"No," I said. "Frank was sterile. He even had a letter to prove it. Besides, he probably didn't even meet your mother until three or four years after you were born."

Sinkfield stared at Connie Mizelle. "You were saving it, weren't you?" he said. "I mean this is how you were gonna work it. You and Dain. You were gonna blackmail him and sleep with him and kill off his family and then you were gonna hand it to him—the one thing that would push him over the edge—the fact that he'd been fucking his daughter."

"Are you arresting me, Lieutenant?" she said and smiled again.

He shook his head. "No," he said. "I'm not arresting you. Like you said, you're twenty million bucks now and I don't go around arresting twenty million bucks. It doesn't do any good. We haven't even got any evidence. We sure as hell haven't got any witnesses. They're all dead. So I'm not gonna arrest you."

"I think I smell something," she said. "I think I smell something very much like a deal."

Sinkfield nodded. "Yeah, they do have their own smell, don't they?"

Connie Mizelle smiled again. "How much, darling? How much do you have in mind?"

"Half," he said. "What would you say to half?"

She shrugged. "That would be about five million. After taxes and after the lawyers, there'd be about ten million left. Half would be five million for each of us."

"There's one other little thing you'd have to throw in," he said.

"What?"

"You," Sinkfield said. "I'd sorta like to keep you around because you're about the best fuck I ever had in my life."

She smiled again. "Then we have a deal, darling. Of course, there is one small problem."

"What?"

"Mr. Lucas here. What shall we do about Mr. Lucas?"

Sinkfield was no fast-draw artist either. But the short-barreled revolver was suddenly in his hand. "Lucas," he said. "Well, I suppose we would have to get rid of Lucas." He pointed the gun at me. "But we'd have to think up something clever, just like Dain did. What about another suicide-murder? We've already got the suicide." He looked at Connie Mizelle. "You and I could sort of be witnesses, couldn't we?"

"Yes," she said. "Yes, I suppose we could be witnesses—of a kind."

"Go pick up the gun that's on the floor," he said. "Pick it up by its trigger guard with a pencil and hand it to me."

Connie Mizelle took a pencil from the desk, went behind it, picked up the thirty-two as she had been instructed, and handed it to Sinkfield. He took it with his left hand which was now wrapped with a handkerchief. He put his own gun back in its belt holster and transferred the thirty-two to his right hand. The gun was still wrapped with a handkerchief.

"No hard feelings, Lucas," he said.

"Not on your part maybe," I said.

"I never knew I could get so rich so easy," he said.

Connie Mizelle's mouth was open. Her breathing was rapid. She was almost panting. "Get it over with, darling," she whispered. "Kill him. Kill him now."

"All right," Sinkfield said and pulled the trigger. He shot Connie Mizelle three times. He was a very good shot. He shot her once in the heart and twice in the face. By the time she fell to the ground she was no longer pretty.

Sinkfield walked over to where she lay and looked down at her. "You know something?" he said.

"What?"

"I think I really loved her."

I found a chair and sat down. I was shaking. I was shaking all over. Sinkfield looked at me. "You're shaking," he said.

"I know. I can't help it."

He went around the desk, knelt, used the handkerchief to hold the thirty-two while he pressed Ames's dead right hand around it, and then let it fall to the rug. "They aren't going to be too worried about the prints anyhow," he said.

"What're you going to do now?" I said.

"That depends on you," he said. "On whether you'll go along or not. She really wanted me to kill you, you know."

"I know."

"She'd of gotten off," he said. "With twenty million dollars, she'd of gotten off."

"Maybe," I said.

"You don't like it, huh?"

"No," I said. "I don't like it."

"You don't have to like it to go along."

"I know," I said.

"Well?"

"All right," I said. "I'll go along."

# 29

The following undated letter was found among the effects of Constance Jean Mizelle by Lt. David Sinkfield. He found it rolled up inside a shower-curtain rod.

Dear Connie:

By the time you get this I will be dead and gone and I just wanted you to know that I love you and wish I could have done more for you, but I done what I could under the circumstances.

You must be surprised to find a gun in this package. Well, I've had this gun for a long time since before you were born. I always kept in in this hollow Bible. I seen a hollow Bible in a picture show once and it seemed like a good place to hide something.

Well, this gun was used by me and a man you never heard of to do something horrible and terrible. On August 14, 1945 we held up a liquor store and killed the owner. Or the man I was with did. We were both awful drunk because we were celebrating the end of the war and we run out of money and liquor and so we decided to go get some and what happened is what I already told you about. This old clipping tells the whole story.

Now I got a surprise for you. The man's name is Robert F. Ames. He's a United States Senator in Washington from Indiana. He's also a Democrat although that don't mean anything. He's also very rich!!! Or his wife is. I have read about him and his wife in the newspapers and magazines and a few times I even seen him on TV.

But here's my real surprise. Robert F. Ames is your real father. Isn't that something? You ought to be able to figure out a way to use that little piece of information. I know I could if I was in your shoes. God knows I have tried to figure out some way to maybe make him pay me a little money, but I never figured out any that wouldn't get me in trouble too.

Well, honey, that's about it. It's all I got to leave you but I didn't want to go without leaving you something. Be a good girl. And if you can't be good, be careful.

All my love and kisses,
Gwen

# 30

F ive days later Frank Size used the eraser end of a yellow pencil to push the fifty-three pages back across the desk at me. He was frowning when he shook his head and said, "There's nothing in it for me."

"It's what happened," I said.

"I'm not saying you didn't do a good job. You got the Mizelle woman down pretty good. And the senator killing her and then himself with the same gun he'd used to kill that guy out in Los Angeles—you did that real nice, too. But there's nothing in there that the wire services haven't already moved. It reads like a murder mystery, for Christ's sake."

"I guess that's what it was," I said. "A murder mystery."

He shook his head again. Disappointment was written all over his face. "It's just not my kind of stuff."

"It's what there is," I said.

He chewed his lower lip for a moment and then

said, "But what was it like, him living with her? What was it really like?"

"I don't know," I said.

"Well, shit, what do you *think* it was like?"

"I think he liked it," I said. "I think he liked it because finally there was someone who knew what he had done back in forty-five. That must have been a relief of some sort. I think he liked her telling him what to do. He had a couple of sex quirks and I imagine that she took care of those for him in fine style. And I suppose every so often she would take him into the library where she'd take the Bible down and open it up and let him look at the pistol just as a reminder of her authority. Or maybe as punishment when he'd been bad, if he ever was. I don't know. All I know is that he knew where the gun was."

Size kept on frowning. "You sure there's not something else—something that nobody else has got? Something about the Mizelle woman maybe?"

"No, there's nothing else. You got three good columns out of it. That's probably all it was worth."

He shook his head. "But what was she like, the Mizelle woman? I mean really like?"

I think I must have shrugged. "She was just a girl who went for the big time and missed. But not by much."

"That doesn't tell me what she was like," he said.

"It's the best I can do."

"You sure you're not leaving something out?" he said. "Some real garbage that I could use?"

"No, I didn't leave anything out."

"And you're not forgetting anything?"

"Just this," I said. "I'd almost forgotten this." I handed him a single sheet of paper. It was folded.

"What's this?" he said, unfolding the sheet.

"My resignation."

"Ah, hell, Deke, you don't have to quit. I didn't mean it like that."

"I know," I said.

"I'll put you on another one," he said.

"No," I said. "I don't think so."

"What're you going to do?"

"I don't know," I said. "I think I might teach. History. I know a lot of history."

"No kidding?" he said. "Where you going to teach?"

"Paramount U," I said.

Frank Size shook his head. "I don't think I ever heard of it."

"No," I said. "Not too many people have."